Lunar Eclipse

Alona Kimchi
Lunar Eclipse

TRANSLATED BY
Yael Lotan

The Toby Press, *London*

First published in 2000 by
The Toby Press *Ltd, London*
www.tobypress.com

Originally published in Hebrew as *Ani Anastasia*
Copyright © Keter Publishing House Ltd, Jerusalem 1996

The right of Alona Kimchi to be identified as the author of this work has been asserted by her in accordance with the Copyright, Designs & Patents Act 1988

Translation copyright © Yael Lotan 2000

All rights reserved. No part of this publication may be reproduced, stored in a retrieval system, or transmitted, in any form or by any means, electronic, mechanical, photocopying, recording or otherwise, without the prior permission of the publishers.

ISBN 1 902881 28 1 (C)
ISBN 1 902881 29 X (PB)

A CIP catalogue record for this title is available from the British Library

Designed by Fresh Produce, London

Typeset in Garamond by
Rowland Phototypesetting Ltd., Bury St Edmunds

Printed and bound in Great Britain by
St Edmundsbury Press Ltd., Bury St Edmunds

For
Efrat, Michal, Micky and Yvonne

Contents

Movies 1

Lunar Eclipse 39

Berlin Diaries 85

We'd Talk About Love 177

*Nightmare Poem,
or The Unrealized Cure of Mor Alkabetz* 217

Movies

1

There was a time last winter when Shahar and I didn't get on at all. I was out of work and Shahar's business was on the skids. He was losing money and kept quarrelling with his partner Doron, but he couldn't cut and run, for all sorts of reasons I didn't really understand. So he'd leave in the morning and come back in the evening with a long face and didn't even have the patience to share his problems with me, and frankly I wasn't too interested. I was waiting for a reply from the Foundation regarding a script I'd submitted about the Golem and the connection between Prague and Jerusalem. I waited, even though I had a feeling that it was sure to be rejected. I used to sleep most of the day, and when I was awake I'd be wondering what was going to happen to me and what I'd do, but I had no answers so

I'd go back to sleep on the living-room couch. I'd close all the blinds and turn the radiator on full blast, to make it easier to fall asleep. I'd curl up in a duvet with a slipcover that I didn't change for weeks, and though it wasn't visibly dirty you could tell that it was filthy, but I simply didn't have the strength to change it, because it's one of the things I've always hated to do, and during that lousy period I just couldn't cope with it. I used to say to myself, if I changed the slipcover I'd have to change the bed linen, and then generally start tidying up and cleaning the place. So I left it on.

I'd get up before Shahar returned, fold the duvet, chuck it back into the bedroom and sort things out a bit so the place wouldn't look revolting—empty ashtrays and all that. From a sense of obligation. I thought that now that I was dependent on Shahar for money and everything, I should try to be a good wife. It made me sick to think this way, but that's what came into my mind.

When Shahar was home he spent most of the time playing with his Nintendo, and became a real champion in all kinds of games. When he got tired of it, we'd order a movie through Home Cinema, or find something to watch on the movie channel. Usually stupid movies, and we'd seen most of them at the cinema over the years, but we didn't care, as long as they tired us out and made the time pass till we could go to bed. Once in a while we started to talk about what was going to happen to us, but it was usually the same conversation which didn't lead anywhere. Shahar didn't know if he should sell his share of the business or not, and I'd say I didn't know what I'd do with a degree in film-making, and maybe I should try to look for some work in television, because now that we have the Second Channel and all the cables, there must be lots of jobs in production, and all that kind of thing. But it never led anywhere.

If it rained at night we'd say how nice it was, and how we loved the rain, but it didn't mean much, because nothing ever happened, and it didn't even remind us of fun things from the past—like the trip to Amsterdam when all we did was wander among the canals, high on Ecstasy, kissing and licking like puppies, or my first semester vacation when we got into a kind of sexual frenzy with each other, and Shahar's head only came out from between my legs to smoke a joint. The rain didn't even remind us of that crazy night, at the beginning of our relationship, when I walked from my flat all the way to Shahar's, because I suddenly longed to see his face, and almost drowned in the huge puddles on Frishman, nor the times when I came home late from the university and saw Shahar's outline stuck to the window, waiting. It was just rain.

Often I had a feeling of claustrophobia because we kept all the windows and the veranda blinds shut, and I felt I was suffocating from the hot air from the radiator and passing out from the noise of the rain on the roof, and from knowing that there was nowhere to go.

From time to time we got up to make instant coffee. We both like filter, but we didn't have the patience to wash out the filter jug every time, and didn't want to miss bits of the movies we were watching. When one of us did go, the other would report what had happened in the movie: "He had a flashback about the accident with his wife", or "They arrested the whore in yellow, but Gene Hackman got the parcel he sent from Prague." When the movie finished, I'd suggest to Shahar that we watch another one, and he usually said he didn't have the strength and had had enough and was going to bed, and I'd stay up and watch another movie, even a shitty one about some Argentinians who crashed with their plane on top of a mountain and ate each other to survive, or about American high-school kids in the summer holidays. I couldn't sleep at all at night. I was buzzing with a kind of alertness I didn't know what to do with, and didn't actually want to do anything with it.

On those movie nights we smoked like crazy, finishing a packet of Lucky Strike in a couple of hours, and drank about half a litre of coffee each. Shahar would say he had a pain in the chest and was sure to end up dying of cancer, he smoked so much, and I'd say maybe he should ask himself before every cigarette if he really wanted it, which would make him cut down because then he wouldn't be smoking automatically, or else buy only one packet a day. And he always replied that it wouldn't work, because he also cadged them off his partner, Doron, and when the pressure was on in the business he didn't have the mental energy to think about it. So I'd suggest trying Chinese acupuncture, and he'd say it's a load of rubbish, because in the end you go back to smoking. I also felt that I was falling apart physically, that my body had degenerated completely, but I didn't have the strength to do anything about it. If we did want to cheer ourselves up a little we'd say we should take out a membership at the Gordon swimming-pool again, and what fun it was when we used to go there last summer, what a good feeling we had afterwards whatever we did.

Sometimes in these talks Shahar would say that he got no satisfaction in his life, that he was already twenty-nine and didn't know what next, and I'd say I thought he was great, being independent and making a living, that he was more successful than other people his age and he should try to enjoy the current situation, until he got a new idea or a chance to do something else. He would say that I didn't understand anything because I could only see things through my own prism, that I thought the fact that someone was earning enough to keep himself was cause for satisfaction, but he wasn't made like that. He said he needed something more than simply fulfilling the basic needs of existence if he was to be happy. I saw I was getting on his nerves and he was also getting on mine, but I didn't know what to do about it. Sometimes I told him that I was in despair, that maybe I'd never make movies like I used to fantasize. When he was impatient he'd say that he couldn't cope with these catastrophic ideas, that he wasn't used to carrying on like this and there was always hope. When he was in a better mood he'd say, sure I'd make movies, he had no doubt about it, because I had the talent. That calmed me down even though I knew it wasn't true; it made me feel a bit better and that was all I needed.

2

Another weird thing was, we didn't fuck. Not for months. This was bad, we knew that but didn't make a big issue of it. I couldn't remember when it started and how it went on for so long. Sometimes I thought perhaps it was because we'd been together for four years, and probably every couple got tired of fucking after such a long time. I was sure that they were all pretending, or forcing themselves to fuck because sex is supposed to be part of married life. I concluded that if you looked at it closely, it was just a bodily function, like eating or shitting. For a time we talked about it a lot, because we both held that it's necessary to discuss everything, and also because we were always very close, but the talks didn't get us anywhere either. We found all kinds of explanations, psychological and what not, and sometimes we actually did screw, but chiefly in order not to feel totally off the wall and sort of pay our dues, but it was boring, even though I did come and everything. I told myself that it wasn't necessary, but still felt relieved after it happened. I thought I was making an effort to be normal and that eventually it worked. After a while we stopped talking about it, because how much can you talk? Sometimes Shahar would say it would be nice if we had a kid, and I'd say I still wasn't really and truly ready for it, that first I wanted to fulfil myself, personally and professionally, to feel that I had economic security without being dependent on him, because that's what independence was all about. When he became irritable and I felt he was unhappy with me, I'd say that maybe I would never want a child, it was my right as a woman. I knew it was driving him nuts, because he had this phobia that he couldn't father children. He'd had some hormonal thing when he was small, or so he thought. He said that if it happened today he'd have got hormonal treatment right away. To cheer him up I'd say that he had a big dick, but he said that even if it was true, it was because of his poor physical development, just like a newborn baby has a big dick in relation to his body. He had almost no hair on his chest, and I loved that, but he was afraid. Everything looked to him like a symptom of sterility, because he'd never got anybody pregnant, not any of his girlfriends before me, not even by accident. It bothered him, but I didn't have the strength to think about it and try to help him. I felt this tremendous pressure and didn't know how I was supposed to go on living. I also knew that we loved each other and that everything would work out all right in the end.

    Saturdays were the weirdest days. Friday nights we spent reading the newspapers, then we'd see movies, two and sometimes three, till we fell asleep. Saturday mornings, which began at midday, were really tough. Sometimes when I woke up, even before opening my eyes I'd wonder what it was that was weighing on me, and then I'd remember—it's Saturday. We didn't know what to do. We'd slouch around the house uncombed and unwashed, and didn't have any idea how to occupy ourselves. Sometimes we went to visit Shahar's partner Doron and his wife Bubaleh.

Lunar Eclipse

Bubaleh was pregnant and Doron was looking a bit down, though he was once the handsomest hunk in Tel Aviv, and I'd even screwed him a few times after I met him and Shahar, but that was a long time ago. Nobody ever mentioned it and Bubaleh didn't even know. We'd sit in their living-room and Bubaleh would say she was so sick of the pregnancy and wanted to have the baby already, and that she didn't give a damn and was going to smoke like she always did. Sometimes she drank a glass of whisky and then took my hand and put it on her belly so I could feel the baby getting stoned on the whisky and kicking. Her stomach was smooth and hot, and the umbilicus was misshapen and bulging, like a badly healed scar. It made me sick, but I always let her fool around with my hand and pretended to take an interest, and just waited for her to let go of my hand and stop embarrassing me.

But that was only sometimes. Mostly we stayed home the whole Saturday, until evening came and it began to feel like the start of a new week and we felt better. We'd look for a movie on cable TV and relax. Sometimes I peeped sideways at Shahar and wondered why I really loved him, what we had between us and what was left of what we had in the beginning. I couldn't say. He was still the same Shahar, with dead-straight hair the colour of sand, with the same haircut he had since we first met, the style of an Oxford undergraduate with a long fringe, which he tossed aside with a twitch of the neck that looked like a tic, was still morbidly skinny, and had a speaking voice that made me melt, kind of lazy with soft sibilants. But he was different all the same, though I couldn't say exactly how. I only knew that when I sometimes thought about us breaking up, it seemed like the very worst thing that could happen to me, and I'd rather my whole life was like one long Saturday.

3

That winter was really bad. That's how we were. I didn't feel that it was something dreadful that couldn't be fixed, but the difficulty was always there, like a useless piece of furniture stuck in the house. I was lucky then, because Netta had quit her job as a researcher for a cable TV programme, and we used to go to Lanchner's in the mornings, sit there for hours and chat about all sorts of things. We'd say we ought to think of something we could do together. We'd say maybe we should write a script and submit it to the Foundation. We'd say maybe we should make a pilot for a TV programme of our own. Then we'd eat breakfast, one omelette for both of us and double cream cheese and salad, and then go on to talk about more practical matters. About life. About men. That's when I realized that something was happening to me. Sometimes I overheard myself talking, as if I was a stranger, and couldn't believe it was me. I'd say, "What's the use of men, anyway," or, "I want to be alone." Netta questioned me about the relationship with Shahar, and when I told her a bit about it, she suggested that I should try to seduce him, but subtly, because perhaps he had anxieties about my conspicuous sexuality.

Just thinking about this possiblity gave me a pain in the eyes and a depression. Once Netta speculated that perhaps he was queer, but later concluded it was hardly likely, and I agreed. Trying to understand better, she interviewed me about the details: "What, you don't fuck at all at all? Never ever? Since when?" Her main argument was that you've got to work at these things, because when you've lived together for a significant length of time it didn't happen naturally like it used to. When we got tired of talking we'd stroll up and down Sheinkin Street, go into "The Third Ear" and rummage through the CDs for hours, or visit the boutiques to see what was new. Netta believed that precisely because we weren't earning any money just then we ought to buy dresses and drink imported brandy, so as not to give in to the misery of life and circumstances.

There was one dress shop on King George Street we rather liked. They had all kinds of kooky clothes from London and Amsterdam, both old and new. The saleswoman was called Ore Ben-Ari, and Netta said if that was her real name then she, Netta, was a duchess. Behind her back we called her Whore Ben-Pee. This "whore" was quite pretty and did some commercials and clips. One commercial showed her picking strawberries and putting them into her open, lipsticked mouth, while a young bare-chested guy, a commando type, was splashing her with a hose. When Shahar and I saw this commercial on the Second Channel I said to him, "This is Whore Ben-Pee, I know her, the one from the boutique on King George, where I got you that leather waistcoat," and Shahar said, "Some of your friends are really tacky." I said, "She isn't my friend, and Netta, for example, isn't tacky at all." He didn't answer because he was always a bit scared of Netta, which disturbed him, so I added, "And Netta is not just any friend, she's my very closest friend in all the world." Then he gave in and said, "OK, so I'm sorry."

    Whenever we went into this boutique Whore used to fall on Netta's neck, because she knew her from some television programme that Netta produced and Whore took part in. She called Netta "Nettie" and told me I had a really beautiful face and why didn't I do something with it. Beside the cash register she kept all kinds of coloured stones and crystals, to give her positive energies and success in business. She'd say to Netta, "Nettie, this is the year of the Cancers," because they were both born under Cancer, and she'd say to me, "Come here sometime and I'll draw your astrological map," and "I saw you and your boyfriend walking in the neighbourhood—boy, did you look like lovers!" She was always overflowing with compliments, this Whore. It was an awful habit of hers. But we didn't mind putting up with her bullshit, because she had a nice shop and when we bought something she always gave us a discount, since she considered herself a friend of Netta's, but also because it made us laugh that we called her Whore while she sucked up to us. She was like a private joke between us and part of our regular route.

    After Netta and I separated I'd go home, get under the duvet in the living-room and think all kinds of thoughts—that I had an ugly body and that I didn't know what to do, but mainly I waited for Shahar, because when he was there I felt a lot less lonely. I tried to think about sex and understand what it meant. If it's really as significant as people make out. I tried to break it up into all its components in my mind, and to understand what the fuss was all about, but the more I thought, the more my thoughts became meaningless—a man's dangling penis penetrating a woman's hairy, moist vagina, and that's supposed to give them supreme pleasure. People have killed and betrayed and conquered countries for it. More—a man's dangling penis penetrating a woman's hairy vagina, and that's the symbol of conjugality, that's what determines it. Without it, all the love, all the attachment, longing and devotion lose their meaning and become mere symbiosis or friendship. And then again—a man's dangling penis penetrating a woman's hairy vagina, and that's what makes the relationship into the Real Thing. Without it everything's sterile. It was an absurd idea, and I had no answers. None of it had anything to do with what I myself felt. I loved Shahar awfully and wanted him to come home.

And all the time it rained.

One night I asked Shahar if he didn't miss fucking and if he was attracted to other women. He said he did miss it in theory, but that in fact he didn't know. He said that at this time, when he was muddled about the business and full of worries, it was naturally difficult for him to feel attracted to women. I asked, "And me, are you attracted to me?" He didn't speak for a moment and then mumbled, "As if you're attracted to me." I wondered if he masturbated when he was alone, and had a feeling he didn't. Then he said, "I don't know what it all means. I love you more than I've ever loved anybody in my whole life, that's one thing I'm sure about," and I said, "Me too, but I'm afraid in the end it'll blow up, though I'm pretty used to it by now and I don't really care if we fuck or not," and Shahar said, "Enough of all this worrying, we're only wearing ourselves out," and held me tight.

I knew that no matter what I got used to, the Apocalypse was sure to come, because if fucking could be treated so casually the world wouldn't have made such a huge song and dance about it. It was a defeatist sort of idea, to rely on the experience of unknown others, but it didn't go away. Above all, I hoped that everything would sort itself out in the end—how could it fail to, when two people loved each other so much—and I put on a movie.

The next day we drove out to see Shahar's mum in Caesarea. I loved visiting her, because the place was always clean and she prepared a meal for us. Her walls were covered with lots of paintings, mostly Kadishman's sheep in all kinds of positions, making the place look like some lousy meadow, but after our filthy flat in town this pastoral atmosphere felt just right. Shahar's mum's name was Dinah, a woman almost six foot tall who wore high heels even in the house, smelled of "Opium" and wore huge silver jewellery, and this ornamented tower was topped with a mane of fuzzy red hair like a wig from the Rio carnival. When Dinah was young she almost became a dancer, but as she already had a bum the size of a billiard table, she decided to dedicate herself to studying medicine. She left Shahar's dad, who was a pilot, and married a sugar importer by the name of Einhorn, who insisted on calling Shahar "son", for some reason. Shahar's dad, on the other hand, lived in Thailand. He had a pub for Israelis, and was married to a twenty-year-old Thai beauty who couldn't speak a word of English. His greatest ambition was to come back to Shahar's mum, at least that's what she said. Naturally he didn't stand a chance of going back to Dinah, because Dinah had no use for him. But totally. Out of Shahar's hearing she called him "that flying prick", and when Shahar was around she changed it to the more educational "your dad, the pilot". In addition to this gang, Shahar had a big sister, Noya, who lived in the United States. Noya was married to a well-known crook who'd escaped from the country because of tax fraud which would have put him away for twenty years. His name was Yoram—a most unsuitable name for a crook. When we asked how Yoram and Noya were getting on, Dinah would pull out, like a magician, the latest photos Noya sent her. They showed Noya in huge sunglasses with a little tummy bulging over her bikini pants, barbecuing beside the pool, or Noya with her two little kids playing frisbee on the private beach of the summer house Yoram had bought in Malibu.

For lunch Shahar's mum prepared teriaki chicken, a saddle of lamb in mint and rosemary, a salad made of four kinds of lettuce, salmon mousse and a quiche made with goat's cheese brought especially from Cyprus. She sat opposite me. Bits of chicken stuck between her teeth, salad dressing was smeared on her chin. She didn't notice, and I spent the entire meal staring with concentration at the inside of her mouth, feeling that if I stared long enough, the mess would sort itself out. While chewing, Dinah talked about a new patient she was treating, a man who had breast cancer. She was an oncologist at Geha, and liked to talk about interesting cases at the hospital. We didn't express much interest, so she went on and explained that breast cancer is quite rare in men, and described vividly and in great detail how she operated on him and took out the malignant tumour, and how metastases were found in other parts of his body, and how he was treated with chemotherapy and radiation. Then she wiped her mouth with a starched white cotton napkin and brought in the dessert—a parfait of strawberries in Armagnac, which I couldn't eat. With the coffee came the time for presents. I got a cheese platter and a book about the differences between men and women, with advice on maintaining relationships. I said I didn't need such a book because my relationship with Shahar was excellent, but Dinah insisted: she knew we were happy, she said, but it would be interesting to re-examine things precisely from this mature and contented position. Shahar got a book about aerodynamics, because he was interested in airplanes when he was a little boy, and "Tsar" aftershave by Van Cleef and Arpels, though he never used aftershave, being allergic to alcohol.

When we got back in the evening, I didn't know what to do. Shahar settled down to play with his Nintendo, and I called Netta. While talking on the phone I noticed that the mouthpiece was filthy with greasy black grime, with crumbs of tobacco stuck to it, and it struck me I was too conscious of the disgusting things in life, and what did that mean about my mental state. I realized that it did not mean anything good.

Netta said, "So come to me, if you've nothing better to do."

We usually didn't meet at Netta's, because she didn't allow anybody to smoke in her place; though she herself smoked like a chimney, she didn't want the house to stink. She really cultivated her beautiful house. If you wanted to smoke you had to go out on the balcony and interrupt the conversation, and now in winter it was too cold. All the same I went to her, because the walls of the flat and the beeps of the Nintendo were scrambling my brain. Netta made us coffee in her super-modern espresso machine, and talked nonstop about some journalist she'd met at a party on Friday, and how he told her that he was busy finishing his book, and that Netta shouldn't call him for another week, when he would have finished it, because love muddled him and threw him off. I listened to her with one ear and suddenly said that if I were a man, I'd be totally revolted by strange women because of their shaved parts with the hard little hair bumps in the armpits and around the crotch. Netta looked at me as if I was crazy, and said that maybe it was none of her business, but I really must start fucking again, because I was losing my marbles. I got mad and started to explain that I refused to attribute such significance to fucking, as if everything depended on it, and that I was thoroughly fed up with this meatshop philosophy. Netta was hurt, and then the conversation didn't go too well, so I went home.

    Shahar was sitting watching a movie we'd seen lots of times—*Apocalypse Now*. It's a movie we both liked so I sat beside him on the couch. Shahar said, "I'll never understand why he chose Martin Sheen," and I said, "It was supposed to be Harvey Keitel, but it didn't work out," and Shahar said, "I know, but that was no reason to use this lump. You know, we ought to see the film *Heart of Darkness*, it's about how they made this movie." I said, "Yeah, but it was his wife who shot it, so you don't see him bonking all those Thai girls, that flying prick." Shahar looked at me and for a moment I worried that now he'd find out that's what his mum called his dad behind his back, and suddenly I realized that he knew it anyway. He started to laugh his head off and repeated in a Thai accent, "The flying prick, the flying prick!" And I laughed too and we hugged each other and I gave Shahar a million kisses on his face, his cheeks and his nose, and Shahar stroked my breasts and said, "Your eyes are so lovely," pushed his hand between my legs and added, "But what's most impressive about you is your personality." Then I went to make coffee and when I came back Shahar said, "Robert Duval's found out that Vince is a famous surfer, so now he's organizing the river surfing contest."

    When the movie finished I didn't stay to watch another one, as usual, but went with Shahar to the bedroom. I cleaned my teeth and lay down in bed beside him. He kept on a T-shirt and underpants, and when he turned off the light I started to stroke him gently. It was awfully strange because I hadn't done it for a long time and I was a bit shy, as if Shahar would suddenly discover what a whore I was. I touched him with little flickering strokes, little passes, in a childish way, so as not to alarm him. He also hugged and stroked me a little and then turned his back to me and in a few moments fell asleep. I listened to the sound of the rain, until Shahar started producing little snores with whistles at the end, then I took my duvet, went to the living-room and flopped on the couch. I lay with my eyes open till I heard the early buses, then I ran barefoot to the bathroom to pee and saw that I'd got my period. I looked at my panties which were stained with dark blood and remembered how when Shahar and I first met we fucked when I had my period. I was very moved by it—I was sure that men were disgusted by all these female things. I remember saying to him that I felt the fact that he overcame the disgust and did all the things he did to me was a sign of real love, and he said it wasn't disgusting at all, it was just that up to then I'd been dealing with messed-up guys, and I thought that he was a special kind of man.

My feet were freezing from standing on the bathroom floor. I shoved in a tampon and went back to the couch. Before falling asleep I thought that being a woman is not all it's cracked up to be. I wondered if anyone would ever be attracted to me again.

4

Netta said she was having a party on New Year's Eve and we should come. Shahar didn't want to go because he didn't have the strength to meet people, but I talked him into going even though I didn't really feel like it myself; I thought it would be good for us to go. Before we left, Shahar nagged me about his hair. He felt it looked ugly and he didn't know what to do with with it, he said he ought to get a haircut but didn't know what kind, and that he was fed up with looking like an English choirboy. I helped him to fix his hair with a little water and gel. He put on black Levis and a black pullover and was looking good, except for his chin which was clenched with the nervousness that weakened his face, and the greyish complexion he'd got lately. Because of all these preparations it was pretty late by the time we got to Netta's and all the other guests were already there. I didn't know most of them. They were mainly friends of Netta's from television, and from the time when she lived in Jerusalem. Though Netta was glad to see me and said I was looking marvellous, I felt stressed and lonely and was even glad to see Whore Ben-Pee, who was wearing a tigerskin hat and little tiny specs which made her look like the blow-job secretary. Her eyes looked like the eyes of a little Doberman pinscher, round and shiny, and she didn't stop smiling blissfully, as if she was still being splashed with a hose. She came up to me and Shahar and said, "Oh the handsome lovers!" and then turned to Shahar, though she hardly knew him, and declared that he looked great in black and how nicely his hair had grown. Me she kissed. She had a pleasant smooth cheek and I thought what fun for the guys who might want to fuck Whore with her smooth cheek, and I bet she sucks them diligently when they press her for it and doesn't grumble that she doesn't feel like it or that the taste makes her sick, and doesn't dare to spit in the ashtray after the guy comes, because she's into being a nice person who never creates problems. I was sure her panties were all neatly folded in the wardrobe, not tossed in anyhow like mine, and she never ever hung up a blouse she'd worn back in the closet but always put it straight in the wash. I imagined Whore's pleasant bed with fresh linen, with slipcovers that matched the sheets, and at that moment I desperately wanted to be Whore and to go to her house and get into her fragrant and tidy bed and take an orange, or one of those dumb magazines she reads, or an astrology book, and read a little then turn off the light. The only mess in this idyll would be the orange peel, which I'd leave on the bedside table. A mess which would only emphasize the general perfection.

Whore said, "Come on and dance," and left, and Shahar said she was actually rather sweet and looked a little sad. I thought that was a lot of bollocks, she was about as sad as a broken toilet bowl, but I was so pleased that he was saying something positive about the party that I also said, "Yes, she does seem a bit sad, and she smells nice." Netta came back and shouted, "Why are you guys sticking together, come on, I'll introduce you to people." She pulled me by the hand and introduced me to an American friend of hers from Jerusalem who said he was a poet, brought me wine in a clear plastic cup and asked me about myself and about the movies I wanted to make. I was enjoying it, but worried that Shahar might be suffering, and kept searching around for his black pullover, then I saw him standing and talking with Doron and Bubaleh, looking relaxed and smiling, so I calmed down and let the poet natter at me. After a while the wine went to my head and I told him about the script about the Golem and this thing that Prague people have about the Golem, and the connection between Prague and Jerusalem. He was very interested and asked when I planned to make the movie and I said I was waiting for money from the Foundation and he said he knew some people who might be interested in investing in such a project. Then we went and danced and I whizzed around and carried on, though it was acid house music which I usually can't stand, and all the time I kept worrying that Shahar might be bored, till I got so drunk I didn't care any more. When I got tired of dancing I stood on the balcony and smoked cigarettes with that American and all sorts of people I met at the party, then Shahar came and said in my ear that he'd had enough and he wanted to go home. He said it in such a sweet way, sounding childish, intentionally, because he knew I loved it and I felt I could die from the sweetness and tenderness I felt for him. We said goodbye to Netta and Doron and the American and went home on foot, totally pissed. Suddenly I had a wonderful feeling that everything was really all right, and anything that wasn't would soon be, and that we always worried too much. I said it to Shahar and he said it was true and he was going through a confusing time and hoped I had the patience to put up with him because he intended somehow to come out of it soon. Then we hugged and kissed in the street and when we got home Shahar took my shoes off and undressed me and he himself undressed and we got into bed and hugged and stroked each other and then he turned his back to me and fell asleep. I waited till he started to snore a little and thought how much I loved him and how I'd do anything to make things work out between us, then I took my duvet and went to sleep in the living-room.

5

Two weeks after the New Year's Eve party at Netta's we were sitting watching a movie with Richard Gere as a psychologist and Kim Basinger as his patient, when Doron rang and said that Bubaleh had had a little redhaired baby girl who weighed three and a half kilos, and they were probably going to call her Roi or Leshem. He said that the delivery was easy, that they'd given Bubaleh an epidural in the spine, and that he'd watched the whole thing, and he would be awfully glad if we'd come and sit with him—he couldn't go to sleep because in a few hours he had to go back to the hospital. So we drove over there right away. Doron opened the door, looking scruffy and agitated. His ponytail was loose and his eyes were shining. He poured us all whisky and water and started to tell us about the birth.

He described things that sounded really ghastly and I wondered how poor pathetic Bubaleh had the strength to go through it all, then I thought that she really had no choice. The marvellous part of Doron's story was his description of the moment when the little girl popped out of Bubaleh's purposely-shaved cunt, how the air seemed to freeze and time stopped and they all stood around, silent and moved, looking at this tiny girl and feeling the beating of angels' wings. The revolting part of the story was how in a moment of strain Bubaleh squirted shit straight at the obstetrician, who Doron said wasn't a bit shocked because he was used to it, and anyway, Doron said, nothing is disgusting in childbirth. Pretty soon I began to suffer, because he started to repeat the stories, and when I took out a cigarette he said from now on there was to be no smoking in the house because of the baby. But in the end he got fed up with his own affectation of holiness, so he said what the hell, let's smoke, anyway they won't be here for another three days, so we started smoking like mad to make up for the wait, and to bring back memories of how the three of us used to wander about in Tel Aviv before Doron met Bubaleh, and how Doron couldn't walk through Sheinkin because he had to keep waving hello to all his ex-girlfriends, which is roughly half the population. Then Doron asked if we were hungry and we said we weren't, but all the same he went to the kitchen and made a dip with cheese and garlic and cut up vegetables and salty cheese, put olives in a saucer and honey and made toast and brought everything to the living-room and in the end we were persuaded and ate and drank though it was already about three o'clock in the morning, then Shahar said he was tired, so I hugged Doron whose neck smelled of the sweat he must have sweated in the delivery, and felt that his arms were as strong as ever but he was beginning to grow a paunch. I thought someday I'd fuck him again in memory of the good old days. I enjoyed thinking those whorish thoughts in the middle of the family atmosphere in that place. Shahar slapped him on the back and said, hang on in there, and we drove home.

On the way I tried to talk to Shahar, because I really couldn't figure out how he felt about the event. I said, "It sounds a real tough business, this childbirth bit," and he said, "Uhuh," then I said, "Doron used to be so handsome," and Shahar said nothing till we got home and he went upstairs before me and unlocked the door with his key and waited for me to come in and locked up, and instead of going to sleep in the bedroom he came and sat down in the living-room and said, "Make coffee." I went and made filter coffee because I felt like spoiling him. When I came in with the coffee he was smoking and looked preoccupied, then suddenly he said, without looking at me, "I want to leave home." I was so astonished I only asked "Why?" and he said he felt muddled and that his life was at a dead end. He felt like being a bachelor again, and maybe all this family stuff was too much for him. I didn't speak, because I wanted to ask if he had another girl but I was ashamed to ask and also certain that he didn't, because he'd always loved me so much. I felt that these kinds of question were like the idiotic scenes I'd seen umpteen times in movies, but those people were all screwed up stereotypes—not me and Shahar. All the same, in the end I did ask him. Then he got up and leaned against the wall and said, "Not anyone in particular." Then he came over, touched my cheek, "Hey, don't be sad, sweetheart," and stayed with me a bit longer without speaking till the atmosphere became really unbearable, then he announced, "Well, I'm tired. I've got to sleep," and went to the bedroom. A few minutes later I heard him snoring. I couldn't understand how anyone could sleep after saying such things to a person, and wondered what to do so that my hurting insides wouldn't burst out of my chest and spatter all over the walls.

 I decided to clean the house, something I hadn't done for weeks. I went to the kitchen and started on the piles of greasy dishes in the sink. I fell on them like a prize fighter in the final round before the knockout, and didn't stop till the sink was empty with bits of rotting muck clogging the drain hole in the middle. Then I scoured the gas cooker which was also greasy and filthy, till my fingers became soft, pink and wrinkled from soaking, but I didn't stop there and proceeded to wash the floors throughout the flat, and repeated the operation, and rubbed the tiles with a dry cloth till they shone, then I turned everything out of the kitchen cupboards and tidied up, and dusted the living-room and threw out old newspapers and straightened all the books on the shelves, and then I went and woke up Shahar. He got up and packed some shirts and underwear in a little travelling bag and said, "I'll be in a hotel," and he also said "I'll call you." I said, "All right" and he left.

I was afraid I'd start to cry and wouldn't be able to stop. I sniffed my hands, which stank of cleaning materials, then closed the blinds and pulled out the first video cassette that came into my hand. It was the American version of *The Three Musketeers*, with Kiefer Sutherland as my favourite musketeer, Athos. I fetched my duvet, curled up in it and switched on. Later Doron rang to ask if we'd like to come with him to the hospital to see Bubaleh and little Roi-Leshem. I told him, "Shahar's left home." He didn't know what to say, so he laughed and said, "The kid's freaked out," he also said, "He'll be back in a day," and also, "You're OK, huh? I don't have to worry about you, do I?" I reassured him, "No, Doron, I'm fine, give my love to Bubaleh," and hung up.

6

At lunchtime, when we were sitting in Lanchner's, I said to Netta, "You know what would really be appropriate now—if they called me from the Foundation to say that my Golem script's been accepted, or something," and Netta said, "Damn right it would be appropriate." She also said, "So what did Doron have in the end—a he or a she?" and I said, "A she," and Netta said, "I can't stand that Bubaleh, she's such a cow, and he's also turned into something revolting. But wasn't he gorgeous once?" Netta had also fucked Doron ages ago, but she couldn't remember what it was like because she was drunk, she only remembered throwing up on his carpet. That always made us laugh when we thought about it. Netta said, "You want some more coffee?" and patted my hand. She started on her omelette and said, "What an idiot, he'll be back on all fours before you know it," and then, "How did he look when you asked him if he had someone?" and said, "Who could he have, that nerd? He's lost his marbles, that's all," and also, "It's the forties crisis." I tried to break in and said, "But he's only twenty-nine," but Netta said, "It's the same thing." Then she spread some jam on a piece of roll and said, "You've got to eat something," and said, "Today we're going to get you some new clothes," and said, "Don't worry, it'll be all right," and at that moment, for some reason, I believed her.

 Netta stuck close to me all day and dragged me along all over the place. First we went to some middle-aged boutique in north Dizengoff and bought me a mannish black suit which cost about three months' rent, and Netta insisted on paying half. I thought I looked as if I was dressed up as John Belushi, but Netta rebuked me—she said I didn't know what I was talking about because of the situation, and that I looked like Annie Lennox and it was stunning. Then we went to some production company to nag them about a cheque that they owed Netta. Then we went to the post office to pay bills, then took Netta's cowboy boots to be repaired, then stopped by Netta's landlord to tell him there was a leak in her bathroom because of the old woman upstairs. I even trailed along to her accountant. I couldn't figure out where she got the energy to be funny and to charm everybody, even the pockmarked secretary. I asked her about it and she replied that today she was carrying the load for both of us, and that's why everything she did and said came out sort of dramatic.

In the evening we bought a bottle of Johnny Walker at the Romanian's and went to my place. Netta said, "Whew, isn't it tidy!" seeing all the cleaning up I did the night before to avoid going to pieces. We sat down and put on the Nirvana disk, "Unplugged", that we were both nuts about, and started to drink, and I began to feel nice and warm inside, and that it was all a lot of nonsense and Shahar was sure to come back in a couple of days, and thought that later that night I might look into Dinah's book about keeping up relationships between men and women, in order to understand what had come over him. I thought how much I loved Netta, and how beautiful she was, like Ingrid Bergman. I said this to her and she said, "This is the day to call up old lovers, check them out, so come on, get your phone book and also some more ice from the kitchen." We started to go over the phone book and crossed out the lot, but laughed like mad the whole time. In the end Netta rang Doron, who was already half asleep, and congratulated him on the birth of his daughter. She questioned him about the birth, and when she hung up we remembered again how she threw up at his place and laughed some more. Then Netta lay down on the couch and I on the rug and we were quiet for a bit. It was pretty dark, only the little lamp was on, and I asked Netta what was happening with that journalist she met, and she said, probably nothing, and that she didn't have the strength for this business any more, meaning relations with men. Suddenly she started to talk about her mother who was sick and how she ought to go to her, and it was weighing on her terribly, seeing her parents growing old. I asked again what about that journalist, and she said he simply stopped calling and didn't reply to her messages, because she'd been too frank about it—kept telling him he was terrific and she was thrilled to know him. She said she should have been calculating and mysterious, but she was incapable of it because it wasn't in her nature, and she was beginning to think she'd never have a real love. I said, "He sounds like just another impotent neurotic arsehole," and Netta said, "You're damn right. Put on some music." I crawled over to the stereo on all fours, waggling my bottom like a rabbit with a little tail, to make Netta laugh, and put on Nirvana again, and Netta said she was sure that Kurt Cobain was probably a nasty piece of work, sensitive or no, and also asked me to pour her another whisky and get her cigarettes from her handbag. I did what she asked, then sat down on the rug beside her and rested my head against her legs. I said, "Come to think of it, it's kind of fun being single, when did we last kill a bottle by midnight?" I asked her if she remembered how, when we were in the Pioneer Corps, we both got into bed with that American Negro who told us he'd been in Vietnam, and how he was so drunk he couldn't get it up. In the end the three of us, Netta, the Negro and me, sat up naked in bed and he showed us pictures of his ex-wife and kids in Oklahoma. Netta started to laugh like mad again and said I missed the whole point of the anecdote, which was what I said to her the next day. "You said that all those stories about Negroes having a big dick must be a fantasy of mixed-up white men!" She laughed so hard that she spluttered the whisky out of her mouth on me, and I also started to laugh and said, "Maybe we should become lesbians," and she said it was a damn good idea, and lay back down and asked me to light her a cigarette. Again we were silent and I felt the tears coming up and prickling in my nose and throat. I didn't want to spoil this enchanted evening with Netta, but I couldn't help myself. Suddenly she asked, "What was his name, you remember?" I didn't know who she was talking about. "Whose name?" She said, "The Negro with the small dick, bubblehead!" I said, "Abraham or Washington, or Denzel or Johnson, some Negro name," and sniffled. Netta rose on her elbow, put her cigarette in my mouth and said, "All right, let's call up that arsehole. Don't you want to know what's going on?" meaning Shahar. I didn't have the number of his hotel. Netta took the phone, put it on her stomach and dialled one-four. Then she dialled again and said, "Shahar Neuman's room please," then handed me the receiver, put the phone on the floor and staggered away to the bathroom, tucking in her shirt which was hanging out of her linen trousers that were all wrinkled on her bum.

I heard the phone ringing maybe five times and was going to hang up, then I heard Shahar's voice saying, "Hello". It made me as happy as if I hadn't heard him for ages, though we only parted that morning, and he sounded so familiar and so loved that I began to unwind. I said, "Hi, it's me," and Shahar said, "How are you? I tried to get you all day but you were out." I said, "I spent the whole day going around with Netta," and said, "How're things?" and he said, "OK, I drove around all day, too. I still don't know what's happening to me. Meantime I'm here in the hotel." His voice sounded awfully sweet, not a bit glum like it was in the last few weeks, but somehow it made me feel uneasy. I wanted to understand what was happening to him, so I said, "And how do you feel otherwise?" and he said, "I don't know. Confused. Trying to understand myself," so I said, "You don't have to sound so pathetic," and he said quickly, "Yes, you're right." That's when the warning light came on in my mind—usually if I used the word "pathetic" about him, he'd get mad and yell that I didn't respect his feelings, and here he was so polite and controlled. I decided to move the plot along a bit and said, "I want to come over now." He was quiet for a moment and then said in a very different voice, remote and businesslike, "Why?" and I said, "Because I want to." He was silent, so I said, "I'm coming over."

Just then Netta came out of the bathroom and made faces at me to tell her what he was saying, but I turned away. I felt embarrassed to let her know, though I didn't know why. I said in a low voice into the receiver, "I want to know what's going on with you," and he said, "I don't want to hurt you," and I said, "Try me." He said, "You want me to say that I've got something going?" I felt that this wasn't happening to me but to someone in a lousy movie. My hands began to shake and I said, "What sort of thing?" and he replied, "A man's thing."

The phone was sticking to my sweaty hand like a damp frog, and I threw it at the wall. I heard the sound of smashing plastic. I felt my body jerking uncontrollably, shaking in big, epileptic spasms. Netta rushed over to me, muttering, "Calm down, calm down," and hugged me with all her strength. I tried to push her away and get free, but she held me really tight. I started to scream, "I'll kill him, I'll kill him, tell me what I must do, what I must do," and Netta said "We'll kill him together, but calm down first," and pulled me to the bathroom and turned on the tap and washed my face with water and forced me to drink from the tap, then dried my face hard with the towel till my nose hurt, then we ran downstairs together, me first and Netta trying to keep up with me, saying again and again, "Just be calm, be calm," though by then I wasn't crying. I was completely frozen inside.

We stopped downstairs outside the house and suddenly didn't know what to do. It was horribly quiet, all we could hear was the humming of the electrical wires. Netta said, "It must be about two o'clock in the morning," and also, "You have any idea where that hotel is?" I shook my head and she made me sit on the low yard wall and said, "Sit here a moment, I'll just pop upstairs to phone Doron and find out where it is." Suddenly we saw the lights of a car and it was Shahar. He stopped in front of us and rolled down the window, looked at Netta with hatred and said to me, "Get in the car." Netta ignored him as if he didn't exist and said, "I'll wait for you at home," then mouthed at me so he wouldn't hear, "Just keep calm."

We drove around for a bit and I kept repeating in my mind like a mantra Netta's dumb phrase about keeping calm. Now and then I squinted at Shahar's profile—he was looking straight ahead like a racing driver, but I noticed a nervous tic in his jaw. After driving for a few minutes he stopped on a corner, switched off the engine and said that he'd been with me for four years and wanted to go on, but right now he needed to be alone, and I had to let him be, and I must try to understand him not just through my eyes—as if I had an extra pair of eyes for special occasions.

But there was just one thing on my mind, piercing my brain like a drill. I broke into a little pause in his speech and asked, "So who were you with?" And he answered me in a voice that sounded solemn and serious, like a Southern virgin announcing to her parents the name of her Yankee lover: "I was with Ore." I didn't understand what he was talking about, what ore was he talking about, I said, "What ore?" Then he said in an even more pompous tone, "Ore Ben-Ari," and gave me what I'm sure he thought was a brave look. That's when I understood that he was talking about Whore Ben-Pee.

This realization destroyed what was left of my strength and filled me with black despair. The worst part was the smug way he pronounced her name. As if she was a human being like any other, Sharon Stone or Hannah Senesz or some ordinary girl, and not our private joke, and I realized that if I stayed with him one second longer I'd really kill him. I opened the car door and started to run to the house. He shouted to me, "Come back and hear what I have to say and stop making scenes!" I heard his voice yelling at me furiously from further and further away. It didn't suit his plans one bit, the way I was behaving. It made him feel like a shit. But I didn't stop, I ran down the street as fast as I could, sobbing without tears, my mouth open and a cold wind blowing in my face, cooling my hot cheeks. The street was empty and I could hear my own footsteps echoing, as if an invisible person was running after me, and I started to yell as hard as I could through my gasps, "Netta, Netta, Netta, Netta, Netta, Netta, Netta, Netta, Netta, Netta . . ."

I heard a balcony shutter opening somewhere and a woman's voice saying what's going on, then a Border Guard vehicle passed and slowed down beside me, and a moustached face peered at me through the window and asked in a worried voice if I needed help, but I didn't stop and went on running, yelling Netta's name again and again into the night, as if I was afraid that if I stopped the pain would swamp me and crush me and I'd never get up again.

7

Netta lit cigarettes for me and for herself and gave me one. "The last two," she said. We sat on the couch, huddled together in my filthy duvet which she'd brought from the bedroom. Outside the light was beginning to turn blue. I said to her, "I'll never forget how he said her name, in such an important tone," and Netta said, "You're probably right," and looked at me with her grey eyes without turning away. I felt grateful to her for not saying empty phrases to comfort me. Then in a tired voice she said, "Let's finish the whisky, shall we," and before I could answer, she poured what was left in the bottle into the glasses. I asked her, "How long will it hurt me, I don't have any strength left," and she said, "For a while longer." And I said, "I don't want to love anybody ever again," and Netta said, "Uhuh." Then we were quiet for a long time and suddenly she started to sing in a soft high voice the last song on the Nirvana disk. It was an old blues song which they re-interpreted. *My girl, my girl, don't lie to me, tell me where did you sleep last night* . . . I listened to her quietly till she finished singing the whole song, and didn't say a word, and after a little while I could tell from her breathing that she was asleep. I went on sitting there, wondering what to do next, I couldn't put a movie on because I didn't want to wake Netta, and I thought maybe I should commit suicide, and for the first time in my life suicide didn't seem like an absurd option. I felt so sad for myself and Netta and life and the love with Shahar, which was finished, that I started to cry again, even though I was completely wrung out. Then suddenly a thought flashed through my mind and brought me a tiny little liberating joy, like a draught blowing in, and I began to shake Netta gently till she opened her eyes, terribly sleepy, and I babbled at her excitedly, through my tears: "Isaac, his name was. The Negro. I just remembered. Isaac, that was his name."

Lunar Eclipse

Tonight there will be a total eclipse of the moon.

    A black shadow will cover the moon, then go away.

    We have to wait, it will not be at eight-nine, when they tell me to go sleep. Put me to bed. No, it will be late, almost the middle of night.

    At eleven thirty-eight minutes exactly, a black shadow will come over the moon, cover it up, the shadow of earth, and the moon will go away. Then come back. And I will turn off the light then. Only then.

    He told me about the eclipse, about the moon. He said: "Anastasia, there will be a moon eclipse, that's astronomy, you understand, like you know where the groups of stars are (in Russian—*sozvezdiye*): Cassiopeia, Orion (the one with three stars in his belt), Big Bear, Little Bear, North

Star (you know how to find it), and the stars Sirius (that big one we can see) and Vega. So now you will see a lunar eclipse. It is beautiful."

He likes to do this, to teach me many things, so I will become an intelligent person. He thinks that before he came I learned nothing—what nonsense! And that I can read from age four—that does not count? I can play chess too. I know lots of things without him.

Even before he came, they taught me. She taught me. She.

And grandma and grandpa taught me. Grandma's a teacher, that's what she does, teaches mathematics to low grades. Me she did not teach, because they put me in first grade in another school, so children will not be jealous that she is my grandma. So she taught me other things after school. Took me to classical ballet. They have such a course in the Culture Hall in our city.

We were eleven girls in the course, little girls, called beginners, from kindergarten. Everyone had a round tummy like a watermelon, pushing out the leotard. Because our bodies are still childish, teacher Natalya Petrovna explained. This Natalya Petrovna was a famous ballerina, a prima ballerina, but she's old now, she doesn't have the strength to jump like she did then. Her tummy's also big now, like our tummies, but from old age. There was also Shurik, the pianist, but really he was a student at the Technicum. He played for us because Natalya Petrovna is his private mama.

Much I learned in those ballet lessons. Every movement there has name, in French. Like "plier-relever", which means go down with the bottom then up, or for instance, "arabesque"—leg rising in front and back, but I can't explain it without showing.

Sometimes Shurik played something happy, like a waltz, and we could run around hall free. Every time it was like something different—sometimes like birds, or bees. One time I fell down in this free running-jumping, because I was looking at myself in the big mirror all along the wall until I slipped. I wanted to see if I looked like a real ballerina. When I fell down there was a big fuss, blood came down from my nose, and Shurik carried me in his arms and everybody ran to call grandma. She was drinking tea in the canteen with the other mothers and grandmas. They stuck a wet handkerchief on my nose and said to hold my head back until the blood stops. Then grandma bought me tomato juice and took me home.

Grandma never panicked, because she is a class-teacher in the low grades and has a lot of experience with things like that. She was all right, my grandma, *babushka*. She did not do like other people—catch me, hug me, kiss me with spit. Things that make me uncomfortable. If she wanted to, she hugged me a little and gave me a little slap on my bottom, but friendly. That was how she loved. She also took me to see ballet shows: *Nutcracker, Sleeping Beauty*. On the way to the Culture Hall I wore my everyday shoes, but when we got inside she took out my special shoes for ballet lessons and put them on my feet, so I could look like a ballerina when I watched the ballet.

Because she had experience from being a class-teacher, *babushka* always had all kinds of things ready for emergencies. For instance, if in the middle of the show I was thirsty, she took out of her basket a little water bottle made of orange plastic, poured cold tea into the cap and gave me to drink, so I didn't need to go out and annoy people. But sometimes there was no choice, I had to go out, then she pushed through with her tummy in darkness and whispered aloud, "*Izvinitye, izvinitie pozhalosta,*" which means "Excuse me please" in Russian, and did not give up even if everybody was annoyed, until we got to the lobby and from there to the Culture Hall toilets.

At home also we were not bored. Sometimes she taught me to roll cutlets of minced meat—not all of them, just some little ones, and I myself ate them. So I could learn to be independent. Also she taught me to crack nuts in the door, to say the multiplication table, shape biscuits like dog poo out of dough, dress a pillow in a pillowslip, all such stuff. Sometimes we played chess. Sometime she won the game, sometimes I. That's the kind of lessons we had.

Grandpa, for instance, taught me less, because he worked all day. He was a vet. Not for capitalist doggies and kitties—for cows in the *kolkhoz*. And other useful animals. When he came home in the evening he had a stinky smell like cow poo, and he liked to catch me and scratch me with the prickles of his face, but I did not complain because it was from love.

One day he brought me a guinea-pig. Tarasik I called

him, like the name of the son of Doctor Ossens, our family doctor. It was brownish, nice, but a little smelly. They told me to clean his box every day, for pedagogical reasons. Many things they told me to do not because it was necessary, but for those reasons. I wonder who that pedagogical was who made those stupid things. But it did not go on very long. After some time, maybe one month, Tarasik died. I asked right away for another, because I already knew how to look after the box, but they said it was not human that I forgot him so soon, so I must wait some time and miss him, then I will be glad when the new little one arrives.

After I missed him enough I said to grandpa, "*Ya gotova*"—I'm ready. Then he went to kitchen to ask grandma and she thought a little, looked at me, breathed deep and said, "*Nu*, all right." Then grandpa made me a sign with his thumb to say all right, and said this time it will be a real surprise.

Next day he brought me a little goat, it's called a kid, from the *kolkhoz*. He was all black, this kid, with nice soft fur like silk and shining black eyes. I had lots of plans for him. I thought when he is big I will cut his fur and make a collar for grandma's English coat, and also take him for walks on a leash and show off.

But nothing came of it. Already the next day grandpa took him back to the *kolkhoz*. This kid had a difficult character. Much more difficult than Tarasik. He did not stay inside the box and at night he made damage everywhere—he ate curtains, chewed and spat newspaper, and left little balls of goat poo all over house. So they took him back to the *kolkhoz*. There he can make a mess all right. Simply, some animals should grow up outside, that's all.

* * *

Now that we've been in Israel a year and nine months, he thinks he has to teach me everything. Responsible, he is. Pedagogical. And she? She doesn't count. It's his decision. And why? Because she's not pedagogical. She spoilt me all the time. That's what he thinks. That I've been reading from the age of four and know French songs by heart and play chess, that doesn't count in her favour. It's nothing to him. Only he knows everything.

Daddy doesn't count at all, because he's dead. Even though my hair is like his and my nose is like his, that doesn't matter. He's now instead of my daddy. But I will never ever call him daddy. Even if they torture me in the inquisition! Only Yacov. That's his name and that's how it will stay. She also calls him Yacov, and also Yashinka. Yashinka is from love. Like my name from love is Nastenka or Nastochka. He calls me simply Nastya.

Since she married him and took me with them to Israel everything is different. Now nothing is done for no reason. Everything is pedagogical. Even when we go to the sea. Our sea here is Akko. It's called the Date Palms Beach, even though there are no date palms. That's just to make people come. Capitalist advertising.

In our city, Lvov, there was no sea. If we wanted to go to the sea we had to go to Odessa, on a plane. Every summer she took a holiday from work, took me, her sister, Auntie Xenia, with her twins Misha and Lonchik, her best friend Galya with her fat daughter Sofochka, and a rubber mattress, half red and half blue, for sailing on the sea, then we would fly on a plane.

It wasn't bad at all in Odessa. We found a room in the house of an Odessa family (Auntie Xenia said they were anti-Semites, that means they hate Jews, that means us, but were ashamed to show it because it is not accepted) and we rented it, one room for all of us. One on top of the other— three in the bed and the others on mattresses on the floor. But it didn't matter, because it was an adventure. And the main thing, the main thing was the sea.

Every morning the mothers woke us up. We cleaned our teeth and went out. The sea was usually far from the place where we stayed, sometimes we walked half an hour or more, but we liked it. The twins ran in front, then me, and a long way behind me, almost stuck to the mothers, fat Sofochka with her yellow bucket.

The mothers walked last, carrying baskets with food for the whole day: fruit, tomatoes, hardboiled eggs, and their rubber mattress that they like to float on in the water, like pickled cucumbers.

Me and the twins liked to be in the water, even though I don't know how to swim so well, just a little so I won't drown. She always looked at me in the water and laughed, like it was a joke or something, and her breasts wobbled like an earthquake. She also said I was swimming "doggie style". I was a bit offended, but it was better than being like Sofochka, who couldn't swim at all and just sat in the water like a salt herring.

Now the business with the sea is not at all like it was there. Funny it is not. That's for sure. Here in Israel you don't need to fly on a plane to go anywhere, because everything is near and there is sea in every city, even the little ones. At first I thought that was very nice, but that's because I didn't how things were going to be. Now we even go to the sea for pedagogical reasons. He wants to have a good influence on me. And on her.

Like for instance, we never go to the sea to swim, or to tan. Now he explains: "This the Crusaders built, this the Turks, this is a lighthouse and that's an ancient breakwater. That's Napoleon's hill. This is hummus-falafel, national Arab food..."

And she. She listens the whole time. She is interested. And she says to me, "Come Nastenka, listen to what Yacov is saying, it's very interesting..."

In the water even "doggie style" doesn't matter, and already it's impossible simply to bathe. He teaches me to swim. Grabs my tummy and says, Go like this with the arms, to the sides, and breathe in through the nose, breathe out through the mouth. He shakes me, confuses me. And all the time I'm swallowing water! Why can't I breathe in the sea like I always do?

When he leaves me alone I try to get away a little. I walk down the beach. I write the word "Help!" on a bus ticket that I took out of her bag, look through the rubbish of the sea, find an empty Coca Cola bottle, put the ticket inside and stop up the hole with tar. Maybe pirates will find it, or something, and save me from this situation.

Suddenly I hear yells. I turn around—he and she are waving to me, like policemen in the traffic. I don't make problems, I walk back to them. He says why do I throw bottles into the sea. Making it dirty. Dirtying his precious Israel. He is looking at her, and she looks right and left and says I have tar all over me. Pedagogical.

Suddenly she also cares about this Israel. In Russia she didn't care at all. Like for instance, when grandpa listened to Hebrew radio on "Kol Israel from Jerusalem", she always made a sour face and bulged her eyes like grapes, and she always said, "*Papa, ya tebya umoliayu,*" which means in Russian, Daddy, I beg you! Because she suffered from the shrieks and noises on that Israeli radio. It was simply that the Russians didn't want Jews to listen to that Israeli radio, so they messed up the radio waves: trrrrr-trrrr, bee-beep, bee-beep.

Now suddenly she's also interested. Now she's also a Zionist.

After the sea we don't go straight home. We go for a walk in the streets of Akko. He talk and talks: "This is Crusaders, this is Turks." And me, I'm thirsty, and hungry too. It's lunchtime. In Odessa, for example, when it was lunchtime we ate. And before and after. But here everything's different. Once I saw a movie about the Crusaders, where they ate all kinds of chickens and cow legs. They drank wine. Also in the book *Ivanhoe* the Crusaders ate every little while. About the Turks I don't know much, but

Lunar Eclipse

I'm sure they also ate a lot, hummus-falafel and sheep. My head is like a carousel of words. I repeat them and repeat them until they lose their meaning and become funny, nothing to do with what they say: Turks Crusaders, Turks Crusaders. It's so hot. We pass by a stall with colas, or a restaurant where people are eating, such a good smell. And he says to her, "You see, Masha, this is a little oriental restaurant, this is a typical oriental café." In the end I say to her quietly, "Mama, I'm thirsty," whispering to her in Russian, and she says very quickly, "Hold on. We'll soon be home."

He says buying in the street is disgusting, dirty and full of germs. That's what he's used to from Russia. Probably nobody bought him anything in Russia. Maybe because he's such an unpleasant person, nobody wanted to buy him anything. For me they did buy in the street in Russia, and how they did! Grandma bought me sodas, watermelon seeds, anything. Also ice cream and Russian popsicle. A red rooster on a stick. That kind of stuff.

Now we're "new immigrants". "New immigrants" is like tourists, but for always. And they don't have much money. That's why they don't buy me anything in the street. Also because grandma isn't here. Thinking about it gives me a pain in the nose. A sensitivity. It's from longing. When we were on the way to Israel I thought it would be interesting. I thought there would be experiences, adventures. In the El Al plane I repeated quietly the words I learned from a booklet for immigrants that we got: "*Oleh, Sokhnut, Mercaz klitah, Oleh, Sokhnut, Mercaz klitah*"

(Immigrant, Jewish Agency, Reception centre), till she said to me, "What's the matter with you, Nastya, are you mad, what are you mumbling there?"

It's from nerves, she told me. She was nervous the whole journey to Israel because in the beginning we lost Yacov. Really. When we were in Vienna, which was our transfer city between Russia and Israel, Yacov got lost. They looked for him all day, until the evening, even the Vienna police, and people from the Jewish Agency, and Zena the interpreter, and she and I also looked. And she had such a long face from worry, the corners of her mouth went down, like a mask in the book on mythology. In the end he came back by himself. On foot. To the palace. It turned out he went into a shop for geography books. Suddenly, in the middle of Vienna, he felt like reading a geography book, turning a Viennese globe, making his horizons wider. I didn't understand it at all, because in Vienna the books are all in German, anyway, so how could he read them? How? I asked her about it, and she said he knew a little Yiddish which is a bit like German. She also said I must not be a poisonous child. So after that I didn't ask any more questions, but I still don't understand why he had to widen his horizons in Vienna, just when her nerves were so-so. If I can try to behave myself then so can he. After the time when he got lost she remained nervous, and all the time held my hand and his elbow, as if it was me that got lost in Vienna. But I'm always afraid to get lost, and anyway it's not necessary to widen horizons just when you're on your way to Israel.

But that was a long time ago . . . Now I'm dreaming about when the streets and the mosques and the views of Akko will finish so we can go home at last.

"Crusaders, Turks." My sandals are hurting me, I have a painful boil on my big toe, a bubble thing with water inside. And it's so hot. Something to drink is what I want, just to drink. She's even a little sorry for me, she says, maybe we'll find a tap with water on the way, then you'll drink. But there isn't any tap. The air is so white, I can see stars, trying to suck a little spit from my mouth, but my tongue is dry. "This from the Crusaders, that from the Turks. Here Napoleon spat and there Napoleon shat" (he did not say that, I'm making it up to make myself laugh). We go into the market. He is never tired, from the moment we reached Israel he has lots of energy. From happiness, probably. He keeps teaching us—"*bazarchik*", he says, which means a little market in Russian. And of course "Crusaders, Turks" . . . The light is hot and all around are smells, smells and colours and talking in that Arabic that I don't understand at all. Now he's telling us about the Arabs and their customs. The customs of the Arabs are really awful, sadistic. Like for instance not to eat for a whole month on account of their god. What do they want a god for—to help them or to make their life like a labour camp, a gulag in Siberia in Solzhenitzyn (one of those cultural-pedagogical types who hates Russia and writes books that he and she read all the time). Then Yacov gets tired of history and starts on botany—explains all sorts of things about the vegetables of the Arabs. "Look what peaches," he says to her, "what grapes." They're just like those, he says, showing off, that they had in Samarkand, the city where he and his mother hid in the war. Me, if I was in that war, I wouldn't have run away, I would have fought with the partisans, in the forests. The Battalion's Daughter, I'd have been. It's known, there were such kids that the partisans were crazy about, joked with them, adopted them to be everybody's kids, and taught them to let the Nazis have six bullets between the eyes, with a Mauser. But him, he was in Samarkand with his mama and the peaches. She explained to me once that everybody ran away from the Nazis, even she and her family, grandma and grandpa and everybody. Simply because they were Jews and the Nazis made soap out of Jews, and he was also a Jew and his mama too. They didn't want to be made into shampoo so they had to run away, because it seems the Russian partisans were not too crazy about Jews either. That's how all this Zionism came about, obviously.

I'm only a Jew by half. Her half. My daddy was a Russian, but I was told not to yak about it to anybody, because here in Israel it's best if everybody is a Jew. They don't like the Russian Jews, the Israelis don't, because of the accent and the style and the clothes. And all kinds of things to do with the religious that I don't really understand. So I mind her and I don't yak about being half-Russian, even though it's something like a lie, when you think about it.

It turns out that Akko is a big city. At least like Samarkand or New York or something. It doesn't end. You walk and walk and still it never ends. I close my eyes, walk after them, thinking about how these Arabs can live without eating for a whole month. I haven't eaten since this morning and already I'm almost finished. Suddenly I feel sick like on a plane, a smell got into my nose, something disgusting, smells like dead fish. It's a special fish shop of Arabs. The fishes lie dead in three boxes of green plastic with some stinky warm water and a little ice. I hear him: "*Nu*, Masha, just look at these sardines, just look at these lobsters!" I try to see the lobsters but suddenly everything goes black before my eyes and awfully quiet in my ears, only her voice from far away, like an echo. "*Oy Nastenka, dushinka, shto s toboi.*" Then a long, long note, I think it's called C-sharp, and then I didn't hear anything.

* * *

Now nothing is like it used to be. Such a strange life. If somebody asked me to explain I'd be confused, but nobody's asking.

I don't have to explain anything to her, because she's here too and can see everything with her own eyes. At least some of the time. When she's not at work. He, for instance, is never at work, because he still hasn't found any. In Russia he was a history teacher, but he still doesn't know enough Hebrew to teach, so he's looking for something else.

In Russia she said that he knew Hebrew. First-rate. A real genius in Hebrew (she said), and now suddenly he knows nothing. His Hebrew shrank like laundry the moment he got to Israel. She says that's because he's modest, that he knows much more than he shows. In Russia when he came to visit us he always brought a fat blue book. A Hebrew–Russian, Russian–Hebrew Dictionary that somebody called Shapiro wrote. So that's what we called it—Shapiro ("Nastya, where's Shapiro, Nastya, put Shapiro against the door so it won't slam, Nastya, don't crack nuts with Shapiro, it's a book for heaven's sake.") He never came to us without Shapiro. Just in case he felt like studying a little Hebrew in our house. But when he came he didn't study any Hebrew—he sat with her on the balcony, or went for a walk with her, and grandma made me sit in the kitchen and drink tea, sigh and say that he's not a bad man just "*zanoda*", which means a nuisance and a bore. But if she's happy with him it doesn't matter, and I must watch my mouth and never dare to tell on her for saying these things. She also said in Russian, "When there's no songbird, even the three-dots (I knew it meant arse) is a nightingale." And she sighed some more.

And she? Well, she was really pleased with him. Really. She didn't notice he was *zanoda*, and when she heard him ringing the doorbell she ran with her arms and tits and her fat stomach, you'd think there was a fire, to open the door to him. She must have been very lonely since daddy died so even Yacov Zanoda looked all right, because of her mental state. She talked about him like he was at least Gerard Philippe, or Yves Montand or Solzhenitzyn. She really fell in love with him.

Like for instance one day she said that he was a Zionist. That's a kind of man who wants to go to Israel and also thinks that all Jews should go to Israel, perhaps so he won't be bored there. There was a time I also wanted to go to Israel, before I knew how it would turn out. I asked her if I was Zionist too. She told me to stop pretending.

Only he was a Zionist. Even his name was Zionist—Yacov. She said it was an ancient Hebrew name. I don't have an ancient Hebrew name but an ancient Russian one—Anastasia. That's the name my daddy chose for me. Even before I was born. If I was born a boy they'd have called me Innokenti. That's what could have happened to me if I wasn't born a girl. So maybe I have a little luck.

The only thing he teaches me that I like is about the stars. It's called astronomy. Sometimes in the evening he takes me for a walk. Mostly in summer, then you can see the stars really well. We go to the main road leading to Akko, sit on the bench in the bus-stop, raise our heads and he explains.

What's interesting about stars is that even though they're far away and have nothing to do with people, they're like people, only much more beautiful. They have names of Greek people, not of Russians or Zionists—not Yacov, Hayim, Anastasia, Tolik, Marina, Zena, Sasha, but names of gods and heroes from mythology: Sirius, Canopus, Pollux, Arcturus, Vega.

The most boring star is the earth. Full of troubles and can't really be seen, because it's stuck here under our feet and we're on top of it. I imagine to myself that she is the sun and I'm the moon, grandpa and grandma are Mizar and Alkaid in the Big Bear, my cousins the twins are Castor and Pollux, my uncle Alyosha is Aldebaran in Taurus and my auntie Xenia is the shiny Betelgeuse in Orion.

Yacov is the earth. That's it. I know that the cosmonauts who saw earth from space said it was a beautiful shiny blue, but I'm not a cosmonaut, I'm Anastasia Demidov and in my eyes the earth looks dirty, brown and doesn't belong to the family of stars.

The star I love best of all is the North Star. Only you have to know how to find it. There is a line, an imaginary line that you have to pass through the Big Bear, stick close to it with your eyes, and then you find it, small and shiny, and with it you'll never get lost. This is something all the adventurers and discoverers know.

I haven't given the North Star to anybody yet. I use it for myself. I have a system: I stand by the window when it's night, don't turn on the light (so he won't catch me and make a big fuss), find the blue star, start looking at it, concentrate on it very hard, with my heart and stomach, but without an effort (it's a special way), and don't think about anything. Then very slowly everything begins to disappear—my body, the room, the whole world, until there's nothing left except my thought and it. And then I am not, but still I am. It's very hard to explain.

* * *

Yes, there's a lot of things I can't explain. When I think about it I get a heaviness in the chest and stomach. For instance his habits. With the toilet for instance, with broken glass.

He hates dirt. Not all dirt, but especially my dirt and the dirt of the toilet. When he comes out of the toilet he shuts the door with his elbow, then opens the bathroom door with his elbow, and the tap also—that's the hardest part—with his elbow. Pushing it bit by bit. Then he washes his hands very well with soap.

She and I must also do it this way. "He's sensitive about cleanliness," she says, and she explains that it's a good thing. It's a good quality that helps us to keep the place in order. As if without this quality everything will be filthy. Also when you flush the toilet you must press down the handle with the elbow, so there won't be any germs on it. Also when you come in from outside you mustn't touch anything before you wash your hands with soap. You soap twice, then rinse, then dry your hands with a special hand-towel (God forbid you should use the one for the face—shock horror!) Only then you can do other things—drink water, touch things, live.

Once I came home with them from the clinic. I was terribly thirsty. Here in Israel it's so hot, you get thirsty all the time. I ran to the bathroom, washed my hands and ran quickly to the fridge to drink cold water. Suddenly he shouts, full of hate, angry: "She didn't wash her hands." "She" he calls me, as if I'm not there. And I say, "Yes I did, honestly." Then she comes in and says in a sweet voice—but with fear in it—to please him, "She washed, Yankele, she did wash." But he doesn't believe us, looks very angry, says, "Not true. Liar."

But me, it was known at home, in Russia, I never lie.

It's a principle with me, and even when I tried a few times—like that time when I ruined her Polish lipstick—it didn't work. My face got hot and my voice went up and down and stammered, so I don't even try to lie. But he doesn't know anything about me. What can he know about me? He's not of our family. He's a stranger. He thinks bad things about me, and he says again, "Liar." I put up my hands so he can smell the soap on them, but he moves back quickly, his face shows that I disgust him, and he goes out of the kitchen.

Only she and I remain. She doesn't look at me and I see she's afraid that he will again be bad to her, like every time. He won't talk to her, will try to get rid of her, to drive her out, because of me. Because I'm bad, I don't control myself, don't try hard enough, I'm dirty and a liar. I push my hands into her face, to smell the soap, to know that I did try! She doesn't need to check, she believes me. But what's the use, she's already so sad, her lips are heavy, the corners drag down, and the fear is very hard inside my chest. Now he'll leave her, hurt her, because of me. And she says to me quietly, "Yes, yes, Nastenka, leave now, never mind, go to your room." And now I'm in my room, sitting on the bed, everything inside is so bad, only the light outside is white and grey and hot, and so many hours before night comes.

* * *

This summer there's not much to do, not like last summer. Then there was a lot. They put me in the summer camp at "Kadimah" school. In the morning a bus came and took me and other children to the summer camp. Most of the children were new immigrants. Some Russian, like me, some Georgian, and some were Moroccan, but only a few. They go to another summer camp in a school called the "Mamlakhti" school. They told me it means the same as "kingdom" in Russian. I don't understand why it's called that. There is no kingdom here, there's a government. I know them all from pictures, the ones who are already dead and the ones still living—Moshe Dayan with one eye, Golda, Ben Gurion with the electrical hair, Begin who killed Englishmen with bombs, Peres who talks slowly, Rabin who was handsome once—ordinary people like that. I can't understand it.

When you reach the school you get a chocolate drink in a plastic bag, a roll and a pear, sometimes a plum. Then you can play in the yard, then you sing some songs in Hebrew, go to the pool—in short, a pretty good place.

I had a friend there—fat Yana from the second floor in my building. Yana is two years older than me. She's starting sixth grade this year. She even has little tits and some hairs on her pom, because she's well developed. Sometimes she lets me come into the toilet with her and shows me the hairs. She has maybe ten hairs, but it's better than me, I don't have any at all.

Fat Yana is also from Russia, from Vilna. She's learning to play the piano. She's got a piano at home—shiny, made of brown wood and covered with lacquer. All the furniture in their house is nice and covered with such lacquer. They also have pictures on the walls, one of Yana's mother, Faina Filipovna, when she was young and supposed to be beautiful, one of Yana's parents—Faina Filipovna and Alik on the day they got married, and the biggest picture is embroidered in coloured threads and shows a shepherd and shepherdess and all kinds of sheep and goats under trees. This picture is called "Gobelin". The shepherd and shepherdess are wearing fancy clothes, she in a kind of big round ball dress and he in ballet tights. It's not clear why they dress like this to look after sheep and goats. I remember that goat kid I had and what a mess he made, with his poos and everything, so I can't understand it. Maybe they put on these clothes specially on the day they were embroidered on the Gobelin.

But the most beautiful picture in Yana's house is the face of a woman on a piece of metal. You can only see her in profile. On her head she has a hat like an upside-down bucket decorated with patterns. It seems she's an Egyptian goddess called Nefertiti. Yana said people still think she's the most beautiful woman in the world even though she's been dead maybe a thousand years. Talking about the Egyptians, Yana told me that they want to blow up Israel and push their thingie between the legs of all the Israeli girls, and stick a knife in the back too. Yacov says that once, in the time of that Nefertiti, the Egyptians and all the other Arabs were really cultured and invented mathematics and astronomy, but they must have gone bad since that time. Yana thinks it's because of the heat, and that since coming to Israel her daddy Alik is also nervous, drinks a lot of brandy and beats Faina Filipovna. It's all from this Israeli heat.

After coming back from the day camp I used to go to Yana's and sit on the sofa while she practised on the piano. Most of the Russian children practise on the piano, but not me, because when I was very young they tested me and found that I don't have a musical ear and don't have a talent in that direction, but more for literature and chess. Yana has a good musical ear, what they call perfect pitch, but it's not such a wonderful thing, because she has to practise for two hours every day, while I can do anything I want. Mostly she hates to practise, and sometimes she lies and says she played. Then her mum said I should sit there so Yana won't be bored, and watch by the clock to see exactly how long she played, and if she played less time I should tell on her.

Once Yacov said that Yana has no talent. As if he knows anything about it. In our place we never listen to music, because it makes a noise and bothers other people. Only when she comes to my room to talk to me we put classical records on the gramophone, the kind even Yana can't play because she's only been learning for two years, and you have to learn the piano all your life, or at least ten years, before you're worth anything.

Yana plays when her parents are not at home, they're at work. Her mum works in a milk plant in Haifa and her dad in an army factory. Sometimes Yana says, "Tell my mum that I played, and meantime we'll have fun," and sometimes I say all right. So we go to her room and Yana takes out of the shoe drawer a packet of "Time" cigarettes. She smokes without breathing it in, and I also tried, but the two times I tried I saw darkness and stars before my eyes and got sweaty all over, so Yana said she wouldn't let me smoke again because I was breathing the smoke into my lungs which is dangerous because I'm too small. After she finishes smoking she makes the air smell nice like roses with spray they have in the toilet, and we play cards. There is a Russian game called *Podkidnoi Durak*, a grown-up game. In our house there are no cards, because that's for simple, primitive people and drunks. We only have chess, but thanks to Yana I can already play well. When we play we curse, the way Yana showed me: "*Yob tvoye mat*" and "*pizda mat*", like her dad curses when he plays with her uncles on Saturdays. When we get bored with the cards we put on Yana's mum's make-up—lipstick, blue eyeshadow, and look out the window for the guy that Yana loves, Victor-Cat. She's really in love with him, even though he's from the Caucasus which is not supposed to be good. Yana's mum told us that people from the Caucasus are primitive and stinky. I don't know when she had a chance to smell them. This Victor-Cat is a big person, he's fourteen or more, and he's not stinky at all. I know because once I stood behind him in the grocery and sniffed, and he had a nice smell of soap and cigarettes. He doesn't know that Yana's in love with him, doesn't even know she's called Yana, or even that she exists. But she doesn't care, we spy on him from the window and that's enough for her. Sometimes we close the blinds in the room, making night in the middle of the day, and tell fortunes. We tie a pair of scissors to a Bible and ask it questions. If it turns right, the answer is yes, if left it's no. These fortunes tell us that Yana will marry Victor-Cat and they'll have three children, two boys and one girl, a Ford Escort car and a stereo. I don't ask my fortunes, because I'm not in love yet, so there nothing to ask about.

There are others things we can do, like for instance search very carefully in her parents' room, and sometimes we find this Russian paper that's called *Club*. It's boring like all newspapers, but in the middle pages there are chapters of a story for grown-ups with such things in it, you can't believe! Everything about love and nakedness, with all the details. The hero there, a guy called Timor, he must be really handsome, he puts his prick into all the girls in the story. There's Claudia, the blonde, and Natasha with straight hair, and all kinds of others. But sometimes Yana plays the piano and I listen and even close my eyes.

* * *

Summer camp finished but there was still a lot of summer left before school started. A whole month. Yana's parents sent her to her uncle and aunt in Kfar Sava, so she won't be in the streets all day. I don't have any uncles in Israel, only mum's friends in a town called Bat-Yam, so I ran around in the streets a lot and she started to worry about me, said I was turning into a street child. She doesn't understand that in Israel it's not like in Russia, she thinks I'll become like that boy Gavroche from *Les Miserables*, or like the hooligans in the *Pedagogical Poem*.

But I stay outside all the time, as much as possible, even though it's hot and there's nothing to do. I do everything not to be in the house with him. Already in the morning when she goes to work I feel it. I get all tense inside. I lie on my bed in the room trying to read, but my ears are listening the whole time—what he's doing, where he's going, which door he's opening or closing. The whole time I feel something bad is going to happen, in a minute he'll find out I did something bad, then he won't even tell me, just wait till she comes home and will talk to her quietly in the kitchen or in their room, then it will be very quiet in the house, a scary quiet, and I won't know what happened, what crime I did and what he will do to her because of me. Maybe he will divorce her and we'll be alone in Israel without anybody, no grandpa and grandma, no Auntie Xenia, nothing. She is so afraid to be left alone. Since daddy died she's been afraid of it, it's the reaction of her soul.

When daddy died I was five and a bit. It was April and the whole city smelled of lilac. Blue lilac and white lilac, with a strong smell like perfume, only stronger. It can even make you feel weak if you smell it too much, or even faint. All the bushes were full of flowers, but especially the lilacs. That's how our city is in spring, and it's really really beautiful. But to me, that lilac smell is the smell of daddy's sickness, the smell of his death. Exactly when he died I didn't know, he was a long time in the hospital. I didn't see him a month or two months, and they didn't tell me anything and I didn't ask. If people don't tell you can't ask, you won't hear any secrets, you'll only have guesses. They didn't take me to the funeral either, because I was too little. Only in the evening, when they came back, grandma said he was dead now and I could cry if I wanted to, but I should also be glad for him, because he had a lot of pain and now it stopped. But I didn't cry. I just sat in my toy corner on my little chair and didn't know what to do, I just thought about her. About her pain. And I hoped she would call me.

It was long after this that I saw pictures from the funeral. Some pictures showed them all walking and holding flowers, and some showed him alone, lying in a coffin. I found the pictures in her drawer, in a special black envelope. He's lying inside the coffin and doesn't look like he's sleeping, but kind of ugly, it's his face but not his face. Greyish. He's dressed in a suit and there are flowers around him. I don't understand why if he was dead he needed a suit. I didn't ask, because the pictures were secret and I was afraid she'd be annoyed, or even worse, that she'd start to cry and wouldn't be able to stop, then lie on her bed, frozen, with eyes like a teddy-bear's, open and made of glass, and won't talk to anybody for days or months or ever.

That's just how it was after the funeral and she went into her room and his, but they didn't let me go in, they only filled the house with flowers. That lilac in every flowerpot, in every vase, and my head was spinning from the smell of it, and all I wanted to do was go to her, but grandma didn't let me, she only said, "Go on, Nastenka, read a book, mummy is sad today." But when her friends came, from work and others, they allowed them to go in. I tried to peep in—carefully, so they wouldn't notice—to see what she was doing in the room, what they were talking about, and why nobody said anything to me, but I couldn't see because they always closed the door behind them.

After a few days or maybe weeks, I'm not sure, people stopped coming, But she still lay there in the room with her eyes not moving, like she was dead and not him. Grandma tried to take me in to her and get her to talk to me, to notice me. She said to her, "Look Mashinka, here's Nastya, say a word to her now, you mustn't torment the child like this." But she didn't want to speak to me, she just turned her head sometimes and looked at me as if she didn't know me, and didn't say a word.

Grandma worried about me. I could see she did. She brought me cherries, a plastic dog that barked, books made of cardboard that you can build houses with, but there was no need. I knew that now that she was lying there like someone dead I had to be responsible. If I didn't watch over her something awful might happen. Even at night when I lay in my bed, which they moved into grandma and grandpa's room, I couldn't sleep. I closed my eyes and pretended to be sleeping, but in my heart I was awake and protected her from where I was lying. I thought, "Maybe she'll call me suddenly. I have to be prepared." And waited.

She didn't call me for a long time, I don't know how long, until one day it was really summer and she came out on the balcony and said to grandma that she felt like soup. Chicken soup, she meant. Grandma clapped her hands and ran quickly to buy a chicken. And she sat in that kind of armchair they call a chaise longue and saw me standing there and looked at me, she even made a movement with her mouth, kind of a smile, her skin was hanging on her like a rag, and I went to her and she patted my head and put her hand on my shoulder and said, "*Nu*, Nastenka, so we're alone now." I couldn't say a word because I felt snot filling my throat, so I pressed myself to her and pushed my head into her tits and smelled her smell—not perfume like it used to be—the smell of her despair, like dust, and I hid my face in her and said to myself that from now on I'm going to look after her all my life, really well, so she will never have a despair again, it was my responsibility now. That's what I decided.

Then when grandma came back I went to the kitchen, took some milk and wrote this vow in secret ink with a safety pin, folded the paper and hid it deep in the pot of the climbing vine, to make sure there was no way back. That's how it was.

* * *

So that's how it is now. Because of that, I try to be really good, to be clean, not annoying or moody, not make dirt. I have a responsibility to do everything so he will be nice to her, won't punish her with silence, won't hate, and most important, that he won't leave her.

But it's very hard. I don't feel I'm really succeeding. Maybe because I got used to being bad when we were still in Russia, maybe grandma spoilt me till I became bad. Now he's educating me over again. He scares me. If only he would find a job and wouldn't be home all the time. Sniffing, checking, to see if something's been touched, if something is broken.

After day-camp finished and Yana went away I stayed home, because she said I mustn't run around in the street like the trash. Scared to come out of my room, I hear him walking around barefoot, snuffling, and it makes me feel horrible. A few days ago I went to the kitchen to wash a peach for myself, they told me they're good for the health. Suddenly he came in quietly, and I was so startled I turned around and boom!—I knocked over a glass that was on the counter. And him, he's even more afraid of glass and needles than of germs. God help us if a glass breaks, he'll crawl on the floor all day and look for slivers until night comes. And you mustn't walk where it happened, he keeps crawling around and looking for the broken bits. He's so afraid of anything sharp. All our scissors are kept on top of a tall wardrobe, because he's afraid. Her sewing-box must not be touched, because there are pins and needles in it, and if she wants to sew something, for instance a button, she has to tell him and he watches her, and then he spends half the night checking if a needle didn't drop on the floor, even if any fool can see that nothing fell.

When I dropped that glass he went white, his eyes were so awful I can't describe them, and his face went crazy. I was so scared I almost fainted, like always, because I don't know what's going to happen. If he beat me I'd know what to expect, not like this cold fear, but he never beats me, and I know that the punishment will be terrible, I just don't know what it will be. I bent down right away to pick up the pieces, but he came up and grabbed my shoulder with such hate, like a scorpion or a crab, that it really hurts. Nobody ever hated me so much. My teeth went click-click-click together, and the sweat came out in my armpits, smelling of fear, and I could feel my whole body trembling, and he said, "Go to your room, I'll clean up," and turned on the tap to wash the hand which grabbed me. I ran to my room, shut the door and sat on my bed, waiting for the trembling to stop, thinking what I'd say to her when she came home from work, how I'd explain to her why I was such a piece of filth, how I'd explain.

After many hours she came home, I heard her key in the door. I knew that her face was tired and shiny, and I stuck my ear to the door to hear what he was saying to her quietly in a tight voice. Then she came in to me and her eyes were like the desert, like hamseen, and she said, "You must learn to be careful." I ran to her, "Mummy, *mamochka, milaya,* darling, forgive me, forgive me, *izvini menya, ya bolshe nye budu,* I'll never ever break a glass again!" She hugged me a little but her eyes were a desert, hamseen, and I knew that now he would leave her because of me. It's all over, here comes the terrible end, it's happening—everything will be sucked into a black hole, the sun and the moon, Andromeda and Cassiopeia, Centaurus and the Southern Cross, spinning around like an enormous whirlpool, a rain of huge asteroids will fall down, and everything will drown, will disappear, will be erased, like the world never existed.

Lunar Eclipse

> *. . . Anastasia*
> *evening sun*
> *clear dewdrop*
> *drop of my blood*
> *my tear . . .*

That's a poem she wrote about me. Once. Still in Russia. Also—

> *. . . Madonna eyes of mine*
> *light of my soul . . .*

—also about me.

There was more, and other poems, but that's all I remember.

* * *

Since that summer with the day-camp another year has passed. All kinds of things happened. First of all, I stopped going to the class of new immigrants and went into fourth grade with all the Zionist Israelis, mainly Moroccans, and one other Russian girl, Irochka, who's now my best friend. They brought in a new class teacher, Zipporah, with hair like an old woman even though she's really young. They told me it's a special colour they do at the hairdressers, they even pay for it, it's called "platinum streaks".

In the beginning it was so-so. Everybody in class hated me and Irochka, and said all kinds of things about us. About me they said I was fucking Prosper Ben-Hamo in the fishponds of the kibbutz near us, and that he paid me a *lira* each time, and all kinds of things that I never heard before. After school we had to run home, because some criminals from our class ran after us yelling words like "whore", "*yinan abuk*", "*akhu sharmouta*", and also, "I'll fuck your mother".

We used to run home like Indians, like Chingachgook the big snake, the last of the Mohicans, like poison arrows, like Apache tomahawks, hide in Irochka's house and read Gogol's *Ukrainian Stories,* stories like "Viy" and "Evenings in a Village Near Dikanka". Life was not impossible.

Yacov started to study something about helping old people, social work. He likes to help all kinds of old women, those who came to Israel on their own. He carries their bags from the market, talks to them in Yiddish: "*Vus makhstu*", "*Zei gezunt.*" It's his hobby, helping old women. Only her and me he doesn't help. But at least he isn't home the whole time, and I also have somewhere to go. Now the pressure is mainly about toilet paper. He's been complaining that she and I waste too much toilet paper. It finishes too quickly. So I try to do my number one at school and not to drink too much when I come home, so I won't have to pee, only if I really must.

But one day there was a change. A kind of change I didn't expect, and because of it other things happened. One day she came home from work and said, "Nastya, get ready, there's a special bazaar for immigrants." On the way she said that Jews in America sent all kinds of clothes they didn't need any more, to help the new immigrants in Israel. A Zionist favour, it was. And this bazaar of clothes was at the house of Missis Berta, the manager of the old people's club.

When we went into the bazaar I felt so happy. Since we came to Israel they didn't buy me any new clothes, and all the clothes from Russia were already small on me, and here were all kinds of clothes which were really fashionable! Flared trousers—what they call "cloche" in Russian—jeans jackets, flowered shirts with wide collars, even one dress made of fur like a tiger, but it was huge.

She looked and looked and found me a blue suit made of something called gaberdine. When I tried it on I knew it was just right for me, and everybody—all the old women and Irochka and her mum who were also there—said that I looked pretty.

The next day I wore the suit at school and even Zipporah, the class teacher, said, "Congratulations, Anastasia," and said me and Irochka were in charge of the class decorations. She told us to make a corner about Early Man. We had to paint all kinds of Neanderthals on cartridge paper and stick them in a sandbox.

After that things began to change. They stopped chasing us after school and cursing us, I started to do homework. I got an A-minus in Bible and an A in maths. Everybody asked us to draw all kinds of things—girls, animals, a palm tree with a monkey on it. And we did everything they asked for. We didn't keep a grudge.

Some Russian boys in the neighbourhood, and some

Georgians, started to whistle at me when I passed. Even that Victor-Cat that Yana was in love with asked me once if I wanted a Marlboro cigarette, but I didn't. Irochka is really advanced in the business of love—she's in love with her neighbour Arkadi from fifth grade, and even I stopped falling in love with all kinds of imaginary people like Sherlock Holmes or the Count of Monte Cristo, and started to take a real interest in Amnon Reich from 5B. Sometimes Irochka and I sat in my room and talked about these boys, who said what, who kept looking at us. We painted posters for the class and all the time we shared secrets, compared experiences, consulted each other, until one day when we were preparing the corner for the Eleventh of Adar, with Trumpeldor and the lion, Yacov overheard our talk. I don't know how I could have been so careless. For weeks afterwards before going to sleep I tried to remember what we said, in what words, about who. But by then it wouldn't have made any difference.

That evening she came into my room when it was completely dark, without turning on the light, and said in a hard voice that Yacov told her everything. That I only talk about boys, that I'm twisted, disgusting, sick, that she was ashamed of me, and that next time I should at least keep my voice down. Then she left. My heart felt like raw minced meat, and my face felt hot as if I sat beside the stove. I threw myself on my bed and lay there in my clothes until morning. The fear was like feeling sick, like vomit, filling me all over, every hair, every eyelash. I heard the voices of the birds and felt the cool sun when it came up, but I couldn't move, I just said in my heart: "God God God God, don't let him leave her now, make him forgive, just forgive . . ."

He didn't leave her, not that time, not any other time. Once I saw her standing beside his desk—the desk that he never wrote anything on—and she was crying. "Why?" I asked, and she said he wanted to leave her, and I asked, "Because of me?", so she looked at me and said, "Also." I hugged her around her stomach and said, "Don't worry, I'm with you," like she used to say to me when I cried, but she only said, "Leave it, Nastya, leave it now, we'll talk later."

He didn't leave her, but I didn't learn anything from it. I was only nine and a half, that's all.

Memories crawl all over me like ants on a tree: the day I lost a purse with twenty *lirot* in it near the kibbutz fishponds and came home after dark, dusty and scratched from searching for it, and she was helpless, at least as frightened as me, she couldn't save me, she was weak. I understood.

Or the time I cracked seeds in secret before bed, and fell asleep without hiding the shells. He burst into my room in the morning and I woke up on the floor—he pulled the sheet down with me, his face all twisted, but he controlled himself not to beat me, filthy me, a little shit germ. He didn't leave her even when I left a knife smeared with chocolate-spread in the sink, or when I finished all the pickled cucumbers, when they discovered that I was reading *Lolita*, which they kept hidden on top of the wardrobe in their room. But I knew very well, like a sharp knife I knew it, that a disaster was coming and I must find a way to save her.

When April came, yes April again, she took me to have my picture taken by a photographer. She dressed me in the American suit. She told me to wash my hair with shampoo so it would look full and rich, not greasy and stuck to my head like always. We took the bus to the commercial centre not far from us, where there are good shops, with perfumes, clothes, a cinema with movies, and no new immigrants at all, only Israeli Zionists from Germany or Poland.

In our town in Russia there were also Poles, because the town used to be part of Poland before Hitler made war. I had a Polish nurse called Musya. Grandpa brought her from the madhouse near his *kolkhoz*. They told me she used to be crazy but now she was supposed to be with normal people, that she was good at scrubbing pots and could do the shopping and the washing. After she finished all the polishing in the house she used to walk with me, show me things. Once she took me to see a little pig being slaughtered near the vegetable market—the Lenin market. This pig, this piglet, screamed like a person, very loud. I wanted us to buy it and take it home, to save it and also to play with it a little. But Musya said that we were zhids and zhids were forbidden to play with pigs—that is, me and my grandpa and grandma. Forbidden. She explained to me that zhids crucified Jesus, which is the god of the Poles, and showed me a picture of a naked man hanging on a cross, blood coming out of his hands and feet, on his head a painful garland of thorns, and instead of underpants a kind of special rag to cover up. This Jesus, she said, wanted the best for everybody, for the Poles, the French, the Americans, because he was the son of the main god, but the zhids were annoyed that he was trying to help and hung him on a cross. But he didn't die, he flew up to the sky, to be with the daddy god, and everybody who loved him became a Christian, except the zhids, who remained obstinate against him and did all kinds of wicked things, like putting the blood of Christian children in their Passover matza.

I asked Musya if I could stop being a zhid, because I really didn't like that business with the matza and the children, but she said not while I was small, but she could teach me a Polish prayer which would help me in the meantime, because otherwise I might go to hell. In hell I'd be grabbed by devils with horns and they would fry me with the other zhids in boiling oil like chips, and the suffering goes on for ever, because in hell you can't even die, you're already dead. I had to say the prayer every day before going to sleep. To stand on my knees in my nightie, look at the sky where this Jesus lived, and most of all make it come from the heart. It's also allowed to ask for things, she said.

I decided first of all to ask Jesus to make us stop being zhids, this would be a good start. I didn't want to bother him too much, but already the first time grandma saw me and said, "What's the matter, Nastenka, what are you doing?" I didn't want to tell her but she was suspicious and called everybody, so I told them everything. I wanted to explain about Jesus and all the bad things that happened to him, but they wanted to hear about the zhids, especially about the matza and the blood of children, so in the end I told them everything, like a rotten spy.

After that Musya didn't walk with me any more, only helped Grandma in the kitchen, until one night she started to scream that all kinds of people were hiding in the house, Nazis and zhids, and they want to do all sorts of things to her, then came the medical van—"*skoroya pomoch*"—and she was taken away for good.

In Kiryat Motzkin we went to the shop of a photographer, which in Russian is called "atelier". The photographer made me sit this way and that and told me to smile, but I couldn't. She said to me, "*Nu*, Nastya, what's the matter now, *shto s toboi*, smile!" but I couldn't manage a smile, my whole face felt like rubber, like it wasn't my face at all, and my mouth didn't move. She and the photographer tried to make me laugh, jumped, made faces, noises—nothing helped, until she found a trick, she made a noise with her mouth like a fart, and I started to laugh and the photographer photographed me.

After a week I heard Irochka calling me from downstairs. I looked out of the window and she yelled to me that she was just back with her mum from Kiryat Motzkin, where they saw my picture in a huge size in the photographer's window. At first I didn't believe her, but later I took a little money and went with her to the "atelier" and saw myself in a huge picture, in the new suit and everything.

Lunar Eclipse

The news about it flew all over the place. At school even sixth grade kids came up to me and talked to me seriously, said compliments and asked questions. I answered everything, only not that I laughed because of the noise like a fart, because that was a secret between her and me, like all the things that are just inside our house and can't be told to anybody.

When the printed pictures arrived, I was so happy I thought the first chance I'd show them even to Yacov, to prove to him that I'm a good and decent person, and it would be a chance to show her that I have good intentions and I'm making friends with him, the way she liked. I waited for the right chance and it came.

One morning I woke up with a terrible tummy ache. They thought it was an upset stomach and sent me three times to the toilet, but nothing came out. Then she said I was constipated and told me to take a laxative pill and stay home. I lay quietly and waited for him to come home from the social work studies. When I heard him coming in I was afraid, and thought I'd show him the pictures when my stomach trouble stopped. I went to the toilet and sat down. It was a really bad constipation, and because I was bored I played with the toilet paper, running it into the bowl between my legs. It passed the time and at last the poo came out. That's when the awful thing happened. I flushed but nothing went down. The bowl was blocked. I waited for the tank to fill up and tried again—nothing. All the poo and paper were still in the bowl. I heard him knocking on the toilet door. "What's going on there?" I didn't answer, just felt that I was starting to sweat, to feel weak and the fear was pressing on my heart. I tried to flush again but everything stayed. I pulled the handle again and again, until he yelled, "Anastasia, are you sleeping or what?" Then I had no choice. I came out. My mouth was dry and I almost couldn't move my tongue. "The bowl is blocked and there's a lot of my germs in it."

He didn't say anything, just waited for me to finish washing my hands and go to my room. After some time, could be a few minutes or a year, he called me. I saw him bending over the bowl holding a huge lump of wet dirty paper. I went to him, like somebody condemned to death. I felt part of my face twitching by itself. He turned to me, raised his hand with the lump and pushed it hard into my face.

I don't remember what happened after that, how I washed my face and got back to my room. I just remember that I sat on the bed and didn't move until it got dark. She came home later than usual, I heard her in the hall, laughing and talking with him in a low voice. Then she came into my room and she was strange and sort of solemn, and said to me, "What's the matter, Nastenka, why are you sitting in the dark?" She turned on the light and closed the wire-net in the window against the mosquitoes. Then she sat down beside me, hugged me and said, "I want to tell you something, it's still a secret, only our family must know." She patted my head, tidied my hair with her fingers, took a deep breath and said, "You'll have a little brother or sister, but not for a long time, about eight months from now . . .

Nu, why are you silent like a fish, aren't you glad?" And all the time she was smiling and playing with my hair, until I hugged her and pushed my head into her neck, the way I liked, and said from in there in a funny voice, "I'm glad, mummy, *ya ochen ochen rada,* very very glad." Then she pushed me away a little and said, "Then why are you crying, such nonsense!" but she also cried, and laughed the whole time, then went to make supper, and I was thinking which star to choose for the new baby, but there was only one choice that suited.

After I decided I went to the window, I drew an imaginary line through the Big Bear till I reached it, and didn't take my eyes off it until everything disappeared except this star, and I said in my heart, "I'm waiting for you, little one, we'll have a wonderful time together."

* * *

Since she got pregnant many things are better at home. Everybody's trying to be nice. Even Yacov. When the summer holidays began they put me in a day-camp of the religious, because they forgot to put me down for the regular one and by the time they remembered there was no room. The day-camp of the religious is nice, only we don't go to the swimming-pool. Every morning we meet in a classroom in the religious school and sing songs. They're not bad songs, only I don't understand the words, so I sing more-or-less. The language of the religious is not like regular Hebrew. Like for instance, "*Odavinu Odavinu hai, Hamisrael Hamisrael Hamisrael hai.*" I've no idea who this Odavinu is, and

Lunar Eclipse

I'm ashamed to ask, because I've been singing it for days, so it's like I sang without understanding, I might as well keep quiet. We also sing songs I've known for a long time, like for instance "Hava Nagilah" that we learned when we first came, but now I think about it, I don't really know who this Hava is, maybe somebody like Golda Meir. Then we paint a little—that double Torah with the commandments, a pirate ship with sails, or a dove, or an old man with a *shofar*. What I like to draw best is girls, also a pirate ship with sails, even though it's not the right thing for this day-camp. The instructor said it was very nice and that I have a talent for drawing—as if I didn't know!

I come home from the day-camp in the early afternoon. Yacov is again at home all day—he left that social thing because he was giving too much of his time to some old women and didn't have time left for other old women, so they fired him. She said it was because he was a serious and strict person, not a superficial one like the others.

Maybe because he doesn't have anybody else to look after, he decided to change his attitude to me. Like for instance he bought me binoculars made of black plastic in case I wanted to watch migrating birds. Only he doesn't know that birds are the animals I hate most of all, they really make me sick, especially if I have to hold one—their eyes are round and evil. He bought me a book in Russian—*The Invisible Man* by Herbert Wells, even though I had it from Russia. He also got me the next part of *The Three Musketeers*—"Twenty Years On"—and allowed me to read until midnight, because he had to take it back the next day.

(Since they decided that I'm wicked and sick, I'm supposed to turn off the light in my room at nine-thirty exactly.)

I hate his presents, at least as much as I hate him, but I behave really well. I say "Thank you", make an effort, wash my hands all the time. Now all the dishes in our kitchen are made of plastic, so he's not so worried about things breaking. He also keeps on trying to explain things to me, to teach me or tell me boring stories about how it was with his mother in the war in the town of Samarkand in Asia, what kind of peaches they had there and what kind of grapes. Such a bore! But I go along with it because it makes her very happy.

The thing that's really awful now is that he's decided to teach me to exercise out of a little book of his that was made for officers in the Red Army. I hate all exercises, except ballet, but I don't resist even though it's awfully annoying—all kinds of exercises: "Inhale–Exhale", "Swallows", "Running on the spot".

"Swallows" is worst of all. You have to stand on one foot, stretch out your arms and raise the other leg backwards. Lately he's been sticking close to me from behind, as if to make it easier for me, and even sometimes when I'm standing at the window in my room he comes in and presses hard against me, but I try to slip away gently, so he won't be offended or annoyed and things will be bad again at home.

So this is how it is at home these days. Everything is easy. She's happy so I am too. It's never been so pleasant since we became a family, a summer like this. This morning

Lunar Eclipse

he came into my room and said, "Anastasia, tonight at exactly eleven thirty-eight there will be a lunar eclipse, so you can go to bed late, not at nine-thirty." Then he stayed in my room and yakked about astronomy, but I was so happy I didn't mind.

I've started to plan in my mind how we'll go out tonight, the three of us. He will lecture us about stars, and I'll walk next to her, and she will be happy that everything is so wonderful, that there is peace between us, and I'll listen to her happiness, quietly quietly, and feel that it's me, the magic fairy, who did all this, who arranged everything, who behaved so beautifully. And there will be a smell of grasses from the fields and a smell of the sea, and we'll be calm and radiant like a new constellation.

Berlin Diaries

I shall never get out of this! There are two of me now:
This new absolutely white person and the old yellow
    one,
And the white person is certainly the superior one . . .
Without me, she wouldn't exist, so of course she was
    grateful.
I gave her a soul, I bloomed out of her as a rose
Blooms out of a vase of not very valuable porcelain . . .
Sylvia Plath

Lunar Eclipse

1

The funniest thing about this ward is the fuss they make about the names of things. It makes them incredibly touchy. Say I call the people on this ward "loonies". Straight and to the point. Loonies! What should I call them? Patients? The mentally disabled? Clients? It freaks me out, these pompous names. They make up names for them like 1980s rock groups—Adam and the Ants, the Sex Pistols and the Sick from the State Sanatorium. So sad. Even Shakespeare said names were crap. A rose is a rose is a rose and all that. It's this kind of touchiness that did for Romeo and Juliet. But here nobody gives a damn about Romeo and Juliet, or anything else except the level of dopamine in their messed-up brains.

Like a couple of weeks ago, for instance, there was a ward meeting and they brought in two nerdy new interns, to show them a day in the ward. Everbody talked their usual rubbish. After a minute I lost my rag and I knew that if granny, the old German from the anorexics room, started whingeing again: "Why isn't there more time for occupational therapy," we'd never get anywhere. So I stood up and said in the name of all the loonies, especially the younger generation (that's me, the younger generation, and the anorexics—the others all have one foot in the grave), I'm asking, begging the management, pretty-please, to connect the ward telly to cable.

And didn't the shit hit the fan. The head nurse goes:

"Galli, you're hurting the patients," and so on. She says to me, "Speak for yourself," like I'm allowed to call myself a loony but not the others. Wasserman looks at me and at Avishag, and Avishag waggles her eyebrows at me like a flamenco dancer, and the suburban anorexics start whispering and giggling together, this being all they're up to, more than that they can't manage. In other words, the ward meeting was down the toilet.

I really don't get it. I don't want to hurt anybody, honest, but I ask you—that orthodox cow who washes her hands all day long and shrieks like a siren if anybody touches her, she'll be more normal if I call her a patient? By this time she could commit the perfect murder, she's got no fingerprints left, but she still goes on washing her hands like some fucking gynaecologist. Avishag says it's because of social pressures. So what is she sick with? What kind of illness? Bnai Brak Stress? A loony is what she is, and I don't think it's an insult. Maybe if Wasserman and the others, the head nurse too, could learn to think that loony is like human being, only more special, it wouldn't sound like such a terrible insult.

Actually, it's not just a matter of opinion. It's a question of a sense of humour. These people don't have a sense of humour worth a damn. They think humour is when you tell jokes—"An American, a Frenchman and an Israeli are flying on a plane," that kind of crap. If you don't warn them, here comes a joke, they'll never see it. But OK, that's the stuck-up staff, the trouble is, they're infecting the loonies with their hang-ups. Even Avishag loses her funny bone when she's with the loonies and starts to act like a social worker.

But come to think of it, what do I know. Maybe life really leans so heavy on some people it bends them, crunches them up, like a sumo wrestler. Even me, with all the satisfaction I have in this ward, even I sometimes get mixed up, like that time with Ironside, for example, that robocop.

A couple of weeks ago they brought in this girl in a wheelchair. Stays in pyjamas all day long, don't talk to nobody. Pretty face, delicate, yellow hair with brown roots. I figure it's time to get properly acquainted, so I go over to ask her what's wrong with her. Que pasa, this and that. She says nothing. OK, if that's how you want it, forget it. I left her alone, went to eat bread and jam in the staff kitchen. Saturday the visitors came. Saturday is a pain in the arse sort of day, like Yom Kippur. The relatives of the loonies come for a visit—pained faces, to atone for not keeping the loonies at home but throwing them into—dear oh dear—a government institution. So, to suck up to the loonies and their own conscience, the relatives come loaded with bribes—chocolate, shampoo, newspapers, women's magazines, family-size bottles of Coca-Cola, home-made hamburgers in plastic boxes, all that shit. One of the anorexics got a huge teddybear. God knows what she's gonna do with it. Hug it at night and remember her fucked-up childhood? Practise sex? Hand to hand combat? This goody-goody act turns my stomach. They also brought her a Benetton tracksuit and a basket with all kinds of soaps and coloured balls that you put in the bath, to soften the skin sort of thing. Where do they imagine she's gonna take that bath—where they wash the old women from Ward Four? Me, I wouldn't go there if you paid me, with all the grey hairs from their old cunts sticking to the sides. But the anorexic solved the problem neatly—she put the whole basket thing on top of her bedside cupboard like an ornament. Like, you know, flowers and fruit arrangement. Group portrait of anorexic with soap. Yuk.

I wouldn't have given it much thought, I'm used to it—these Saturday visits always piss me off—but suddenly I see the anorexic talking to that new Ironside. What do you know, a new twist in the plot. With me no, with the anorexic yes? Ironside is crying and holding the anorexic's hand—my my, a moment of intimacy, and then the anorexic runs off and comes back with her basket. I thought, what a cow, showing off her soaps. But surprise—she pushes the damn basket into Ironside's arms, would you believe a present, and Ironside shakes her head, "no no no", she can't accept, but her hands are around the basket, and both of them are crying! Tears. Emotions, you know. They're friends, you know. I thought my ribs would crack from laughing.

Before they came round with the evening medication I went up to the anorexic and asked her nicely, "What's with that Ironside? Shouldn't she be in a rehab centre, not this place?" She looks at me like I'm a cockroach and doesn't answer. Off she goes to sit on the bed of the other anorexic, and they start whispering together, the snobs, because they've already been through every youth ward and they feel like they're at least Jim Morrison. I didn't care, I stood and watched them, sucking a "Mozart" chocolate ball that the old German woman gave me, sucking it real loud to make them puke, but suddenly I had enough of all this hush-hush crap and went straight to Ironside. I said, "What's the matter with you?" She doesn't answer. I say again, "Talk to me, or I'll throw a fit." She makes a suffering face but still doesn't answer. So I grab her wagon and give it a shake, lightly, a gentle hint as Avishag would call it. "Look here," I tell her, "you should answer when people talk to you. Here I'm giving you a little hint about what's going to happen if you don't respond, see. I can send you from here straight to rehab, no trouble at all." She got the point. She comes off her high horse and opens her mouth. And what do you know—three times she jumped from a tall building and didn't die, but now her whole body's held together with clamps. My god, a real robocop. And why did she do all that? 'Cause she didn't get enough warmth and love from mum and dad and her hubby.

Oh come off it. Honestly, what the hell is she on about? A robocop tries to commit suicide three times and fails? It's either sci-fi or some religious-mystical waffle, or else she jumped from the ground floor. I said to her, "You listen to me, Ilana (that's her name, Ilana), the next time you jump, do it from a higher floor. Especially now, with the wheelchair, you'd better take the lift, you hear." Then out of the blue she says to me, quietly like, her lips trembling: "You know, always, in the most awful moments, when everything looks washed out, I still have a tiny foolish little hope that perhaps somebody will save me. Not from death. From pain. So maybe that's why I always survive, like that little toy man that always bounces back up."

It made me blow a fuse, this talk. I felt my chest crowding up, my head got heavy, and my thoughts turned ugly and boring and started going around in circles. I gave her wheelchair a hard shove and dumped her on her side. She spilt out on the floor like a rag doll. I thought, how come all those clamps holding her together don't make a metal noise, why is she so pulpy soft with her unwashed hair and crumpled hospital pyjamas? She lay there without moving, probably scared of me, so I gave her a kick too, in the stomach. But she still didn't speak.

That really tore it, her silence. The weight on my heart must have been a hundred tons, I felt I was choking, and my thoughts were driving me crazy, round and round, blocked up and hurting. I tried to look for Avishag, but she was in the television room with all the others. I went to my room, took out the old deodorant packaging, turned back the top of the box and took out a fresh razorblade— I hate infections, see. I cut the vein on the left as deep as I could, diagonally, and sat and watched the dark line of the cut swelling up and thick heavy drops begin to fall down on the floor tiles. My head began to ease up and I started to take deep, deep breaths—aah, aah. Then I went to look for Avishag, but I fell in the corridor. It was November, and cold. It was freezing.

2

The person I like best on the ward is Anita, the redhead. She came from Belgium originally, ages ago, that's why she's got this Eurovision-style name. She's been here longest, almost a year, and she's also the most normal. I say to her, "Hey, Anita, why're you hanging around in this place at the tax-payer's expense? Go back to your pretty flat in Beersheba, your kids will come to visit you there—it'll be nearer for them." Then she says, "I have anxiety attacks," and that sort of nonsense. Or else she says, "Piss off, Galli, go read a book."

But I can't manage to read. Since being here my concentration is shot to pieces. I can't concentrate on a thing, on account of the nerves of this condition. But even if I could read, I wouldn't read in this place. Next thing they'll come on to me with the educational bit. It's bad enough when they pressure me about occupational therapy. Let them think I can't concentrate. Anita, though, she concentrates like mad. Sometimes she reads for days on end, or plays the kind of card games you play with yourself. I don't have the patience for this kind of stuff. I think when you play a game you play to win, otherwise it's just like wanking. I said this to Anita, and she said, "What's wrong with wanking?" Like she's broadminded. But she's all right, this broad, and I love her best of all the loonies because she's open-minded.

Here on our ward nobody wanks—nobody feels up

to it. It's a depression clinic, isn't it. But next door, in the mixed ward, they all wank like there's no tomorrow. A regular wankers' ward, that is. Yesterday I went in there to get an envelope for Anita and saw Savyon, the graphic artist, the one whose boyfriend left her, sitting there with her hand in her panties, like in kindergarten. I said something about envelopes and she said, "Look in the drawer," like everything's cool. I decided to have a chat, to get to the bottom of this perv behaviour that could have a bad effect on the other loonies. I asked her if it wouldn't make more sense to try and get her boyfriend back, instead of sitting twiddling her cunt in broad daylight and in front of a bunch of lunatic old women, as if everybody around her is morning mist and don't have any feelings. So she said that first of all, he didn't want to come back, secondly, a woman shouldn't depend on a man, and thirdly, I should take the envelopes and piss off, and stop bugging her. I took the envelopes and nicked twenty shekels, too, but she was so busy she didn't notice.

In the evening I asked Anita if she thought a woman could manage without a man, and she said that's the modern idea, but she personally hates to be without men. "There's not even half a man on this ward," I pointed out. Then Anita says that's the only difference between this ward and paradise. I said, "Too right it is."

I'm thinking about Jay. I can manage without Jay. But Jay is not even a man—a man is an ugly thing, hairy, with a nasty outlook on life, like Anita's daughter's husband, or Wasserman, or those sort of relatives who visit the ward.

But Jay is incredibly beautiful. When I asked Avishag to go and meet him instead of me, that time he came for a week, 'cause I didn't want him to see me looking fat and neglected, I kept nagging her to tell me how he looked. And didn't she describe him! The words she used—fancy words, sure, but also the kind that made me want to rush out and find him and do all the wild things I used to do to him after opening his fly.

But that was donkeys ago, Jay's gone back to his town, to Londonderry, to his mother and sister. I hardly think about him any more, not like the days when as soon as I got into bed and turned off the light I'd go to pieces, and no matter what I was thinking about, good or bad, I'd cry my eyes out. I don't know why, but the thing that made me cry the most was remembering how I'd say to Jay, "Are you English, Jay?" and he'd say, "No I'm not," and I'd say, "So if you're not English, how come you speak English?" It was a dumb joke, but it always got his goat, he has this Irish national pride and goes all childish when he gets mad, and it always made me laugh my head off. I can't explain it, but even now sometimes it makes me laugh a bit.

Sometimes I think about what's going to happen, but such thoughts pressurize me something terrible. The scariest thought is that nothing will happen. Like, that's what life's all about. I don't mean on the ward, I mean in general. To me, this ward is actually the nicest part of life. Here you can be anything you want and feel, and nobody sits in judgement. People outside think that the people inside are nothing but garbage. They also think that a place like this ward is a garbage bin. They think people are tortured here, they get filled with poisonous medications and electrified. It's true there are medications, but who said you've got to swallow them if you don't want to? I don't have to tell you about keeping a pill in your mouth, between the lips and the gums, do I? Every movie with even five minutes about a psych ward shows this trick, 'cause of its social implications, like the revolt of the individual loony against the establishment.

About electricity. I've seen people turn into human beings after a bit of electricity. Really fucked-up depressives, the kind that don't even have the energy to top themselves, start walking around the ward with a happy face from morning, like they're just back from the ashram of Rajneesh in Pune, after a month of meditating and fucking.

But what do I know about other people. Everybody's free to think what they like. For me, life on the ward is the only life there is. When I was outside it came to me, I don't know how far back, that I didn't have enough strength to breathe. I used to feel so tired I didn't know how I could still be alive. And I couldn't calm down. My head was working overtime. Going round and round in circles. I'd cut myself to get some rest, 'cause when you have wounds that people can see they let you rest. But it looked really bad and people were saying I was a loony. And all the time I tried to be what I wanted, until I didn't have any will left. None at all. So I erased everything, little by little. I kept the notebook, so that I'd remember from time to time who I was and where I was, and what I thought, and who I loved and who loved me. That kind of nonsense.

It's good here. I never had it so good. I grant you some things are lacking, like there's no chance of meeting somebody like Jay. But outside also I only met one Jay, and he had all that gentile stuff, and had to go back to Ireland, and I know I wouldn't have gone with him. Like, what would I do over there, what would I shine at?

Here on the ward you don't have to shine at anything. Here everybody is messed up, officially out of the race, and they don't have to knock themselves out for anything. Granted some of these idiots don't appreciate what a gift it is to be here. Some of them fantasize about coming out of the depression and going home and starting the dolce vita. They don't understand that the outside world will kick them right back inside, back into their own bottomless pit. They can't get it into their heads that their own weak little souls go everywhere with them, no matter where they run.

Berlin Diaries

"Avigail," she wrings her scrawny hands. The fingers are loaded with the impossible rings designed for her by that arthritic Yemenite in Rosh Ha'ayin.

Again.

"Avigail, answer me, will you—my blood-pressure's up."

Her earrings tinkle like the bells of Notre Dame. A tiny, invisible Quasimodo makes them swing even when her chin freezes in mid-air and her head is still. She waits.

I'm lying here on the floor like a bitch. Like a bitch who's just had pups. Pressing my thighs, my belly, to the Italian marble floor. Trying to strain every trace of coolness from the heat. I stick to the air and the air sticks to me. Esmeralda being humiliated, interrogated. But she won't have an air-conditioner in the house. She doesn't like artificial air.

"She won't answer, not if you go on with this Avigail—Avigail." That's Allon. I roll my head, press my cheek to the marble. Open a slit between my eyelashes. Shirtless as he works, the romantic snob. Standing in front of the easel like Schwarzenegger in front of a gaggle of religious schoolgirls.

She tries again: "Can't I try to find out why she quit school? I'm still your mother, despite all this liberalism you've established here. Or does that no longer hold either?"

This time he doesn't answer. She's managed to exhaust him too.

The night brings no relief. The same humid air standing still. Breathing it is like dipping your face in a bowl of tepid soapy water. Allon puts out a bare foot and drags the fan closer, turns it to face him.

"Sonofobitch, leave the fan alone, turn it back the way it was, you selfish bastard." I've become practical, I'm exclusively practical nowadays.

"Avigail! Why is she so foul-mouthed? Why are you so foul-mouthed, I'd like to know? Why doesn't she answer, what's the matter with her? I don't know what to think, what to say, I no longer know anything."

Lunar Eclipse

The imported cane armchair creaks when she stands up. She goes up to Allon and stands behind him. He hates people to look before he's finished. I know that, she knows that. But she doesn't care. Right now she wants explanations. He shoves the brush into her hand. Takes out a crushed packet of Luckies, lights two, one for her, one for himself. Leans on the balcony railing with his back to her. The upper part of his back is freckled. A pale, unfriendly back.

"But why, what's wrong with her?" she insists.

But she shouldn't have touched him, shouldn't have stroked his sweaty back.

"All right, my darling, let me explain what's wrong with her." He sounds dangerously casual. She has brought it upon herself, but I'm a bit sorry for her anyway. For the last two weeks this conversation has recurred with minor variations about twice daily. He slides his hand through her folded arm. Mother and son arm-in-arm on the well-tended veranda. He inhales the smoke. "She's not feeling too well, Mum, you understand. A bit depressed. She's got such a sensitive nervous system, don't you know?" Wicked Cheshire cat. Calmly he smokes, his eyes narrowed.

I pick myself up from the veranda floor. Go inside. Drink water in the kitchen. Peck at the insides of a huge half-watermelon without taking it out of the fridge. Fragments of their conversation: "Just to understand why . . . why . . . why . . . I've a right to know . . . Quitting school . . . What Dr Fischbein said . . . such talent . . . irrelevant . . . What do you mean, she worked for him? . . . What

Boaz? . . . irrelevant . . . and why suicidal tendencies? . . . Irrelevant, I tell you . . . So she doesn't want to . . . She's incapable . . ."

Inadvisable to go back into your childhood room, when you haven't lived in it for years. A faint smell of mothballs thickens the heat, almost solidifies it. I sit down to write in the notebook Allon bought me the day he came in a taxi to pick me up from Boaz's house in the Yemenite Quarter. Poor Boaz, he was petrified. At Bezalel they hushed it up—a third-year student pushing light drugs in the school yard. Anyway, I couldn't have stayed another day there. After three weeks of idleness I slit my veins with a Japanese knife. Poor Boaz, he had no idea what he'd got himself into. A loony courier. That's all he needed. The business was going down the drain anyway, what with the police raiding every acid party. Couldn't believe his bad luck. He found Allon's number in my phone book. Searched through my bag, the little crud. Allon came, and all he said was, "Keep going like this, and the scars will come up to your armpit." He sat and watched me as I packed. The taxi was waiting outside, but he didn't rush me. We drove to Mum's place.

I lie down and stare at the lamp with the Japanese paper lampshade. It'll be three weeks before the Prozac begins to take effect, but I can already imagine the calm that will begin to dissolve into my brain cells. I close my eyes. Sinking, sinking. When will the white rabbit arrive with its teeny-tiny white gloves? Patience, Alice, patience. Tomorrow and tomorrow. Signifying nothing. Sinking.

Allon is talking to me from the darkness. When did he come in, when did he turn off the light? When did he start talking? He didn't bother to wake me in any normal way. He sits in the dark, talking quietly, in that patronizing, nasal tone . . . The pain inside me reeks of mothballs. He also wants to understand. He asks am I never going to speak anymore. Calls me Galli. Galli he calls me.

He talks about purpose. His voice echoes from afar, from the other end of the room. I can smell the scent of shampoo on his wet hair. Showered, clear-headed Allon talking to his terminated sister about purpose. When he finishes and leaves the room I'll turn on the light and write down for him what he wants to know about me, though he knows it all anyhow. Through the crack of the door, before he shuts it after him, I hear the faint sawing of an Elizabethan cello. Our mother is a heroine of a movie that will never be made, a movie about a woman with silver chandelier earrings listening to Vivaldi on a summer night in a stinking Mediterranean city . . .

Sweeter than kiddush wine, wiser than Socrates, nobler than Emperor Hadrian, blessings upon thee, Allon! You speak of purpose? Oh Allon Allon, Etruscan statuette that you are, with my brains and your beauty what shall we not achieve? Happy the man capable of believing that anything has a purpose!

You're right, dear poppet, purpose is an essential component in performing any action to perfection. Overcoming obstacles in your path and bringing the undertaking to completion. But what, in your opinion, makes a person wish to do a thing? And, more interestingly—what is it that causes the person to rise and do the thing he desires?

I say—

that thing is God's special grace for a spiderling that got caught in its own web. It is a moment beyond comprehension. Unfortunately God does not always grant his wondrous grace at the appropriate time, and the waiting can be unbearably long. Then, while you're waiting, you begin to perceive that there is no purpose. None. Consequently, there is also no reason to do anything whatsoever, starting from fighting for your existence to moving your arm, opening your eyes, or changing your position in bed . . .

Then comes the silence.

You know that it is supposed to terrify, yet you no longer feel the fear itself but only its shadow, an imitation of a feeling that used to drive you on. A two-dimensional reproduction. An insulting reminder of the emotional flesh-and-blood that you once were.

And yet, would you believe it, that reminder succeeds in keeping you alive. And sometimes, as you lie in the dark, you listen to the dull thudding of your heart. Blindly faithful, life's metronome continues to carry out its God-given mission, unburdened by questions of purpose and cause.

These days, my dear Allon, I find myself envying it. Envying my heart. That organic mass of muscles, arteries and veins. A stupid pump that simply goes on doing what it was designed to do. Signifying nothing.

3

What I like best about this ward is its name: the Clinic for Depression. Not like the usual ugly name, "Psychiatric Clinic", or as it was called at home when I was little—a madhouse. Incidentally, I'm sure the name makes all the difference to the loonies. When your address is something like "The Locked Ward, Be'er Yaacov", then between the macramé and the needlework you'll feel like bashing the duty nurse on the head with a chair, or alternatively, play with yourself while staring at the duty nurse. But here in the Clinic for Depression it's a different story altogether. With a name like that you feel obligated.

For instance, here when they do the electric, you don't find people sitting on a bench outside and announcing every time someone is rolled out: "Here comes so-and-so—got electrified." Also, you won't find any violent loonies here, or the kind who bother the hell out of you. Here even somebody who feels violent gets balanced.

Like for instance, the day before yesterday, Izrailov, the guy with the pills, was driving me up the wall. There was a quiz on television and they said anybody who guessed the answer should send it to the television in Jerusalem. They gave the other details, like the name of the street and the number, things you must write down or you'll forget them in a second. Right away I knew this time I was sure to win, no question about it. Generally, anything to do with music I win hands down. That's my territory. There isn't a song I don't know word for word, even the lousiest lyrics. Anyway, as soon as they gave the address I rushed to find a pen or something to write with, went to the nurses' station but only Izrailov was there, organizing the cart with the medications. I spoke to him nicely at first. I said, "Izrailov, quick, I need a favour, give me something to write with before I forget everything." He says, "I don't have anything." So I say again, "Izrailov, baby, lend me a pen, I'll just write something down and give it back." So he says again that he doesn't have anything, which pissed me off, 'cause I saw he had a pencil in the pocket of his smock and meantime I was starting to forget. So I grabbed the night-nurse's lamp, a kind of big flashlight thing which the duty nurse at night uses to see if the loonies are sleeping all right, and brought it down on Izrailov's head. A bullseye hit at close quarters, you could call it. Smashed his glasses to bits, and his nose became a fountain. In a second the head nurse was there, and Avishag, and the Russian Sofia, and the head nurse got an injection ready, to calm me down, as they call it. A real cuckoo's nest, that scene. I push her away, 'cause I'm scared stiff of needles, Sofia and Avishag are trying to hold me still, like Border Patrol grabbing a terrorist, and the head aims the needle—only doing her duty, right? I say to her, "Hijo de puta"—'cause she's Argentinian—"Oh come on, leave me alone and I'll calm down by myself, you're just getting me worked up. Leave me alone and I'll cool down, I'll be an angel, I'll even beg Izrailov's pardon, even though he's an arsehole and doesn't deserve it." But she acted like she was deaf, stuck the needle in my right arm, and I didn't dare push her and make the needle slip. Then I said to her, "I'll kill you," but she looked at me as if I was a cockroach and went away. Her arse under the smock wobbled like two fatsos screwing. I wanted to yell something after her but I felt the tears coming up so I shut my mouth. Sofia the Russian went to help Izrailov and Avishag said, "Come, Galli, lie down in the room. Here's this week's *Woman's Magazine*." I wanted to say I'd had it up to here with her, to stop playing the good cop, but my head began to go woozy so I lay down like she said.

Before falling asleep I thought about Bono, and how Avishag said that she'd like to sit on his face. So I pictured Avishag sitting on Bono's face, her smock rolled up, puffing on a fag. I stroked his legs and her face and fell asleep.

That's what I call balance. In Abrabanel for a trick like this they tie you up like a parcel, without the dishy U2 singer for dessert. In this nice atmosphere even a loony can become a human being.

Berlin Diaries

Such a pleasant lassitude seeps into your limbs when you start your synthetic glide out of depression. At twenty thousand feet above the Mediterranean Allon looks and feels much less adult and perfect, and I even remember that he's junior. Yes, my junior by two crucial years. In the days when I lived on contraceptive pills and passed my time, shod in vicious high heels, with paratroopers—he spent his nights on the Italian-marble balcony reading bad translations of Rilke and battling against acne.

We must look like a weird couple, but who cares. Allon is busy sniffing my wrists and the insides of my elbows. Not to worry—it's not deviate lust. Right now I'm modelling perfumes. That's right. In the duty-free at Ben Gurion Airport he squirted on me every aftershave that cost more than a hundred dollars, and now he's testing them to decide which of them he'll buy in the duty-free in Munich, before we change for Berlin. He wrote down in tiny script on his medical insurance policy which scent was sprayed where: "Galli left neck—Farenheit; Allon inside right arm—new Calvin Klein; Allon right shoulder—Tsar; Galli left hand—Zeno Davidoff..."

He pushes his nose behind my left ear. An odour of the sea and watermelon and those furry yellow flowers, how come I don't remember their name. That's Kenzo, pet, Kenzo, I tell him before his finger with the paint-rimmed nail starts hunting through his miniature notes. "So this is it!" he declares triumphantly. "That's what it is."

It was his idea. Some things you can't take away from him. We're going to Berlin. Using the money that was unfrozen, Dad's money. And it was his decision. Because now we're rich kids. Or should I say prosperous? To us this is rich.

She shed tears as big as marbles. They plopped off her cheeks, something unreal, an operatic effect on a woman whose life is an opera. The libretto may be a little trivial, but that's what librettos are like. Opera's grandeur against life's petty realism.

But why Berlin of all places? (earrings swinging wildly), isn't that where they roast Turks? Neo-Nazi skinheads with bicycle chains lie in ambush for Israeli kids in the underground stations? *Achtung kinderlach!* Bloodthirsty Palestinian students disguised as room-service waiters carry compact explosive charges in their rectums which were stretched by Israeli Mossad interrogators. Mum, Mum, we don't want to hear about what the Nazis did to us in the Holocaust. Don't want to think about grandpa and grandma standing naked with their backs to the firing-squad on the edge of the trench in Babi Yar. Especially since grandpa and grandma died a natural death, he of cancer at the Meir Hospital, and she of old age in the old house with the orange grove in Zichron Yaacov. Our blue eyes, inherited from Dad, look forward to the future. So what if Avigail was thrown out of Bezalel because she doesn't want to be an artist. She needs to be watched over. Handled carefully, as you'd handle the exposed innards of a futuristic computer program. Mustn't sweat over her, or infect her with viruses. She suffers from clinical depression with an increasing risk of psychotic breakdown. You've seen with your own made-up eyes what that dear, dear (in both senses) Dr Fishbein wrote to the District Physician. She needs to think a little. To decide in a civilized environment what kind of genius she's going to be. And Allon is already a genius. And over there higher studies are free, from national guilt and economic prosperity. And we'll write a lot and phone. Avigail likes to write and Allon has bought her a notebook with a fancy leather cover decorated with an ancient Mexican god. Ichu Michu Machu Pichu.

Nor did we forget you. Now you're free to visit your sister in South Africa. You always dreamed about it. Here is your opportunity. Rest, have long chats in the kitchen far into the night. Eat steaks for breakfast, like those racist fascists do. But anyway why should you care, you're apolitical, you think Negroes have human rights, a sense of rhythm and interesting music. Give reality a shake, suck up to fate a little—maybe it will be good to us, and if not, at least we'll be good to it. But you'll have to install an air-conditioner in the flat if you want to let it for an appropriate, operatic rent. Go, Mum, go, Hansel and Gretel.

The lights in the plane are dimmed. Beside us, the smokers, a queue of hopeful pissers is forming. Allon is listening to popular opera on his headset while I stare at Tom Hanks' weak features on the video screens, listen to the noise of the engines that are holding us up in the sky and rubbing against the ozone, breathing in the blend of masculine scents covering all my exposed body parts, and sinking.

Berlin Diaries

Before evening falls in Berlin there is a heavy smell of soot. Coal soot. They heat the houses with coal and the smell clings to the air molecules with a deathly grip.

But I'm a rundown person. I internalize the essence of this city and the nation inhabiting it via the trivial details. That's why I'm thrilled primarily by those miniature bottles of shampoo, the shoe-horn, the glasses and tiny ashtrays, all inscribed in elegant but restrained script: Hotel Unter den Linden.

Uber alles, no doubt.

You can't be in Berlin without thinking about Berlin. You can't be in Berlin without placing yourself in Berlin as in an already-painted picture with a special vacant space kept for you on the canvas. When I pull back the curtain in my room all I see is a huge grey windowless wall of an industrial building, yet it doesn't feel sombre. In some strange way I seem to belong here. Achtung, pet.

We keep teasing our collective national memories. I have no particular interest in the Holocaust, but it's simply here. The war is here. Allon: I'm told breakfast at the Reichstag is worth a try—they give you a good strawberry cake. Achtung, Allon! He's trying to overcome the morbid notions with revolting jokes. When I take a shower he advises me piously not to use the local soap, because you never know what it's made of. My baby brother is dying to fuck an East German woman. Allon (at the Reichstag café, his face full of strawberry cake): Tear up her pussy, come on her face! He thinks when one Jew screws one German he's screwing all of history, spraying good Semitic semen on the Third Reich, while singing Ave Maria. It's always easier to humiliate a single person—nations are not so easily humiliated. It takes more than contempt to bring down a nation.

We take a taxi to Checkpoint Charlie. Allon, the stingy little Yid, an infant Elder of Zion, is trying to economize. He's thinking about the future, about studies, God knows what. I tell him to cut it out, we've got enough money for several months, but he frowns and presses against the window. I pay. When we get there we buy flags, helmets, heavy army boots, Red Army decorations, pieces of the wall. I chat with the American soldiers while Allon gets bored and jealous. The younger one asks where we're staying and at once gets a warm invitation to our Unter den Linden. He's from Minnesota and looks like he has some black blood. The handsomest guy we've seen since coming to Berlin. Achtung, baby!

Achtung, Galli.

Allon's nagging me, "When are we going to Alexanderplatz?" Bargain-basement intellectual. These last few days have restored me to the older sister's proper place, and I catch myself treating him like a pedigree pup that refuses to learn where to do its business. I know it's nasty, but he really can be very trying sometimes. I'd prefer him to handle his famous sanity more naturally. I've always felt that nonchalance is best suited to our God-given gifts. But this is my brother's way, and since of the two of us he's the gifted one, he does have the right to choose any style he wishes. There's something almost religious, a touch of pagan dedication, about the way he celebrates being what he is. And is he energetic! Sometimes when I look at him happiness itself seems vulgar. But that's only envy. He's a good lad and it's not his fault that he hasn't got the sensitivities that come with his sister's wretchedness. And sometimes I find him touching—determined to visit every Berlin location that's ever been mentioned in world literature. While I chiefly want to visit the Zoo Station on account of Bono and company.

Depression? Who's depressed? I'm not depressed, I'm in Berlin.

Berlin Diaries

"Can he read and write?" Allon is stuffing his face with oatmeal porridge mixed with blackberry jam, his favourite Berlin breakfast, while gazing at my swarthy friend through the dark glass of the dining-room. The evil midget is gloating at the sight of the brave soldier stuck in the revolving door of the hotel exit. "A hard day's night, was it?"

"He's a quarter Negro and a quarter Indian, can't remember what tribe, he has a skull tattoo on his shoulder, and you make me sick with your mouth full of porridge." I turn back to the shopping-centres guide.

People I meet on trips are forever a kind of stage-set in a show seen that evening, and so they remain in my memory. Exotic, colourful, capable of being summed up in seven adjectives.

Actually, it's a loathsome mannerism. A mannerism

of travelling romantics. I think I picked up this low style from the Hungarian I met in Jerusalem, who used to tell a foolish tale about a young gypsy woman who was so beautiful it was hard to walk down the street with her. Her name was Salome, naturally. She could hardly be called Sarah or Jane or something earthy of that sort. The Hungarian and Salome wandered all over Europe, drunk with love, blind with desire and other sicknesses. They slept on all kinds of beaches, under a variety of palm-trees and fir-trees, or in attics in roadside inns that were crowded but charming, with tough, fat landladies whose hearts melted at the sight of their wild young love.

They subsisted on cheeses bought in neighbourhood supermarkets and cheap wine. But oh, l'amour, l'amour.

The festivity ended when one day they were eating some kind of cheese and sipping red wine, the Hungarian spilling drops of it on Salome's lower belly and lapping it up with his tongue which he then inserted (I'm not exaggerating—the Hungarian was given to soft porn). Sensuous Salome was about to perform a similar service for the Hungarian, when suddenly, oh dear, Salome begins to swell up and become breathless. The persistent Hungarian went on tonguing her between her legs until he realized that those were not ordinary gypsy sex moans but an ominous sign. Fortunately for Salome, the Hungarian quickly abandoned the prospect of sexual congress by the sea, sharpened his wits, rolled up his sleeves, heaved her over his shoulder in the classic Hollywood style we call "flour-sack", and hurried to the nearest hospital. There the emergency staff diagnosed a powerful allergy to the aforesaid damned cheese which they had been feasting on.

At this stage in the story the Hungarian would pause to utter a tiny, heartbreaking sigh, then with a Jack-London, tough guy's self-control would light an unfiltered Gauloise and stare at some indefinite spot in space which in the circumstances served for the horizon.

At this stage in the performance it was best to move directly to the Hungarian's knees and tempt him to stroke my thighs, because that's what he was really good at. And that's how I learned from him what makes bad stories and what makes good sex.

In the evening we come out of the gypsy flea market. Allon leans against a lamp-post to tie the laces of his Doc Martens, and catches me studying the arse of an unusually handsome Aryan guy carrying a baby with a blue woollen hat on his shoulders. "Sometimes," he says dreamily, "you remind me of that redheaded Hungarian you used to see in your first year. He was pretty intelligent, only his stories about girls were too much. And with that accent! How about taking a picture of me in front of Hitler's bunker before it gets dark?"

4

The rains started at night. I was woken up by the rattling window panes and the rain banging on the blinds. The wind was yowling outside. At first I went on lying with my eyes shut, listening to the sound effects of real winter, waiting for the next thunder, till suddenly I heard a strange noise, like a little child or a mouse. An irritating sort of twitter—"ee-ee-ee-ee". It woke me up completely.

I sat on the bed in the dark, trying to work out what was going on. I saw that the handwashing orthodox woman was rolled up in her blanket over her head like in a sleeping-bag. Marcelle the depressive was dead to the world—she was electrified in the afternoon. Everything was quiet like a cemetery, and outside a downpour.

Then I saw the old German. She was standing up beside her bed in a white flannel nightie, with her hair sticking out all around like a witch. I could see her face in the light of the fluorescent strips outside.

I couldn't see her eyes, they were like deep black wounds. Like holes in her face. So I crept a bit closer, to check her out. On her bedside cupboard lay the sweater she was knitting, a glass with her false teeth, and a carton of the smelly menthol fags she smokes. Nothing that could be making that noise, not a transistor, nothing. I wanted to go back to bed, but first I went up to take a cigarette, and then I realized it was she who was making the noise with her toothless old mouth—"ee-ee-ee-ee".

I said, "Hey, granny, put a sock in it. It's enough to drive us crazy, that dial tone you're making. You'll wake everybody." But she cut me dead and kept going, "ee-ee-ee-ee". I thought I'd make her lie down. I took her by her skeleton arms and pushed her a little towards the bed. But she didn't bend her knees, her whole body was stiff. I put my arms around her and lifted her a few centimetres in the air. She was light, like a little girl, but she got away from me and stood up again like a waxwork, staring at the window through those black wounds, and twittering.

I tried to speak to her again, in Yiddish. I said to her, "Kish mir in tokhes," and "shayna maidale", but she didn't react. I switched to German: "Ich liebe dich," and "Achtung", but the weirdo didn't even turn her head. I stood beside her a bit longer, smoking the menthol ciggie and puffing the smoke in her face. I tried to remember other words I used to know but couldn't, so I went to the nurses' station to call the night nurse to give her a shot or something, before I flipped my lid completely. I found only Sofia the Russian. She was sitting in her chair fast asleep, and I had to grab her fat shoulder and shake her hard before she understood who and where she was. I said to her, "It looks like granny's gone right off her head, so take care of her—scientifically, you know how, 'cause it's impossible to sleep. And it's scary." Sofia took the flashlight and hurried to the room, and on the way there chewed my brain with why I never sleep at night and maybe they should increase my dose of—, so I told her that their shitty medications don't work on my brain, anyway, then I stood beside her and held the flashlight while she gave granny a shot and talked to her quietly in Russian, and if I wasn't so jumpy I might have laughed, 'cause granny came from Germany, from Berlin, but I didn't say anything and after a bit the old woman began to calm down. At first she just lay down but went on with the "ee-ee-ee-ee", but then Sofia went sshhhh for a long while and stroked her arm till she calmed down completely and fell asleep. Then Sofia took the flashlight and hissed at me like a snake to go to sleep right away, but I knew that the night was a dead loss.

I stood by the window and watched the rain washing the path, bending the oleander bushes down, falling across the lighted places around the lamps. A wall of rain, a waterfall of rain. I thought about Jay.

I tried to remember what he was like the last time we met, but it escaped my mind completely. I couldn't remember when it was and how, and where, and what we said. The harder I tried the more I got upset and frustrated, till I became tense as hell, a Stratocaster string, and knew that I had to stop thinking, stop poking around inside my own head. Granny was sleeping but was still twittering quietly in her sleep and I felt I was going starkers from the rain and her twitters and because I couldn't remember that time with Jay, and I thought about the time granny came from Berlin, maybe a million years ago, and said to myself that if I didn't forget, I'd ask her some day if she remembers anything and if she knew the hotel Unter den Linden. And I thought about Berlin and the smell that was in the air, and Allon and me. But it was all blurry, like it didn't happen to me, like it was somebody else's life, a stranger's.

I threw the fag on the floor, said one more "Achtung" to granny and went quietly out into the corridor. I thought I'd walk the length of it, to calm down, but it was dark like a Negro's arsehole and cold. A hospital by night is the pits. You know there's lots of people around and every one of them is somehow wacky. They lie in the special beds with the head raised, with disturbances in their beta waves and REM. They hardly dream they're so full of drugs, and nobody cares what they do dream, 'cause there aren't enough Jungian therapists for everybody. When I reached the bathroom at the far end I went inside. I shut the door quietly, so Sofia won't hear, and turned on the light. I looked at the big mirror stuck to the wall. I saw a fat girl in too-big pink hospital pyjamas, scruffy, with bulging pimples on the forehead, small, deepset eyes, and greasy hair pulled behind the ears and hanging down like a rag. A real paintbox, only the kind used for Pollock's paintings. I tried to comb myself a bit with my fingers, then made a face like I was smiling. It looked horrible. I felt anger building up in my chest but didn't know against who, only felt my forehead and upper lip starting to sweat, so I turned it against Anita, how she always says to me, "So young and pretty," that kind of crud. Old people's natter. The kind of things people say when they don't really look at you any more, just remember you vaguely, even though you're right there under their noses.

I pressed my face to the face in the reflection till the

nose was squashed. The white areas in the eyes were yellow and full of blood vessels, the pupils the size of fleas and around them a green stain with yellow puddles. I said "Achtung", stepped back and spat a fat gob at the creature in the mirror.

That felt better and I decided to go back and walk around the corridor quietly, try to find someone who was awake. Some loony with a worldview, or stories about fucks. Even the anorexics would have been welcome company tonight. I wouldn't mind talking a while about how the little one manages to throw up three hours after meals, when nobody's watching her, and how the big one was a promising violinist in a children's philharmonic and was the daughter of millionaires from Ein Hod, who demanded too much of her so she became Baby Biafra.

But they were asleep. Everybody was sleeping. The rain stopped raving and came down at a steady rate, like toothache. Once this kind of background could put me to sleep right away. Out like a light. Generally, I used to be able to sleep. I've forgotten how it felt to push my head into the pillow, feel the sweetness of the clean bedlinen, the good laundry smell, think about something cool and drop off. I think I've been awake for weeks, may be months. Maybe always. It's like I never slept in my whole life. I decided to do something that would tire me out. I went back to the room, opened the window that looks out on the big lawn, and climbed out. The air was freezing cold and I felt I was getting soaked through. I stood on the path under a lamp and raised my face. I let the rain wash away the mug that was in the bathroom mirror, clean the ugliness off me like it was just a coat of dirt. The smell of wet dust banished the smells of cooking and disinfectants that are always there like tombstones. I took deep breaths and after standing there for a while with my face up like a dog looking at the moon, suddenly, frame after frame, like a picture developing in a darkroom, I began to remember the last meeting with Jay. I remembered we drove north from Dublin, towards Belfast. I remembered I was driving, which was madly confusing because of the left side, and Jay kept asking if I wanted him to take over but I wouldn't. And I remembered how we stopped on the sea shore. And I remembered that there was a kind of Irish light which lit up everything golden grey, and I remember the tide was out and the beach was empty and naked and I gathered big flat shells into a supermarket bag, and I remembered saying to Jay, the Atlantic is so beautiful, and he said it was the Irish Sea, and I said no, it's the Atlantic Ocean, and we almost had a big argument, but then we stopped and simply stood there and looked at the horizon as if we were hypnotized.

I remembered that we walked quietly back to the car and Jay said I should drop him off in the nearest town, because I had to get back to Dublin in time for the flight, so I left him near some pub and waited for him to find out when his bus was due, and he came back and told me to drive off, to be sure I would make it in time, and I remembered that there was this kind of thin, nagging kind of rain, not like this one but the kind that never stops and pricks the face like needles, and his face was wet when he bent down to the car window. He didn't smile, just looked at me like I was a complicated equation in physics.

I got completely soaked and it was really cold. My panties under the pyjamas stuck to my arse. I thought what weird luck that one rain can remind you of another rain. I sneezed, climbed back into the room and shut the window. The water dripped off me, making little puddles on the floor. I shivered. I sat beside my bedside cupboard, slipped my hand underneath and very carefully and quietly pulled out the plywood base, and took the Berlin notebook out of the hidey hole. I held it in my hand for maybe an hour or more. I felt the nice leather cover with my fingertips, and the Mexican god engraved on the front. I didn't read, 'cause it was dark and anyway I didn't need to.

I remembered everything. I let things come up, wash over me and melt away until the next wave. I didn't take part in any event, just watched it closely and quietly from the side, till it took its place in my memory and vanished and another wave of events, words and sensations came up. It went on and on like this till I knew that I'd been over everything, and my mind emptied. I couldn't think of another thing even if I wanted to. But I didn't. The knowledge was already inside me. I read the notebook without opening it. The work was done. I put the notebook back and lay in bed in the wet pyjamas. I didn't think. I waited for morning to come.

When Izrailov came in with the medications cart I knew it was seven, though it was still dark outside. Hospital breakfast smells announce the start of another day better than any insignificant, moody sunbeam. I took my tablets, a big white one, a little smooth one, also white, and another yellow one, and swallowed them and drank water from the little cup he gave me. Like I should.

After breakfast I knocked on Wasserman's door. I went in before he answered. I said this to him: "Doctor Wasserman, I hope you won't freak out when you hear this, but I've decided to tell you the truth. Up to now I've been dumping all the medications I was getting. I held them in my mouth till Izrailov moved on, then spat them out in the toilet. But now I'm awfully sorry, Doctor Wasserman, I swear to God. I'm asking you to forgive me and I want to start proper treatment and get well."

He looked at me without speaking, passed his hand on his forehead and his hair, which he combs in a kind of flap over his bald patch, and I expected him to start yakking at me, but he only looked at me with terribly tired eyes, like an old monkey, and said, "All right."

Then he thought a bit more and decided it probably wasn't enough for my mixed-up mind to take in, so he said, "If this happens again, you'll have to get the medications by transfusion, and that doesn't belong in the open ward."

I nodded and went out.

Berlin Diaries

Berlin days, such sweetness. We've been here for weeks and it feel like eternity and at the same time like a flash of a second. Allon says that proves we're having a ball. I've found a pharmacy where I can buy Prozac with my Israeli prescription. Nightclubs at night, wandering through the museums and streets by day. Life is like a quiet, calm river. My usual reality is slowly dissolving in my consciousness, passing before my inner vision. Ontological games. Pretend games. Everything melts. Only Berlin exists. And the illness. The illness dormant inside. It's always there, it reminds you of its existence when you open your eyes in the morning. It rustles inside like a snake slithering from the heap of dry leaves in which it had rested during your night's sleep, lying in ambush for your waking hours.

Berlin Diaries

Ho ho, a letter from Lucia di Lammermoor! My dear, dear mother. As a matter of fact, letters arrive from Her Operatic Personage every week, but they are addressed to Allon— that was the agreement, she would write to him and he would reply on behalf of both of us, because he's responsible and I'm a nut. But this time she actually added a page for Foolish Avigail. She has plenty of free time and likes to cogitate. And since she refuses to view existential occurrence in general, and mine in particular, as a chaotic mass of events, but seeks the determinist Kantian order, she is forever searching for cause and effect. In other words, now that my morbid insanity, or is it my insane morbidity, are soundly, Berlinly asleep, could I not explain why I am so unhappy despite all the efforts made and all the natural blessings which were showered upon me from Olympus, disguised as a loving family, talent, favourable circumstances and similar goodies. Oh mother, heavy-earringed mother!

I tell Allon to reply in my name, I pick up my coat and go out. A pale high sky and the sooty smell. Chased by the winds, chasing the winds. Not to think, not to think about anything.

So many colours of misery. So many ways for the buds of madness to grow. So many nuances of falling darkness. Literature has managed to play with a fairly comprehensive vocabulary, psychology somewhat less. Depression is the formal name. I personally suffer various sensations of pain, emptiness, anxiety, fear. Each of them has a multitude of faces. But despite all these, and despite their rigid fatefulness, I believe that the natural state—or should I say the primary state—of Man in general and mine in particular, is a good one. Here, I suppose, is a side that is contiguous with my mother's ambitious rectangle.

Oh if only I could rid myself of the pretension to understand the other!

Yes. The Apocalypse according to Galli.

Maybe I'll drop her a few lines after all.

5

Since I confessed my sins to Wasserman and started taking the medications again, I've been feeling rotten. The first thing they did was start bringing me down from the high I was on. I heard Wasserman yelling at Izrailov and the nurses in the conference room: "She's been hypomanic for two months and you tell me she's on a twenty milligram dose! It would have been enough to sedate an elephant, if it were true. I want you to watch her for an hour after she gets the medication, just as you do in the youth ward. Anyone would think this was your first week in the job!" Later he said to Izrailov: "Yudah, I want to go on relying on you like I always did."

And so it was. After giving me the medication either Sofia or Izrailov sat beside me for nearly an hour, to make sure I swallowed it. It was an awful waste of manpower, 'cause I swallowed it right away and didn't try to fool around, but what really mattered to them was to look good to Wasserman.

First it was lithium like once before, but then they changed it for some shit that in one week dropped me into such a depression I couldn't move from so much suffering. I lay on the bed feeling like somebody died, like I'd been raped, like the Nazis came, while outside everything was as usual. The sun was shining, the old women were knitting, and Izrailov was sitting beside me looking like a camel and picking his nose when he thought I wasn't looking. Wasserman talked to me every day, but I couldn't explain what I was feeling. One day I felt so bad, I knocked my head against the wall till I opened my forehead, and Wasserman said, "Strange, so it must be a type of depression after all. A very strange reaction to Teril." Marvellous, isn't it?

So now they've added something for the depression. Something new. Some fancy drug that recently arrived from America, and I can already tell it's not worth shit. It's called Moclobomide, but I call it Bonnie and Clyde. It's not a bit like the real Bonnie and Clyde, at most like Sofia and Izrailov trying to rob the JNF donations box. But would they take my word for it? Wasserman says to me, "It hasn't even been two weeks." But with my experience I don't need to chew my pillow for a whole month to know what works and what's rubbish. 'Cause when it works, after just a few days you feel like there's a puppy in your brain licking you, and you begin to feel sort of slow and nice.

But right now I don't have the strength to quarrel with them. I've no strength inside. Washed out. Scared to move an inch without them. I even said to Wasserman yesterday in a pathetic voice, "Help me," and that kind of nonsense, 'cause I was dying from the pain inside me, but he said, "Galli, you know there's nothing more to do, just wait patiently." So I cried like a moron, and kept saying it won't work and so on, but he was finishing his shift, and in the end they gave me Valium and I again got up in the morning feeling like a steamroller went over me. Why do they keep handing out this Valium, this old people's medicine, which gives you a headache and makes you even more depressed?

These days I can't be bothered with anybody, and it's better this way, 'cause no matter what anybody says to me I think it's against me, and even if it sounds all right the moment they say it, afterwards when I'm in bed I start interpreting it and discover that it was all against me, and that what they were really saying is that I'm nothing but muck, and were trying to humiliate me. So I try not to talk to anybody, not even with Anita and Avishag, but in the end I break down and go around nagging everybody about how lousy I feel. Then I hate myself something rotten. I hate myself right now. And everybody else. Even people I used to be so cosy with, even them I can't stand, I think about the bad things they did to me, and why I never defended myself and hurt them back. Even Jay. When I was down the toilet and being really difficult, crying or breaking things, right away he felt sorry for himself, poor thing, what a hard life he was having. Then I'd feel awfully guilty and think what a shitty person I am who can't pull herself together.

When they told me, here on the ward, that it wasn't really in my power, it was the finest thing ever happened to me. Suddenly everything went all quiet inside. A cemetery. And I was content to be in the cemetery the whole time. I pictured myself lying wrapped up in that white stuff that the orthodox use to wrap dead bodies, and people came to my grave and put flowers on it, carnations or roses, and also the little stones they put down in funerals, and it made me feel so good I wanted to melt into these thoughts like an ice cream out of the freezer, sweet and soft. Then I forgot everything. I fell asleep inside.

6

Granny died the night Jesus was born. She went to bed after lunch and when I went to call her in the evening to watch the Christian programmes on Arabic television, I saw she was lying with her eyes shut but sort of strangely, uncomfortable like, her blanket was on the floor and her mouth was crooked and drooling on the pillow.

I knew right away. I can't even say why. To make sure, I called her a few times, then I stopped. I covered her with the blanket and then climbed on her bed, lit a smelly menthol cigarette from the packet on the cupboard, wiped her mouth with the pyjamas sleeve, and sat on there till Avishag came to see why I didn't show up and found us. Suddenly I knew that what's past is really dead. Like this granny was an archaeological remnant of Berlin, a piece of the wall with graffiti on it, a dying echo in a cave.

After that I stopped eating altogether. I swallowed my pills and that's about all I could swallow. Every day Wasserman came on his rounds, sat on my bed and buggered my brain, saying if I went on like this they'd have to feed me intravenously. Avishag also tried to talk to me, brought me things from the stall outside, pitta with hummus, mango nectar, sandwiches, a vegetable omelette.

All the things I like best, but nothing turned me on. It even made me sick and I couldn't understand how I ever did eat anything. I was unbelievably tired, didn't even think, just felt full of a pain that pinned me to the bed like a heavy weight. Then Wasserman told me they were going to try electricity.

    He must have thought I was a primitive in these matters, since I didn't even look at him, so right away he started to explain that it's really not dangerous at all, in spite of what people think, and that I must have seen what a good effect it had on some of the people on the ward. Actually, it's better, much more effective than the medications I was getting, and even less troublesome than the stuff I used to get, 'cause it hasn't got any side effects.

    That day, when he finished his rounds, he came back to take me to the operating theatre where they do this famous electricity, and showed me everything: special gadgets that show the whole time what condition the electrified person is in while getting the bang. Just then the room looked to me like a NASA space lab, or a cabin in Star Trek, even though I knew that it's just a room for minor operations.

    I was thinking, Oh no, Galli, here it comes, I thought, like in the movies, and imagined the male nurses jumping on me and grabbing me by the arms and legs, pushing a rubber stopper in my mouth so I won't swallow my tongue, then connecting me up with wires and cables like a generator, and Wasserman would press something and then buzzzzzz and twitches and shaking, and my eyes rolling over like billiard balls, and then I'm dead. Just like that, splattered like a flattened steak on the stainless steel table. But I didn't feel any fear. I even thought, terrific. I thought, what sweet liberation, by Moses and Aaron and the God of Israel. Wasserman must have thought I wasn't impressed enough, so he put his hand on my shoulder, like he was going to do a Yemenite folk dance, and said, "Why don't you say something, Galli? Ask questions. It's very important that you have everything clear, so you won't worry unnecessarily, because there's nothing to worry about."

But I had no questions. I just didn't understand how electricity can put you in such a good state of mind, scientifically speaking. Why, for instance, when you happen to get an electric shock you don't have one hell of a high? How is such a thing possible? Why not every time you feel cheesed off you don't stick your finger in the socket and get a trip? But I didn't say anything, I just wanted him to let me go back and get into bed.

Turned out it wasn't so simple. When we left the operating room he told me to come to his office for another chat. I didn't know what more there was to say about things that are so straightforward. It turned out I also had to be clear about the legal side, and sign a paper saying I agree. I said, sure, and then came the knockout punch: "Keep in mind, Galli, that by law a member of your family must also sign."

I felt I was going pale and my hands started to shake in a panic. I searched my mind quickly for words. Then I told them I didn't have any family, that my dad bought it in the Yom Kippur War, my brother Allon settled in Berlin, and my mother has no idea I'm in this place, and she'd die if she found out. It would simply finish her off after all this time that she didn't see me and never got a call from me, 'cause I had nothing good to say for myself since our last meeting.

I think I started to cry. I begged them to leave my family out of it, to find some way around it without anybody else, just me. I suppose he saw that I was desperate, so he said, "OK, Galli, it's tricky, but I promise I'll check with the management of the Psychiatric Section to see what can be done." He also said, "Go wash your face."

Berlin Diaries

Cause and effect? What a bore.

When I was small I could draw well. When my brother Allon grew a little, it turned out that he was also good at drawing. The woman with the earrings realized she had two real wunderkinds. Her existential frustration was about to end, and the bells of salvation began to ring. Expensive paints were bought, the best private teachers hired, we were told we were rare children and our future looked especially bright, like a canvas by Kandinsky.

Now, years, achievements, failures and tears later, each of us in his turn and individual style, withdrew from commitment. That is to say, in exchange for other, equally glittering commitments, this time to ourselves, because even without Apollo's stooge watching over us, we no longer knew how else to live. And in the light of that known and resolved past of ours, Allon committed an act of betrayal. Oh yes, in those Berlin days, which were supposed to be a creative break from all that was troubling us, my baby brother polluted himself with an act of villainy. He went and bought himself an easel, canvases and paints. Now his room is filthy and untidy and the chambermaids hate it, because they never know what belongs there and what can be thrown away, but the management is on our side, which he says is all that matters. Permanent guests at the hotel, artists. We'll have paid thousands of dollars by the time we leave. He says it soothes him, the little traitor, and by the way, he's decided to stay here and study. Now the search is on for a suitable college and a flat. I wish I could say, what about me?

When I paint I can't stop watching myself paint, which makes the whole thing revoltingly self-conscious. I suppose for certain painters this continuous, violent observation becomes a fascinating process in itself, but it makes me ill. Sometimes it gets so bad I feel confused and physically weakened, watching me watching myself watching me. Perhaps all kinds of eccentric poets, writers or film-makers find sufficient interest in continuing to move around in such self-conscious circles, but it's devastating me.

I should like just once, if only for one second, to see the world as it is, not through my eyes observing my eyes observing the world.

Like Cézanne!

Because this is not the end of the nightmare—as well as that observation which I call the dizzying one, there is another kind, called God's observation of the worm, which happens whenever I see with terrible clarity every move I make, and thereby lose any chance of evaluating those moves. At every moment I know how interesting, simple or manipulative I intended to be. It's an observation known to anyone who's ever tried to do anything, it is the castrating goddess of creative people which keeps armies of psychological parasites in business.

These are my problems for today, quite aside from the ghastly environmental nuisance represented by Allon, who's gone crazy and decided that while he is neither painting nor earning he's going to learn German in two months. And since he famously does not recognize the limitations of the human mind, he goes straight to the top, to the classics, and for the last two days he has been muttering selected quotes from Schopenhauer, terrifying shop girls and taxi drivers. He doesn't stop chewing his thumb and staring into space like someone under hypnosis, which is exactly the sort of stupid artist's mannerism that drives me round the bend. But I treat him patiently, wasn't he the visionary of this journey, and console myself thinking about our new friend, Mo Nevin Hayes, the handsome plumpish saxophonist, who's expected at any moment to take us to buy coke. What a life! No more Boaz and his lousy grass. Long live money! This city is magic, why I can't I simply breathe and exist?

7

He really took care of business, this Wasserman. Consulted and checked and pulled strings and made me sign more papers, and faxed Allon's college in Berlin and got him to sign—which was irregular, he being younger than me—and they took blood from my finger and vein and checked my heart with that jumpy zigzag diagram, and asked questions about all the illnesses I ever had, and filled more and more forms, and the first day without rain, when some of the loonies actually went outside to catch a little sun in the area beside the ward, I was taken for the first treatment.

First thing in the morning, Avishag showed up, looking solemn in a new vampire-style lipstick, and smiled the whole time we were walking down the corridor, and didn't stop babbling about what an excellent doctor Wasserman is, how much trouble he took to get permission for me, and how much experience he's got in cases like mine, and experience in general and in electricity in particular (she made him out a regular Edison-class genius), and I mustn't worry. I could tell she was more nervous than me, perhaps on account of that woman from the mixed ward who got an eye stuck shut after a bad electrical session, leaving her like a cyclops, which made her go nuts again, and I knew from Anita that the woman's family were going to sue Wasserman and all his bosses. I tried not to think about it and hummed quietly to myself, "Who's gonna ride your wild horses" from U2, to block out the worry.

Wasserman was waiting for us in the operating theatre, with two other guys in medical costume. They explained everything again, that I mustn't be afraid, that I should understand that it's all scientific and humane. Humane. In short, that my physical and mental rights are fully protected: complete anaesthesia, complete muscle relaxation, some drying stuff so I don't choke on my spit. Five-star electrification, no less. Avishag helped me to put on a gown open in the back with nothing underneath, introduced the anaesthetist, a guy called Nimrod, and he came at me with a needle designed by Dr Mengele, into the vein. Through this enormous needle, Nimrod said cheerfully, he was going to pump in all the relaxing and sleep-making stuffs and I won't feel anything at all, at all. Before losing myself completely I tried to hold on to the picture of Avishag who was hanging around helping, her lipstick looking crimson and sick like a skin ulcer, and the black hairs sprouting from the nose of the anaesthetist Nimrod, and all the while Wasserman was talking quietly to the other guy, probably an intern, who was looking at Wasserman with flower eyes and his mouth hanging open with concentration, and I lay there trying not to think about what was happening, my heart going tacka tacka boom boom, and Bono's sweet voice going far away in my head: "Ya ya sha la la, ya ya sha la la, who's gonna ride your wild horses, who's gonna fall in your blue sea . . ."

When I woke up the first thing I felt, before I opened my eyes, was Avishag's scent in my nose, Christian Something, and saw her face over me, only upside down, and she said, "So it went all right." I said, "I'm thirsty," 'cause I was never so thirsty in my whole life. She said, "No problem," and helped me to sit up on the bed and gave me water in a plastic hospital cup, and I swallowed it in one gulp and asked for more, and the weirdest thing was that even though I was woozy and weak, I felt that something inside was sort of lighter. Sort of airy. But I didn't know what. I said, "Right, I want to go back to my room, but hey, Avishag, get me a pyjama bottom or my arse will drive the horny loonies right up the wall. Poor things."

Berlin Diaries

We struck it lucky today—handsome Mo Nevin Hayes found a flat for Allon to share with two cute Turkish girls from Limassol. I get on well with them and perhaps I'll go home via Cyprus, to wash off the Berlin soot in the Mediterranean and eat squid. Allon is hysterical. He's submitted all his documents and his amazing portfolio from Bezalal, and I'm sure he'll be accepted, but he's jumpy, keeps nagging Ted with his anxieties, and practising German words. I think Allon's so good, what's he got to learn? Probably film-making, he says. But what about me? Even narco-man Mo Nevin Hayes is leaving for Paris, where he's found a drummer to play with him, a magnificent Negro from Montgomery, Alabama, and he'll probably stay there, because the Parisians are jazz-mad, always have been, and anyway he hates Chicago, where he was born and grew up.

I ask again, what about me. I even envy Mo. And why not—he's so American, such a virtuoso, and looks terrific in evening clothes. Galli the envious. I even envy a cat crossing the street. Everything that isn't me. The gods love them all more than they love me. I alone know that. But all the same—what about me?

It's pretty obvious, in fact. I must go back and start doing something astounding and exceptional. This is it, the time has come to pay my debts, to pay the tax on the knowledge that was so carefully instilled, even branded, in me, that I'm to experience life only from the chariot of the gods, with the muses licking my neck. The woman with the earrings is waiting impatiently. I can foresee the failure, terrifyingly approaching like a tornado. I am sated with Berlin, sated with fantasies, dreadful moods attack me every day. The future looks so murky. Insoluble.

But maybe this is it. Maybe that's all there is?

I always had a vague feeling that soon all this would be over and real life would begin. But it actually began way back, didn't it? It began when I was expelled into the light of the delivery room, mucky with blood and amniotic fluid and the rest of the gunk that fills the placenta of the gravid Homo sapiens female. Ugly, blind and wet, I encountered the world. How loathsome. Loathsome and hopeless.

8

Today I laughed my head off. I was talking with Avishag and it turns out she thought Jay was an English volunteer-tourist type I met at a soldiers' bus-stop. It knocked me over. I said to her, "But you met him, didn't you? You asked him questions, talked to him, didn't you? Couldn't you tell he was Irish?" Then she says he told her he was a friend of mine from London and was working as a volunteer in a kibbutz in the north.

I thought Jay would have been very pleased. He always wanted to disguise himself, to make up stories, because he felt miserable about not being in the IRA, like his two brothers who were killed and his cousins.

The cousin he was most proud of was Bobby Sands, who offed himself by going on a hunger strike in an English prison in '82. Everybody was upset about starving Sands, except the Queen, who obviously wasn't impressed. Jay himself couldn't join up—he was his mother's only living child except his sister, and his mum, who's crazy about him, made him swear that he'd never go near the organization. It seems there was a nasty rumour about the dead brothers, who weren't protected like they should have been.

Originally he said that he wanted to get away from Derry, and had a job in England before going to Berlin, but after we got married and he came to Israel with me, I realized that he was pretty restless. One night, after we finished half a litre of Lebanese arak left over from Cyprus, he mumbled something about a training camp in Libya that he was considering. I fell on him with questions and interrogations, but he wriggled out and didn't say anything more. I knew he was lying to me and plotting things, but I had no way to check up on him, till one time he didn't come home for two days, just called at night to say he was staying with an Arab friend he knew from London. When he came back we had a dingdong battle. I freaked out, I suddenly realized he was capable of scooting off without a word. I tore the phone out of the wall and slammed it on his head, then he also got mad and said he was planning to go to Libya but not for long, and I must keep quiet or he would kill me, and if I kept my mouth shut and behaved myself, we would go to Ireland after he came back.

I couldn't believe my ears. I screamed that nobody could possibly want to recruit a pudding like him to the Irish intifada—he'd only be a liability. I saw his face going weak from the hurt, because deep inside he knew I was right.

He was always hurt, was Jay. Madly sensitive. I think it's an Irish quality. Even his skin was terribly sensitive. Two mosquito bites and he looked like he went into bee-keeping without proper training. I loved that. I loved it to death. I kissed him and bit him and loved to see the red marks on his skin for days afterwards. Like medals.

Seeing that he was hurt, I made a long speech. About real strength of character, and what we generally look for in life and what we specifically, that is him and me, were looking for. I said we both had a tendency to look too much into the abyss, till it pulls us in like heroin, each to his own personal destruction, and that we should look after each other, or else what will we have left. I knew I was being a whore, but I pushed all his buttons. I told him he must be his own man for ever, that belonging to something beyond the personal in this day and age was the same as surrender or slavery. I talked about his brothers, that I never met, and about Sands. I talked about the great loneliness that we have to accept. I couldn't stop talking. I looked at his hands—long, nervous, hothouse orchids. I thought I succeeded in keeping him with me for ever, because I was so old and wise.

Later we lay side by side, without touching, in the dark, on our backs, and Jay asked me to get him an apple from the kitchen balcony, and when I brought it he ate it in the dark, making hrrup-hrrup noises, then he gave me the core to put in the ashtray, which was on my side, but I didn't put it in the ashtray, I put it in my mouth and tasted Jay together with the apple, and thought about how nervous he was and also how amazing that we're married. I thought he was full of shit, 'cause he was living on me and didn't have anything to do himself, certainly not in this country, and I hoped everything would sort itself out. Then I think I fell asleep. Yeah, I'm sure I fell asleep then.

In those days I could still sleep.

Here also I've been sleeping lately. Actually sleeping well. Eating, too. Twice a week I get electricity. My body has gone all soft. Not shrinking, not stiff. My shoulders are flexible, I keep moving them this way and that. I walk around the corridor and rooms being sociable and nice, a real angel. I don't disrupt ward meetings, don't yell, don't interrupt other people when they speak, not even the big anorexic when she starts her usual spiel about her shitty parents in Ain Hod and how she feels like a hippopotamus even though she's a skeleton. So let her feel fat, why should I care. Let them all feel and say and do whatever turns them on, I don't bother them any more. I go to occupational therapy and take part—I don't get shirty about the classical music, I scrawl and paint childish blobs any way I like, with happy colours. Move over, Joan Miró. I help the embroidering old women to thread their needles, take an interest in their emboidery patterns, what kind of flower is this, what sort of thread. Shower every day without being reminded. Wash my hair with the Flex shampoo with conditioner that Avishag bought for me. Clean, tidy, not a nuisance, don't nag, speak nicely to Wasserman and the head nurse, do crosswords with Anita. And my thoughts are sort of calm, moving along comfortably.

And memories. Suddenly I have memories from before, lots. But not like they used to be, about insults and harm that was done to me. No. Suddenly I remember nice, sweet things. Irish lakes and Berlin nightclubs.

Something's changing.

Berlin Diaries

Before I write one more word about my usual philosophizing, I have to make the announcement of the century. Last night, trailing Mo and Allon to some fashionable pub in Kreuzberg (distinguished by having a deaf-mute owner), I met a splendid young man of the Irish nation. Looks like I'm in love (how humiliating). His name is James Douglas Buchanan, but very cleverly and for the convenience of general humanity, he calls himself Jay. Like a Gaelic (or is it Celtic) knight, he rescued me from the deaf-mute's crematorium and we spent the rest of the night polishing off a bottle of Glenmorangie I lifted from Allon's room, sitting in the darkened lobby of our dear Unter den Linden and talking about the phenomenal transition of the older Yeats and Bono's disgraceful sellout.

Yes, we slept together.

In the morning I went down for coffee by myself. I can't stay here any more, everything makes me sick.

Except Jay.

9

There's one thing you can't help noticing in movies—any movie that the director thinks is something special, Coppola or Angelopoulos or Cimino, or even any old joker without ambitions, he's sure to stick in a party scene.

It doesn't matter where the movie takes place—Vietnam, the mafia, a hospital or the house of a dead friend—there's always a scene where all the characters get together and then all kinds of shit begins to build up. At first they're all having fun, dancing, eating, fucking in the corners. Then the row breaks out, which of course advances the plot right up to the finishing line.

They especially like to put these scenes in movies about hospitals, it gives them a chance to replace the disgusting atmosphere of the movie with one that's even more disgusting. The director puts on a party with a bunch of hopeless bums trying to have a good time, which gives him a chance to illustrate the misery of being a human being in this cruel world of ours, the atomic dick that life shoves up his arse.

And if the movie is about a hospital for loonies, you can bet it will have such a scene. When it comes, it'll be the tackiest, most pathetic occasion you ever saw—loonies wearing little clown hats, drinking juice, eating cakes prepared by the nurses, and slowly going crackers—every loony in his own way: throwing fits, falling to pieces, goosing the evil head nurse or the maniac shrink, another one commits suicide, others (mostly those in the minor roles) start talking to themselves in the corners and behaving like refined loonies are supposed to behave in movies. Some make speeches, others suddenly discover the truth about themselves and begin to do something they failed to do the whole length of the movie, like stop stammering, start flying, and a lot of that kind of garbage.

It goes without saying that in a real hospital, never mind a madhouse, there aren't any parties. Never. Nobody in the management or staff is crazy enough to produce such events for genuine loonies. The nearest thing to a party here is when there's an Israeli movie on television— *The San'ani Family*, or *Cool Daddy*, then everybody comes to watch it, even Izrailov. But except for that there are no celebrations, 'cause there's nothing to celebrate.

So it was a hell of a surprise when one day the head nurse came in with Sofia and announced there was going to be a party on the second day of Purim. Turns out the relatives of some schizo woman in the mixed ward are an impresario and a singer, and they wished to express their warm regard for the hospital which was treating their batty relative so well.

As it happens, I knew that schizo pretty well, even though she's not in our ward. I used to meet her in the corridor, outside Goren's office, he's the shrink who treats her in his internship—his office is right next to the glass doors of the ward. Her name was Shuli. She was pretty fat, about my age, made up like a clown, always dressed in a jolly green tracksuit. Sometimes when I saw her sitting out there, chain smoking, I'd go out to her to beg a few cigarettes off her and chat, 'cause she's terribly funny. Schizos are usually people it's fun to talk to, they've got this shy, nervous trick that I like, and they talk a lot of nonsense if you've got the patience to open them up, only they're disconnected emotionally from what they're saying, like robots with a screw missing somewhere.

This Shuli was totally messed-up. She was getting a lot of Haloperidol, which made her legs jumpy. They didn't stop swinging and jittering the whole time she sat there, and with that green tracksuit she looked like a fat lettuce leaf shaking in the wind.

Poor thing, she really was a mess. Being in the mixed ward, she was always sexually exploited. She told me without any expression on her face how all kinds of loonies asked her to give them "oral sex", that is, a blow job, in the staff toilets or behind the prefabs by the carpark, and she couldn't say no. Then they'd threaten to tell everybody about her if she didn't do it again, and so it went on and on. She was also bothered by thoughts about God and interstellar creatures, who were God's agents on earth and had nothing to do but keep checking on Shuli to see what sort of crimes she was committing and where, and to plan her punishments.

So this Shuli's relatives, her older sister and her husband, were the jokers who were going to entertain us come Purim.

The head finished the announcement but nobody cared, only Anita said, "I hope there'll be Eretz Israel songs," 'cause that's the kind of songs she likes. And I thought, Ye gods, here comes the messiah, the party scene in the movie that I'm in, and I started to get excited for no good reason.

On the second day of Purim the ward was half empty. The families of the orthodox women took most of them home to spend the holiday with their orthodox kids. All the other loonies were apathetic, as usual, stunned by depression, deformed by the side-effects, and weren't expecting anything. I tried to tell myself that nothing would happen, but something inside me was ready and full of anticipation. Fortunately I wasn't alone—at breakfast Anita sat beside me and said, "Don't forget there's a party today, Galli."

Of course I didn't forget.

Nowadays I remember everything perfectly. Ever since the electric treatment I've been calm beyond belief. Even happy. Everybody's noticed. They say, "You're improving, Galli, great, Galli, well done." Honestly, I'm more contented than I ever was since coming to the ward. Maybe more contented than I've ever been in my life. The suffering's stopped, and there's real calm inside. Days of real happiness that I wish would go on for ever. I could say I always dreamed of it, but it wouldn't be true, because I never knew there were such places for me. But I bet if I'd known, that's what I'd have dreamed about. To be here always, protected and peaceful between these walls, and never come out again.

After breakfast I went to Anita's room to give her a facial to pass the time till the evening. There's this new treatment we've been doing lately. Anita read about it in a woman's magazine. You take all kinds of vegetables and slice them up, lie on the bed, close your eyes and leave them on your face till you get bored, and it's supposed to make your skin look nice and fresh. I brought two tomatoes and half a sliced onion from the kitchen, laid this salad on Anita's face and sat down to wait. I felt that everything had a special solemn kind of meaning, because of the party. Like everything I was doing was a symbol of something secret and more significant.

Then we had black coffee and went for a walk. We walked along the inside road almost to the main gate of the hospital. When we got to the maternity ward building we went inside and walked around the corridor a bit, hoping to see new mothers with their babies, 'cause Anita's crazy about babies. It reminds her of her grandson that her daughter doesn't let her see. But we had no luck and didn't see any babies, only some women in dressing-gowns walking like ducks, which Anita explained was on account of the stitches in their pussies after the childbirth. It made me feel awfully sick, but I asked a lot of questions about childbirth, and the more she explained the more it turned my stomach, about the pains and the water running out of your thingie, and how you lie on your back with your legs wide open and the pain's so bad you don't mind people standing there looking into your cunt, and how they give you an enema and a shave before the birth, and all sorts of horrors like that. Anita didn't understand what's to feel sick about, it's all quite natural, she said. As if nature doesn't have all sorts of disgusting stuff in it. You'd think it's all sweetness and light, you'd think nature's always so wise.

Anita said that I had a distorted view of life, and even felt a bit hurt, as if I was against her personally. Then I said I didn't want to go on talking about it, or I'd be dreaming about myself as this filthy baby pushing out into this rotten world from between the legs of some insignificant woman. Maybe it was because of the peculiar feeling I had all that day, as if I'd already had those thoughts and said those things, as if I'd already seen daisies just like the ones that were growing all over the lawn, as if I'd already waited like this for something—salvation or a catastrophe ready to happen—exactly like I was feeling today. I hoped I'd have a dream that would interpret this mix-up in my head. When we went back to the ward I couldn't eat my lunch and went to the room to sleep.

The show took place in the big lecture room, and the moment I went in I was shocked to see that the place looked just like in that scene in the movies. It was decorated with balloons, and in the corner stood a table brought from the dining-room and on it plastic cups with yellow drinks made from concentrate, and slices of cake, also yellow, on paper napkins. Loonies from all the wards came pouring in and the nurses ran around like traffic wardens, showing them where to sit. I couldn't help noticing that most of the loonies from all the wards were women, mostly old and orthodox. Shuli was there in her green track suit, like a lettuce imported from the Territories. She looked awfully nervous, her legs were jumping, her eyes were twitching with excitement. She came and sat down beside me. I said, "Give us a fag, Shuli," and she told me that when they made the announcement about the show they said there would be no smoking.

Now that's the cruellest thing you can do to loonies. Loonies, no matter in what ward or how spaced out they are, are hooked hard on fags. It's known. They smoke all the time, up to three packs a day, they cadge them from each other, light from each other, search for a light, nick matches, lend lighters, and all the rest of the hassle that goes with smoking. It occupies them, it makes them less nervous. It's one of the big centres of their physical life. To stuff loonies from four wards into one room and not let them smoke, that's about the worst thing you can do to them. And they called it a special show for Purim.

When everybody was sitting down in rows, the head nurse stood up in front of us and announced that the singer Yudit would sing holiday songs and accompany herself with a guitar, and we could join in. Then there would be refreshments and then everyone would go back to their rooms, and she reminded us again that smoking was forbidden.

Then she called the singer, who was sitting on a chair in the corner with a bald guy standing beside her. Shuli explained that this was her sister's husband, Amiram, who was also her agent, and that he also molested Shuli and groped her whenever she visited them. This Shuli must be a real sexy hit with certain types. She attracts pervs like a magnet. I said, "Does your sister know?" and she got even more nervous and said, "No, God forbid," and her legs started to swing very fast like a spinning top, and Anita whispered to me from the other side, "Stop provoking fatty, the show's starting," and pointed at the "stage". The singer Yudit looked just like Shuli, only a lot fatter and taller, and her hair was dyed rust colour. She had on tight jeans, trainers and a huge white sweater, which with all its size looked like it was going to split on her bust. This enlarged

Shuli stepped up to the centre of the floor, supposedly the stage, and said, "Happy Purim to all the friendly patients and the wonderful staff—please join me in a medley of Purim songs." Then she tossed off some crashing chords and started to sing "Purim comes!" I was shocked to see that in a couple of minutes all the loonies were bawling with her, "Masks, rattles!" as if smoking wasn't forbidden and everything was perfect. I looked around, but except for some catatonic old women they were all into the singsong. I saw that I had no partners in rebelling against it, so I decided to go out for a smoke. I said to Shuli, "Hang in there," and started pushing my way out.

One of the male nurses from the mixed ward tried to stop me at the door and the head nurse made signs with her hands like she was trying to hitch a ride. So I moved the wheelchair of Ilana the robocop that was blocking the exit, gave her a sweet smile, touched my crotch to show I needed a piss and slipped out before they could start bullshitting me their arguments.

Only when I stood outside in the dark corridor and heard the loonies' chorus from the other side of the door, I remembered that I forgot to take cigarettes from Shuli. But I couldn't go back in without catching it from the head, so I thought I'd go for a walk through the empty wards till I found somebody who smoked.

The corridors were empty and quiet, not a bit like when everybody's in their rooms. I felt like the last human being after the last atomic bomb. The last loony. I could develop the idea and make it into a book a movie a video, but for some reason I wasn't a bit amused. Just a crummy feeling, a sort of fear around the heart, nagged me and didn't leave off.

I turned to go to Wasserman's office. I hoped it was open so I could lift a few fags from his drawer. This Wasserman's a heavy user of Marlboro Lite, which are yukky, but I already had the habit that you must have if you're on the ward, to smoke whatever you can lay your hands on.

When I reached Wasserman's room I saw a bit of light under the door, and when I went closer I heard people talking in low voices inside. I tried to listen, but they were speaking very quietly and I couldn't make out a word. I didn't know what to do—they could be junkies breaking in to steal drugs, and those are highly nervous types. I thought I should run and call a guard, but then I'd be questioned what I was doing there and it would start a whole hassle. I stood beside the door for a few long minutes till the need for a cigarette got too strong, then I took a deep breath and knocked on the doorpost, and before anyone could say anything, I pushed down the handle and went in.

Wasserman was sitting with half his arse on the corner of his desk, and beside the basin stood Avishag, dressed in a smart leather coat, smoking. They were at least as surprised by me as I was by the sight of this odd couple, as I always thought Avishag couldn't stand Wasserman any more than I did. And anyway what did she have to talk to him about at night, when both of them should have been in their cosy homes, he in his and she in hers. I must have looked stunned, 'cause Avishag was the first to speak, but instead of asking how come I wasn't at Yudit the singer's show, and what I was looking for in Wasserman's room at a time when he wasn't supposed to be there, she said, "Ah, Galli. Come in. You must be looking for cigarettes." I nodded and she took out of her new coat a packet of Marlboro Lite, though she usually smokes plain Noblesse, and offered me the pack. Then she looked at Wasserman and said, "Go on, give her a light," as if he was her husband or something, and he took out a shiny electronic lighter and lit my fag.

I didn't know what to do in this comedy, though I was dying to know what the hell was going on, only I saw that it wasn't a good time to find out. But before I could open my mouth to say "Thanks" and split, Wasserman said, "Come, Galli, sit down a while," and pointed to the chair beside his desk. I looked at Avishag, but she just gave me a funny smile and didn't say anything. Wasserman waited for me to sit down and then asked, "How're you feeling, Galli?" and I replied, "Good, even very good." And he smiled and said, "I'm glad to hear it. You're looking good." By now I was totally confused, and he stopped smiling and said very seriously, "Today we had a meeting of the medical staff and we talked about you. I have something important to tell you—very soon, in a week or two, you'll be discharged."

I suppose he thought I didn't understand, as I didn't say anything, so he repeated, "You understand, Galli? You'll be free to go home, to leave the ward." Then Avishag broke in and said, "Aren't you glad?" and Wasserman said, "Well, she's a bit stunned. I meant to tell you about it in the morning, but since you came here tonight . . ."

I don't know how I managed to stand up, and my voice came out weird, small and rusty. I squeaked in that strange voice: "I got to go. Good night." I almost ran out into the corridor and slammed the door behind me.

I started to run as fast as I could. I passed by the lecture room and heard the loonies singing as if from far away, but I didn't stop till I found myself in the big carpark, which was almost empty, and leaned on a dark car that was wet with dew and took deep breaths of cold air, and there was only one thought in my head. It's all over. I've had the party scene in my own movie. It's all over.

Berlin Diaries

What a parting I had from Allon and Mo. We behaved like millionaires and bought ten grams. Then we went wild and danced in some dump full of tranvestites, till Allon got sick from the tequilas and threw up over everybody.

These last few weeks have been Jay weeks. Days of Jay and nights of Jay. He's here with me in the Unter den Linden, having quit the flat where he'd been living with his English friends before we met. The room is tiny and we're crushed together like puppies in a box. Not bad, not bad at all. Anyway, what difference does it make, I'm leaving. I'm leaving and Jay is coming with me. Yes, yes, he's coming with me to Israel, via Cyprus. There's no joy in Derry. I quite understand that he's got nothing to look for over there at present, just unemployment and more unemployment in a filthy town. He also undertands this. Probably even better than I do. In Israel, I told him, he can live with me in the flat I shared with Allon in Bezalel days—it's paid for for another six months, and we'll find him an easy job, and it's warm, and who wants to separate, who can even bear to think about it.

He said that all Irish people love music and Guinness. I never heard such rot, even guidebooks for tourists would be ashamed to put in such foolishness. He charms me anew with his silliness every day.

This morning, after Allon's farewell orgy, I woke Jay and proposed to him to become my official husband when we get to Cyprus. I got the most enthusiastic acceptance that any suggestion of mine ever met with. We spent all day on the Kurfurstendam, and bought me new platform shoes in red snakeskin. Allon said spitefully that Jay had interesting taste—for a Celtic Neanderthal.

So how can I help being in love with him the way I am?

10

All hell broke loose after the business with the pills.

At first I was in intensive care, with a stomach pump and a catheter and an oxygen mask, intravenous needles in both arms, and Wasserman like the angel of death sitting beside the bed, bullshitting away. He couldn't wait till I got back to the ward, he needed to know right away why I swallowed my whole stock, and how I collected it without anybody knowing. I can hardly answer him. I'm thinking what an asshole, 'cause what's really bugging him is how he was fucked in his own ward. Serious breakdown of control, that was. Frankly, I felt a bit sorry for the Arab doctor on night duty, who's really an intern in pediatrics and only does night duty in our wing to buy lipstick for his wife in the village. What could he do. He was perfectly correct, made the rounds with a flashlight, checked on all the loonies who were sleeping like babies with all the poison that's shoved into them. What else could he do, poor Palestinian doctor, keeping his head down. Like if nobody's playing acid-trance-ambient music and people aren't cutting each other up with knives, everything just fine and dandy, and you can settle down with the sports section of the weekend paper.

A few days after the party scene they told me officially about being discharged. "Sunday, eh?" Wasserman winked at me every time he passed me in the corridor. They were all grinning at me and making jolly faces, and on Friday Sofia brought me a little cake with chocolate cream made with margarine, and on it, in tiny candy beads: "Good luck, Gallinka!" Like they're all sharing in my joy.

Saturday night I decided the time had come. I raised the bed and pulled my whole stock out of the foot. A super collection, a regular museum. I sat on the floor and sorted it into kinds. All of the last year's crud was there. All the tricyclids—Anafranil, Tofranil, Melodil, Imipramine, Deprexan, and then the latest kind: Prozac, Faboxil, Zoloft, and those two pink ones, I forget their names, very easy to swallow thanks to the glucose. I generally prefer the imported kind, 'cause they're usually cute pills, sugar-coated in pretty colours and nicely packed, so I put them in a separate, special pile—Nardil, Paranat, shitty Aurorix and that knockout sonofabitch Teril. I went and got a glass of water and started swallowing. I hoovered them up in batches of ten, fifteen pills and flushed them down with a good drink of water, to send everything down easily so I wouldn't want to throw up. You might say I made good progress, even had a special rhythm that I made up. Chuck in, gulp gulp, swallow some more, gulp gulp again. I got up for some more water and when I came back I started on the mild anxiety-suppressants: Valium, Vaben, Tranxal, Xanax, Lorivan, Modal, then moved on to sleeping pills—Prodormol and two others I can't remember, and from them moved on to Largactil, Perphenan and Moditen, and for dessert I swallowed forty lithium tablets produced by the Ministry of Health, to toast the founders and funders of my favourite ward. At the end of the meal I crawled quickly into bed, and by my reckoning after six hours with that whole pharmacy in my stomach my arse would be ready to be donated to science, except science isn't likely to want such a poisoned arse. As I was going under, I wondered what would happen if they attached my arse, or any other part of my anatomy, to an accident victim, and how it would make him really sick to go about with an arse that was (a) not his own, (b) with complexes and depression, (c) with side-effects. Then I woke up with pipes running out of me like the national water grid. I felt sick as a dog and couldn't take my eyes off the black stuff in the tube that came out of my nose. I thought it was all the poisons from my stomach, but they said it was charcoal which has some cleaning or cleansing function, I didn't quite get it and didn't really try. I was so nauseous I thought I'd die, and slowly began to realize that they'd caught me and ruined everything, and they were actually pleased with themselves for saving my life. Only a lifebelt was missing. It pissed me off terribly, even though I was exhausted and could hardly breathe, and I said to Wasserman, who was already hanging around when I woke up, that they shouldn't think they'd tricked me, that the first chance I got I was going to top myself, and next time with violence, so he'd be fired from the ward, and the old women and all the other loonies would get hysterical, 'cause they can't stand to see blood at all, not even on a tampon—it gives them the willies. So Wasserman said he gathered that I was saying I wanted to be in a locked ward under close supervision with sedation round the clock. He was threatening me. Then he opened his stinking gob and said, "Galli, I'm talking to you as to an adult!"—that's after making threats! But I was knackered, and decided to postpone this conversation for some other time, if ever, 'cause there was an idea nagging at the back of my mind from the moment I opened my eyes, but I couldn't get hold of it, it kept slipping away. Finally I got tired of chasing after it and thought I'd lie quietly and wait for it behind the corner, to catch it when it reached safety. Meantime, from the moment they heard I was awake, all kinds of assholes began to turn up, to bugger my poor worn out brain. The psychologist, the expert on static depression, the head nurse with Katz and Goren, Wasserman's flunkeys, a cute young cardiologist, that if I was in a more solid mental state I wouldn't have minded letting him tap my chest every day before lunch, giving me a chance to tap him, maybe, on his back.

But clear head or not, I was in a really lousy shape. I understood from what they were saying that I'd done some damage to my heart, which burns me up, 'cause that's a real old people's scene.

The next day my head was still ready to burst. They took out the stomach tube and the oxygen, but the intravenous needles were still in and so was the catheter. I felt that if they didn't take it the hell away I'd rip it out and strangle somebody with it. But in fact I couldn't have strangled anybody, or even pulled out the catheter, I was much too weak, a corpse, and only wanted to rest and not have anybody talk to me, and hoped they'd soon send me back to the ward. I couldn't figure out where Avishag was and why she didn't show up. All the shitty nurses from the ward came, Izrailov came, and only she was missing. I didn't want to ask about her. I can't say why, it's like I was afraid they'd tell me something horrible that I wouldn't be able to deal with. I thought I'd find out what was the matter with her as soon as those slags agreed to take me back to the ward. I mean my ward, not the locked one, like that Führer Wasserman had in mind. To my own dear ward, the good-mood ward.

Berlin Diaries

When a man stops loving you his eyes become covered with a dull film like dust. It can happen for various reasons. Boredom, attrition, another woman. But sometimes it happens simply because his own life is in such a mess that it has no room for you. On the contrary, your presence reflects his private chaos in a particularly ruthless mirror. So it seems to me. Possibly there are other reasons that I haven't figured out yet. Maybe I don't care to figure them out. Or maybe there's no need to figure them out, or anything else for that matter. I'm drained.

Oh, and one other thing—don't bring Irish fellows to work in construction in Jerusalem. My husband Jay, for example, hasn't been working for many weeks, though at first the thought of being a common labourer in the Holy City made him look like an orchid in a champagne glass painted by Rossetti.

What an ugly, endless spring. This spring was not painted by Rossetti. This spring is a photograph on a calendar issued by the Ministry of Immigration. It is the smell of an overflowing sewer in the next alley. It's an ugly light over the Nahlaot Quarter at midday. I'm feeling lousy and got some pills from Fishbein, who also happened to mention that in my condition it would be best to go in for observation at a good psychiatric clinic. Maybe he's right, but it's not appropriate these days, while Jay is withdrawing further into himself, alarmed by the strangeness, the isolation, the loneliness, my uncontrolled fits of weeping, my perdition, his own perdition. I made Fishbein swear not to tell Mother that I'm back in the country, in case he ran into her at a concert or wherever they bump into each other.

Just after we arrived in Israel I tried to paint, but now I'm too depressed, too worried, incapable of touching a brush. Bezalel rejected my application to complete the degree course. The work I showed them from my Berlin days and the short time I painted after I returned looked too simplistic, they said, and could not justify allowing me to come back for the final year. I agreed. And naturally a year's absence wasn't enough to soften them about my old narco shenanigans. Anyway, who says I want to go on painting. I only want to feel a little bit better. One teeny bit. To rest from the pain that's starting to compress into gravel.

Fortunately, there's still some money. My husband Jay doesn't think so. He hates my money and buys only cheap Farid cigarettes, though when we met he used to smoke Benson & Hedges. I can't say anything to him about it, because I'm afraid of his grimace of disgust, though he refrains from answering me. I know—he's homesick and I feel like a cruel circus owner who's brought a rare exotic animal from faraway lands. He can't understand what's happening to me, and with typical self-centredness believes that it's because of him. My poor unhappy sweet innocent. If only I could express the clouds of compassion I feel for him. The depths of tenderness. But I'm also lonely and frightened and hard, and don't know what next.

And Berlin? What is it and where? Take a powerful telescope and look into the wrong end. That damp spot in the far end, that crack in the wall of memory.

11

Olé! I'm back on the ward. They're looking after me so delicately, like after a corpse. Only Avishag's not around. And this morning, in process of my general improvement, I caught hold of the slippery idea. I had a flash of it when they took out the intravenous. No one, none of the medical staff, ever explained how they found out I wasn't simply snoozing on my bed with nothing worse than bread and cream-cheese in my stomach. Somebody spotted it in the middle of the night, 'cause if they'd waited till morning they'd have been visiting me under a marble slab in the Holon cemetery. The only explanation is that someone found out while I was sleeping. Someone tried to wake me, didn't succeed, and then the shit hit the fan. That's the only possibility. But who? No one is allowed into the ward at night, and only Russian Sofia and soppy Hisham were watching over the loonies' snores. Maybe I was making noises in the middle of the poisoning, or sweating a lot, and they spotted it when they made their rounds with the flashlight. But as I found out later, all these guesses were crap. When I finally saw Avishag, she said simply, without an unnecessary word, "I found you."

She looked away, like she was watching the ward, but I knew she was afraid to look me in the eye, 'cause she's a thief and Wasserman's flunkey, and a whore, whore, whore. She was afraid to see in my eyes what I looked like last night when I pulled the formica from the underside of the cupboard and tore a fingernail, and even when I knew for sure that the notebook wasn't there, I still went on groping for it, like maybe I missed it, or pushed it in too deep. When I understood, I simply sat down and wet my pants.

That's what she was scared to see, the worm. She was the only one, being my friend, who knew about that notebook. I trusted her. I wanted to share a secret with her, like a little marriage between friends. A blood pact. But now she wanted to shine, to uncover more information about me, to save me. To rub her arse on professional ethics. Left me without a private millimetre in my soul, with my soul's cunt exposed, like what Anita told me about childbirth. Stripped me, shaved me and shone a million watt fluorescent light on me. Except nothing was born, only betrayal and hate.

I looked hard at her, so she'd dream about me at night, and said quietly, like a dying angel, "All right. Take me to watch the news."

Berlin Diaries

The smell of jasmine on the walls of Jericho. The smells of spices and goat turds on the walls of Jerusalem. The smell of the sea in Tel Aviv in July, of sooty chimneys in Berlin, of alien vegetation on the road above County Kerry, a smell of other people's ocean on the shores of the Irish Sea. I gathered huge sea shells in a supermarket bag, because it was low tide, low tide now, and the shore was exposed, naked.

 Beloved, eyes of distant lakes, eyes of Irish lakes and Belfast brown-brick houses. My sweet tender beloved, eyes of distant lakes, my sweet, love of my life.

 I'm learning to drive on the left, I grip the wheel tight because things so easily slip out of my hands, so I'm holding the wheel tight, I haven't much experience, but I can always stop on the verge. I'm taking you home, after we've been to the film festival in Cork. I'm taking you home. You're saying that in a month, tops, you'll be back. Monstrous fat gulls are walking on the sand.

12

Lately I hardly talk to people. Only to the speech therapy woman. I can't even be bothered to bully Avishag, and she's also going through something, I see her walking around looking so-sad, and speaking softly like an actress in a

French movie. But I'm not a bit interested in her anymore. Nothing feels important. I take what they give me, I don't make trouble of any kind. In fact I'm getting what they used to give me at the beginning—Anafranil, and a little Perphenan for sedation (not more than eight milligrams I think, though you never know, with the pills being by themselves, without the packet). On Sundays at three, Tuesdays at eleven-thirty and Fridays at one I have physiotherapy. Sometimes it's with Amalia, and sometimes, mainly on Fridays, with the student. It's nicer with Amalia, maybe because she's a woman, even though you don't have to undress. I think my hand's a bit better, I can move the fingers and can even hold soft, light things that fit. The leg, well, they push it this way, that way, turn, bend, but I don't see any change yet. Amalia says it'll take time, not just exercises.

And the face... The face is clapped out. The whole left side doesn't move. And I can't see anything through that eye. My smile is really terrifying, I saw it in the mirror, but my whole expression's off-putting, like a Nazi or a KGB. That's even when I happen to be feeling positive. In short, I look a godawful mess. But what's really scary is that it doesn't scare me any more, not a bit. In fact, I don't give a damn. That's what's scary. I go to physiotherapy, I do the exercises by myself like they tell me, swing right, swing left, tighten, release, just like they tell me to do, but inside it doesn't move me at all. So help me God.

Then there's the problem with speech. When I woke up in intensive care with the catheters and tubes and all, I felt that my speech was peculiar and the words weren't coming out right, but I was weak as a kitten, so I thought that was why. They said I was in a coma for six days, which was real weird—to think that so much time passed, when I felt in my whole body that it was just a few hours ago. So probably by the time Madam Avishag the Discreet actually arrived, I was already snuffing it. Then when I got a bit stronger they told me that now I'm paralysed on my left side, with a damaged heart, and I'll have to use my left foot to talk, like that sexy hunk. And I'm not allowed to smoke. Why? Because.

But even that doesn't matter. All I want is to stay in the ward. I think about it all day long. It's an open ward, not for incurable loonies. Here the loonies are supposed to recover, meaning, to become halfway normal after a few months and go back to making their families' life a misery. I need to be transferred to a locked ward, but a normal one, not full of wankers and imbeciles.

Only right now I've nobody to talk to, my head is heavy and thick and the thoughts get to the middle then scatter and disappear. To the middle—then drop. To the middle—and boom. To the middle, and that's it, can't sort them in rows. That slag Avishag, why can't she help me think. I must stay in this ward or find another one. I must.

Berlin Diaries

The ground is slipping from under my feet. The ground is slipping, I feel my insides getting foggy. I need to throw up, it helps for a moment. God I'm in such pain, such shit. What's more, ashamed of being in pain. What a miserable comedy...

Boaz says: "So how much money did you and your brother blow on that Berlin trip? You guys are nuts—my God, you could have got a mortgage, bought a flat, rented it out—you'd have something to show for it. You're both nuts."

All day long he smokes grass through a bung made of a small bottle of mineral water half filled with revolting water brown from nicotine, gurgles "glug-glug-glug", his eyes popping while he's trying to hold the smoke a second longer in his lungs. Incidentally, this grass is a great hit and next week we're going to sell all the remaining stuff.

Here we go again, Tel Aviv, summer. Me here. I couldn't bear to stay on alone in the flat in Jerusalem. I waited for Jay at the airport the day he was supposed to come back. I didn't mind wasting those hours. It does me good to see a plane take off through clear tears, I love you terminal bello mio. Boaz gets uppers for me, they keep my head above water most of the time. He's good to me, my pain doesn't frighten him, he even finds it interesting. Something special. He only made me promise not to hurt myself—"Don't go topping yourself again, you nut." It's a condition of letting me stay here. And of course he insists on sleeping with me, though I function like a corpse. But he even finds that attractive. "I'm nuts about your phlegmatic arse."

I'd like to kill the people who glorify pain, who find a dark, elegant beauty in pain! To them, suffering contains a searing, rich existential sense which is well worth the price of some discomfort.

They're brutes. They're ignorant. They've never known the ugliness of pain. Because pain is nothing less than the god of ugliness.

I've always been ashamed of pain. I've always been ashamed of the shame. The crummy sex-appeal of happiness and perfection seduced me too. Who knows shame? But I mean—immense. Dreadful. Searing. Yuk, searing shame, how could I write such a moronic phrase . . . Searing shame, flame, maim, dirty Galli's on the game.

I know shame. It's one of the most revolting emotions that I store in the inventory of my feelings. Emotion means: ugly, sticky, the lower gut . . . A person with emotions is nothing, a zero. Doesn't frighten anyone. Not one. Such a person is flabby, slack, feeble. A pathetic creature moving in obedience to the set of reactions it developed to external stimuli. A trained laboratory rat that runs when a red light comes on and salivates at a green light. What's more, this rat is attached to the student who cleans the lab, it licks his hands when he brings it leftover stinky cheese from his fridge. That's what emotions mean to to me.

But do you know when people acquire a value, when

emotions become worthy of interest and appreciation? You know when people become dangerous?—When they act.

That's it. Emotions without action belong to unintelligent people, to bad poets, to men that women wouldn't piss on, to women who'll never hold key positions in the workplace. To losers. Humanity has always had this basic law. It hasn't always succeeded in weeding out the emotionals, but it certainly tried.

Me, I'm exactly that—an anxious, pink-eyed rat. I can't do anything, I can only feel. I feel everything, like some state-of-the-art radar—every little breeze, every movement of atoms in space. I'm a skinless pink rat. I can hear the gurgle of filth in the sewers, and the fluttering of a butterfly in faraway Shangri-La crushes me with pain. I don't know how to do anything. I don't know how to walk, how to talk. A fat cocoon that will never ever turn into a caterpillar.

I want to scream that I'm in pain, but I'm ashamed. There are people who are driven to act by pain, but pain only causes me pain. I know why people don't confess their pain, why they're afraid to express their misery. They feel that if they spoke, if they defined and localized their misery, it would take on substance. But misery has substance from the start!

I say, "Be clear, Galli, define a purpose." But I have no purpose. The possibilities are too numerous to bear . . .

13

Some weird scenes going on here. Everything's arse-backwards. Now that I'm a KGB face, the phantom of the opera, I get special treatment. Avishag, like I said, is playing it distant, French-movie style, all mournful looks, no more my pal. The whore. When anybody, like for instance Anita, asks what's up with Avishag that I used to latch on to her arse but not any more, I don't answer. It's not my fucking job to explain nothing. I owe no explanation to nobody.

Now that they've found the "diaries", they're trying to creep into my soul. Only for treatment purposes, of course. Got a pile of information, got a swollen head, wrote on my medical file "Avigail Portnoy-Buchanan", like now I'm Jay's official spouse till death etc., which I wish would hurry up. Then it'll be—"the widower Jay Buchanan". Terrific! He'll be able to walk proudly to church with mama. A good Catholic boy without a Zionist-fascist-Jewess estranged wife. Now they also know all about the time in the Yemenite Quarter and that I worked for Boaz. The lot.

You want more? They got hold of my mum and put us together in a room, not alone but with Wasserman, the head nurse, the test psychologist and Avishag. As soon as Mum saw me in the wheelchair with the twisted face and the rest of it, she started to howl like at a funeral, with her mouth open, real loud. I got scared shitless thinking I was going to fall to pieces, 'cause then I'll have had it—they'll take me up and start giving me the hopeful treatment. No way! They'll make me talk like I used to, and I'll try to be something special, Mum's pride. Shirley Temple. So I kept everything bottled up tight. I know from experience that the more I resist the more I remain strong. So I resisted like a tiger. Wasserman started with his usual bullshit from recent days—like if I say, "What's with you?" he goes: "Galli, why do you persist in speaking in such uncouth language? Nobody wants to hurt you, nobody's expecting anything special or unusual from you, I'm only asking you to reconnect to yourself. Can't you see that the only person you're fooling is yourself?"

I spat at him, but the gob fell on the front of my shirt, which pissed me off worse, and I got really stressed by the whole scene with my mum and not being able to budge. I said to him, "Don't bother to smarm me with your fancy talk, asshole. Uncouth?—your crippled sister's uncouth, and don't tell me what I must connect to, or one day I'll connect you to a high tension socket." Then I ran out of things to say to him so I just screamed "Crazy sonofabitch", but it didn't come out too clearly, and also what I said before wasn't too clear, and I felt I was going spare with this scene that they got me into, and making me ashamed before my mother.

She didn't stop crying the whole time. She was totally broken up by the paralysis. Her earrings wobbled in her ears like snot in the nose of a crying child, and she said to me, in that sweet voice she keeps for special occasions, "My girl, my darling love."

I had it up to here with all that crap. I wheeled myself

back to the room and wrote her a letter in fine language. Then I got so scared I swallowed it.

    . . . All right, then, Mum, here come the sober insights to wake us up. The grief-stricken queen, the naked princess with her eyes ripped out, and the prince sleeping on a pea in Central Europe . . . All the myths and fairy tales are at your feet . . . Flame maim blame . . . I'd add "vain", if you hadn't cried so bitterly out there in the conference room . . . But who can judge a grieving mum . . . Clichés and quotes and rub-a-dub-dub . . . The essence of life rub-a-dub-dub . . .

    Love and disillusion . . . Incidentally, in view of that humiliating conference, in company with state officials with power to decide our fate, if you'll allow me, I'll clear up some facts for you. Well then, when I was hospitalized, it was not because of a paranoid psychotic episode, as they said, but as a result of poisoning caused by systematic overuse of Ritalin and uppers, two stimulants and not of the best quality. Naturally, Boaz, being a dope pusher, did not choose to raise the point with the doctor on duty when he brought me in, and since I recovered quickly and went back to my good old depression, I did not see fit to mention this detail to my kindly carers. Incidentally, Boaz is that curly guy with the nose stud who visited you about six months ago, introduced himself as a friend who was going to visit me and Allon in Berlin, and took some books and clothes. I lived with him till the hospital, but we knew each other back in Bezalel days when we were lovers. I hope you're not going to collapse when you hear that he's not a translator from Sanskrit, as he told you. He lied so as to amuse me later. I was in bad shape . . . Love dove shove . . . Now listen carefully, it's very important: I wanted to be here, in the hospital, at every moment, and I still want it. I'm begging you, I'm pleading with you, to avoid making the slightest effort to take me out of here so as to look after me yourself, though I know you'll feel duty-bound to do so. It's hard for me to fight and bargain in the state I'm in, so please please, respect my wishes and don't make it harder for me . . . Love a dub dub . . . Give my love to the prince who's turning over on the Berlin pea, and forgive him with all your heart for lying to you about me for so long. We all meant for the best, only for the best. Right? Burn burn burn. Finally I wish I had a tiny flicker of courage to dare to ask you to forgive me too, but there are no such words, they haven't yet been coined, so I'll say again love a dub dub, and in my mind kiss all the rings on your fingers, one by one, and hide in your made-up eyes, and cry while the tinkling of your earrings puts me to sleep on an eternal, unfading A-minor note. Love love love love love. Avigail.

14

They told me they are moving me to Shalvata, to a locked ward, 'cause I took a fork from the kitchen and stuck it into my left cheek. I couldn't cope with this "maybe it'll get well in time." My arm got real well, the leg's also getting better, slowly, but my mug's a mess—and everything falls out of my mouth, especially bread or anything that needs chewing. Yogurt and cream cheese I can manage OK.

But these days I don't really eat much. I've got no appetite and don't have the patience to chew. I'm getting Anafranil like before, but they said they'd change it for something else, 'cause I've become too phlegmatic and I sleep some ten hours every night, and then in dribs and drabs all day.

In the evening Izrailov handed out the medications, and just as he was leaving Avishag showed up. She said, "Come, Galli, let's go out for a bit." We went out and she wheeled me straight into the bathroom and shut the door and gave me a dramatic look: "Why do you agree to take the medications?" I thought I was going mental, but said to myself, hang on, Galli, let her have it this time. I said, "Tell me, asshole, what are you fucking Wasserman for, if I still have to explain to you that if I wasn't on antidepressants, with half a body gone, half a face paralysed, a clinical mental illness and a shitty nurse like you to look after me, I'd have topped myself long ago? With a bullet, not pills—get it?"

So she started to talk real fast. She couldn't stop. She said she understood about the fear, and about believing that you must be really good and really talented, and that you need to have everything special and just right, and not to be an ordinary person, but one that's really unique, as well as beautiful and interesting and with style. She got into a flat spin and went on and on, and said it was like going to Berlin and being admitted into the top schools and never saying anything stupid, or especially stupid, and never having a bad smell from the mouth or the pussy, and being wicked only in an elegant way, and not hating sex and not giving a damn about anything, but knowing what really matters . . .

She was holding my hands the whole time, and her hands were getting awfully sweaty, till I got the point and stopped her, and forced my face so that the words would come out as clear as possible, and said to her, "I understand what you're saying, and as you can see for yourself, I find my own solutions. I do love staying in psychiatric hospitals. Surely you've observed this fact."

She was a bit stunned, but shook loose in a second and turned on the tap again. She wanted to encourage me to leave the ward and go back to my mum and stop being depressed.

I've never, but never heard such crap—that I should quit this place of my own free will? I bet she'd have tried to get me to wheel myself to university, or she could drive me over there every morning. This was a total failure of communication, total. She couldn't get it into her rectangular brain that I'm really and truly a loony. She was thinking that if a person chooses to be a loony, then she's not really a loony. She was so primitive she didn't understand that it's a matter of choice like everything else. I wanted to get it into her head but I didn't have the strength to keep talking. I took my hands out of hers. They were wet from her sweat, so I dried them on the pyjama trousers and wheeled myself back to the room.

In the morning the psychologist from the group therapy came, and Sofia, and they took me to Shalvata. They dressed me in jeans and made up my face with Sofia's lipstick. It was a great ride, I saw orange groves, and the driver had the radio on full volume, and then there was a musical quiz and I knew the answer right away. It was the opening of Van Morrison's "Moondance". I decided that this time I was definitely going to send a postcard and win. I made a note in my mind to remember the address for replies: "The Broadcasting Corporation, Romema, Jerusalem." I repeated it to myself the whole way to Shalvata, so I'd remember it once and for all.

We'd Talk About Love

A

Wake up with eyes shut. Elisha. Seconds of conscious existence outside reality. Quiet. Pleasant. The mind awake, empty of thought. Candy floss.
    A moment. The mind moving into gear. First sensation. A millstone on the chest.
No explanation. Sensation only. Meantime.
Viscous, sticky weight.
Memory creeps up to join awakening. Noise of concrete mixer. Engine. Vehicle. Another one. Morning. Get up, Elisha, editorial board today. Reality. Memory. In a moment.
    Another second.
Got it.
Mushmush.

Lunar Eclipse

Smack lips. Mouth tastes like shit. Shouldn't smoke so much before sleep. Can hardly breathe.
Mushmush.
A slight change of position.
Meantime memory sharp and nagging—
Mushmush.
Did he come back last night?
Didn't come back last night.
Alley cat.
Yesterday Elisha called the ballet company, ashamed of himself.
The woman says, He hasn't been all week. Since Sunday. And today's Wednesday.
Yeterday he heard but didn't see him.
In the morning, heard coins jingling. Falling out of the pocket of corduroy trousers from Amsterdam.
You crazy, Mushmush? I'm trying to sleep. You need change for a cab, get it out of a cashpoint, pest.
When are you coming back today? Don't know, have to go straight to the shop after the lesson, Itzik won't be there today, after that—I don't know, there's a party somewhere, maybe I'll stop by for a shower, maybe not, taxi's waiting, I took twenty shekels, got to run.
    Didn't stop by to shower.
Elisha waited till two then fell asleep, couldn't hold out. Daytime animal, doesn't function after midnight. Bourgeois. Editorial. Maybe I should buy a computer after all. Decided against it. Man of principle. They all type their rubbish in straight from home to the editor, only Elisha writes by hand

and walks five kilometres on foot. Unbelievably athletic. Toddles into meeting, eye corners sticky from the night's discharge, which he rolls into pills between fingertips. Goddamn daylight. Forgot to close the shutter last night.

    Rising now, to the kitchen.
Mushmush starts with smokes. Two cigarettes. First thing. Staring at junction of wall and ceiling.
Elisha—How will you be a dancer, with such quantities of nicotine in your lungs?
Mushmush—So I won't.
Elisha—You nervous or something?
Mushmush—Just waking up.
Elisha—I don't need to talk to you, no problem.
Mushmush—So shut it.
Elisha—Great, so now I'm a nag.
Mushmush—Make coffee.
Shuffle into living-room, sofa's empty. Didn't come home. Scumbag. Where does he hang out. I'll go over to the shop today. Cheats shamelessly. Doesn't even pretend. Little whore. Let him go and live in Power Park, the bastard. Everything's aching. The whole body. Even toes. Fridge. Cocoa. Now a pudding. Sugar, for energy.

    Fat. Getting fatter. Don't have the strength to think about it any more. The Mushmush is a rail, Bangladesh. Eats like a pig. Gobbles a container of ice cream in the evening in front of the television. Oriental. That's his build. God, such thoughts. Poor Elisha. Attracts bad thoughts like flies. Mushmush is beautiful. Twenty-three. Why would he need a fatso like me? Though I do have something to offer—

I'm refined, cultured, and he? Gutter child. Gutter! Thrown out of every kibbutz in the land, how many years of schooling? No idea, I know nothing about him. For months he wouldn't tell me his real name. Elisha says, What's Mushmush? Are you a cat, a dog, Mushmush, Mushmush—sounds like a husband's nickname for his wife when he wants to play house. But he, usually content to forgo every scrap of independence, digs in his heels—Mushmush. Elisha was ashamed of himself but finally sneaked out the ID card—the boy is innocently cavorting at the ballet, and me . . . What a photo! Uncompromising mugshot, almost artistic in its black and white horror. Oh my Mushmush, aged sixteen, frizzy hair, pimples like tiny volcanoes ornamenting his forehead and some on the chin . . . Nissim Ohana, birth date 1971, father's name Babar, mother's name Joelle, address . . . Oh my tender Nissim Ohana, brown startled Nissim Ohana, jungle boy, Mowgli-monkey, a fawn in flight, a fleeting arrow, my wildest deviation.

B

The mother base—the editorial office.

Elisha thinks: ridiculous to hang about here while the cow types. But can't rely on anyone. Boyarsky says: Hey Elisha, take it easy, why worry, your writing's legible, she types, I check that it's OK, what's an editor for? And Elisha always replies: Ari, me you don't edit, so let's talk about love instead.

He's choking with impatience, she'll never finish, and the boy, where is he, the little tart. Even if he gets out of here in fifteen minutes, there'd be nothing to do. The Mushmush doesn't start working before three. Afternoon shift. Some job he's got—in Itzik's jewellery shop. *Objets d'art*, he calls it, little fool, showing off—art nouveau, art deco, retro. Undoubtedly a potential snob. Earns peanuts. Has a talent for business. All orientals have. Mum. Phoned yesterday and immediately started: I took Sedistal, had a soft motion, long jump just like Carl Lewis. Felt he could strangle her there and then, electrocute her through the wire. Controlled himself. Since Mushmush he's been speaking to her less and less. Mushmush always picks up first. Always. Rushes to the phone as if the place is on fire. Elisha always asks, Why are you running, are you expecting anything in particular? enunciating like a primary school teacher. And Mushmush—I'm expecting something good. Particular enough for you? Fool.

Elisha grins. Mushmush, holding a joint, is chatting with Elisha's mother. You feel pressure in the stomach? he questions, and in the rectum? he investigates, colitis! Showing expertise, not to worry, he comforts, lucky it isn't something worse, he reassures. A fatalist, an angelic cherub, a virtuous saint. I also suffer from pressure in the rectum, he confesses. What a blabbermouth. Giggling with pleasure at making Elisha laugh, the clown, pothead.

And she hasn't a clue. It's forty years since I popped out of her flabby womb, forty years I've been breathing the air of this world, eating the food she cooks, listening to her talk, ageing before her watery eyes. And she neither sees nor hears anything, pathetic human mutation that she is, amazing that she gave birth to me, of all people. A benighted primitive, a Czech.

Eat at her place on Friday. Every Friday. Mushmush came along once, just felt like it. She whined to him that Elisha hadn't settled down. Marriage? Mushmush asks. For instance, she says. Never mind, he assures her, there's plenty of time. Yes, but she'd like to live to see grandchildren, she's a sick woman, who knows how much time she's got. What's the matter with you, Sarah? he scolds, you're still young, everything's still before you, overdoing the flattery a bit, even she won't swallow that—but it seems he underestimated her dumb animality—she swallowed it whole. Watery eyes dripping, she even sniffles, pats him on his head, sighing like a whore under a sailor. Bravo Mushmush. Take home the leftover cholent and carp.

The typist has finished. What a monster, eyes like a carp. Hate everybody today, go down the corridor, step into Boyarsky's room. The creep's busy. On the phone. Authoritative. Childish. I fucked him. No one to talk to to. Go downstairs, cab. Three more hours.

Dizengoff. Maybe run into someone.

The corner of Frishman. Not a soul. Just when you need them. Could go to the shop and ask. Don't want anyone to think there's something wrong. Itzik's an old woman. Hate him, hate everybody. Hate myself. Go home, Elisha, you idiot, go, he'll come home when he feels like, you can't hold him against his will. Maybe he sensed something and panicked? Nonsense, paranoid nonsense, there's no way he could find out. Try not to think, Elisha, not to think. You've worked this out with yourself. No need to wallow in your sinful quagmire every single day. You'll burn in hell for ever. I know, I'll burn, it's my one consolation. But there is no hell, Elisha, you scumbag. There's a good reason, good reason why the beast is sucking at your heart. You'll pay for it. Oh yes, I'll pay for it, I pay for it every second I breathe. Filthy murderer, and what about him? Can't think about it any more, lust won. The body won, that's all. That's it, so crucify me, what can I do, what could I do? Talk, you creep, talk. He has a right to know. Drop it now, enough. Full stop. What have you done, Elisha? Killed a man. Had no choice. If he knew he'd leave. You didn't check, you could have taken precautions without telling him, goddamn condoms. Beneath you, is it? It's done, he'd never have guessed. But supposing he did? Eight and a half months together, he'd have suspected, sure, he'd have split, the coward, the startled doe, Bambi, it would have scared him off. I couldn't risk it. Couldn't take a chance. I love him, I'm dying, dying . . .

No, sweetie, no. You're alive.

You're so very much alive.

C

Gazing into the shop window of a perfumerie. Drifted off again, Elisha. The same thoughts for the umpteenth time. Must snap out of it. Break the cycle. What revolting earrings. Wonder how much for the Yves St Laurent. The little one loves it. Lemony. Lean on the counter. Air-conditioned. Pleasant.

May I help?

(Yes. Drop dead. Ugly mug, orange lipstick melting into wrinkles around the mouth, fleshy.) How much is the St Laurent for men?

(Mushmush's shaved chin.)

Eau de toilette or aftershave?

Aftershave.

(Shaves with my razor, kibbutznik, no sense of privacy.)

No, better the eau de toilette.

It's a little more expensive. Depends what size you want.

(Mushmush's size, nosey. He always cuts himself shaving. No patience. Always in a hurry, hyperactive. Can't sit still for more than ten minutes. From club to club, my slippery Tel Aviv tart.) Forget it.

Thank you, I only wanted to ask.

Drop dead.

Walk down Dizengoff, sweating, two and a half hours to go. Could wait at home, in the air conditioning. Horrible summer. Why not travel. Where. Some place in Europe. What'll I do there. Adventures and experiences.

Look at this street. People. Such boring thoughts. If only it were possible to remain conscious without thinking. Arlozorov. Why don't they change the blowup photographs in Faraj's windows. Ugliness spreading all over life.

Cross the street. Sit down. Cigarette, mineral water. Something to eat? No, not yet. Wait, do you have gefilte fish? All right, with bread. Horseradish. Elbows sticking to the formica, lagoons of sweat under the arms. Perhaps stop by the house after all. Change shirt. Will take at least half an hour, if he walks. By the time he gets there it'll be almost three. How did you find work in an antique jewellery shop, Mushmush—the most antique thing you ever saw was your sneakers. I know Itzik, the owner. Where from? From town. Whore.

Maybe nothing happened. Maybe it's all right. Come on, Elisha. Eight and a half months, fucking, razor blades, toothbrushes, everything warned against.

Anal oral genital
Hand job
Hand job my arse
Mushmush with little children's enemas
Special size for children
Fifty ml
For when little children are constipated
Or when little children practise buggery
Then it is best
To pop into the pharmacy

Mushmush's enemas are in the medicine chest
Plump transparent soldiers in pointy orange caps.
Knights of the round arse. Brilliant Elisha, such scansion, such rhymes.

    Brought paper napkin and cutlery. Where's the gefilte. Hungry. Horseradish.
Oral anal

    Go back to shrink? Two years with Kaplan was enough. And expensive. An hour of confessions. Better become a Christian. But maybe a support group, helpline for the distressed, not an overall repair of the soul. What's called counselling. Counselling. Sounds even more revolting than "contacts". Since Kaplan stopped smoking every exhalation from Elisha's nicotined mouth pushes him closer to his grave. Started to niggle. Surely he can suffer a little for the money he charges. Greedy bastard. Gefilte. Carrot slice too thick, not thin like mother's. Enough! Don't think. Not enough salt. Can sprinkle some. Not the same. She's a gefilte artist. Going into hospital for observation. Colitis. Yesterday three motions. I'll kill her one of these days. Informs me every time there's an opera. Knows I'm interested. That Pavarotti event was too bad. Boring popular hits. Perhaps travel after all. Go to operas. Where's the money for it. Could send in my column. Wouldn't be enough. Europe's expensive. Boyarsky's arse's got too big. Won't pay enough. I taught him everything he knows. Invented him in fact. That little jerk Boyarsky—a newspaper editor, my boss . . . Funny old world. Why don't I have any ambitions? Maybe because I'm an only child.

Didn't need to envy anyone. Ha ha. Finished eating but still hungry. It's stress. Hey, you! Doesn't hear. Wave— hello hello. Finally. What else have you got? Jellied calf's foot your mother

With a lot of gravy on the mash. Heard through her back. Marlboro Lite. Two left. One now, one after the food. Matches. Left them in the perfumerie. Shlemiel. Mother. Don't think. I'll kill her. Friday again the day after tomorrow. I could stop reporting in, as if to a superior officer. Impossible. Why. Because. Subject closed. Don't open it any more. Simply report in every Friday. Period. You can look into everything, except this? Right, I look into everything except this. And Mushmush? My sin, my great sin against my lover is unquestioned, like my little act of charity to my mother. These are my faults and defects in their existential essence. What a firm man you are, Elisha. Vomit me out of myself.

We're dealing with a man who is aware of his own value.

Thinking about Rimbaud. Jean Arthur. What's the point of translating poetry. Let them learn French. Stuck with this translation for six months now. Every time it looks like it's been caught, it gets away. Slippery Arthur. Playing with the language as if he owned it. Sweetheart. A screwed-up kid, little genius. At my age he was worm fodder. His face on a postcard Yoni sent from Amsterdam. Plumpish. Cold eyes, heavy, rounded, pinchable chin, what a pet, God, and Mushmush's chin. Can't pinch Mushmush's chin—bony, tight brown skin. Razor scraped.

Lunar Eclipse

        Trembling hands
totally neurotic
anal oral
he should use his own razor, for heaven's sake
always cuts himself
I did for him.

    Franz dying in my arms. A huge gaunt bird. Plucked eagle. Forty kilos. Doesn't respond to AZT. Nothing for it, begged to die at home. Weak. Can hardly speak. Pain knocked him unconscious. Morphine. Don't carry him to the bathroom, don't tire him out. A bowl of water. A towel cut into washcloths. Armpits, neck. Holocaust and Heroism Day for Elisha Fliedl. Purple-black patches. Kaposi sarcoma. From now on it'll gallop, a few weeks, maybe a bit longer. Radiation treatment. Handfuls of yellow hair. Franz is blond. Blond. Franz's face gone slack, disorganized, undisciplined, like an old man's, get him to swallow the drops, thick white ones, against throat fungus. Foam in corners of mouth. Tissue. Boxes. Nausea after treatment. Kaposi's sarcoma. Franz in profile facing window. Tremulous lips. Diagnosis positive. Sweats so heavily, the bed is soaked by morning. And the fever won't go down, won't go down. Tired all day, diarrhoea, Franz baby, get a check-up, maybe it's the flu, avoids looking in my eyes, heart thumping, and nausea. Stop drawing it out, get a check-up. Franz at the window. In profile. We're done for Elisha darling. This is it. Two years together. I'm done for. I hate you Franz, dirty Nazi, mother, Holocaust, Nazis, murdered us, will come back to murder us, any moment now the next Holocaust,

We'd Talk About Love

Nazis everywhere, dirty Franz what did your father do in the war, killed me, queer, fascist thug, blond Aryan, hanks of hair on pillow, how this body can still draw air into its lungs, bladder infection, antibiotics. A joke, dragging it out, pisses in bed, Elisha, you coward, change the sheets, you wanted to take care of him, God what a fool fool fool, in denial they call it. I've been fucking him for two years, I'm finished, he's finished, afraid of the sheets, stupid Elisha Fliedl. We're finished Franz, we've had it.

My Nordic lover, ageing wise Viking. We talked about death too many nights. We were overheard. A thin smell of Prinz cigarettes on your dry hands. You killed me. I wish I was home. With you. We'd talk about love.

Sorry?
What?
You said something?
No, why?
I thought you said something.
What?
Something like I wish I was home.
Maybe I did.
I also talk to myself sometimes.
You do?
Yes, but at home, not in cafés and that. I live not far from you.
Really?
You're a friend of Mushmush, aren't you?
Where from?
I dance with him in the ballet.

(Hands start to sweat, calm down Elisha, paranoid)
Ah.
He hasn't been in all week. Is he out of town?
(I'll tear you apart right now, shithead)
Yeah, the kibbutz.
Friends?
No, adoptive family.
Shame he's missing class. He should also work out with weights. His arms are a bit weak.
(When did you check out his arms, you ugly fairy creep)
He's working at it.
You're not eating the roast?
I forgot it for a moment. I'm eating it. Yes.
The gefilte here's not much.
Yeah, horrible, no salt, and the carrot slices too thick. Where do you know Mushmush from?
You asked already. He's studying ballet with me. But I know him from before, by sight. He's around a lot.
Oh yes?
Sure. Everybody knows him. He's sweet, you know.
Yeah, he's sociable.
You been together a long time?
Almost a year. Bill, please! I'm terribly late already.
Right. Bye then. Say hello for me.
What did you say your name was?
Amir. Tell him Amir from the ballet. He'll know.
See you (sonofabitch, scum, be grateful I didn't kill you)
I'll tell him.
Bye.

The bill!

I'll never get out of here. She's gone to get change. He smiles. Pretty boy. Seductive little lesbian. Plain to see how he makes his living. What do I care.

D

Smoked the last cigarette, asked an old man for a light. The empty packet's in his hand but can't find a bin, can't dump it in the street. Mother. Shit. Two and a half associations for the whole infinite variety of external events. At least there's some shade in this neighbourhood.

    Food lying heavy in the stomach, starting to be digested, to ferment, to rot. Taste of nicotine moist with saliva. And of meat. Buy chewing-gum. Cigarettes. Matches. Money. Cashpoint. Cross street. Car horns. Drop dead. Cursing all the time, like the market. Friday he went to market with Mushmush. But nobody was cursing. Elisha picked stuff, Mushmush carried bags. The chef and his helper. Charming sight, picturesque. Marvellous Italian meal out of Aharoni's book, fettucini Alfredo. Mushmush says, what's this white stuff? It's the sauce, you primitive, but he goes on: "Spaghetti sauce is supposed to be red." Punk. Wants to provoke the bourgeoisie. Eats a tiramisu, then chips out of a bag, plebeian, man of the people, and two ready answers for everything: "Lay off me," and "Make coffee." What's this business with coffee in this country. These orientals. Mother. Elisha grins. Making myself laugh now. In despair.

This service has been temporarily suspended.

Dizengoff. Go straight to the shop, wait for him there. Will have to chat with Itzik. Perhaps the cashpoint on Nordau-Ben Yehuda, chance to sit in a café, dying for a smoke, chewing-gum, menthol, take away the taste. Try to think about something that develops, Elisha, thought arising from thought accompanied by a continuous input of additional data. All thoughts lead to Mushmush, all roads lead to Mushmush, everything begins and ends with Mushmush, Mushmushon, poisoned doe, deceived in the name of love, lust, porn. Shut it Elisha, pathetic, playing the literary hero. Which book? *The Jungle Book*! Mowgli Mowgli, yes, here too all roads lead to Mushmush.

Why can't the brain defend itself, preserve itself like the body. For instance, the body can jump in one spot till exhausted, then collapse. The brain has the stamina of a marathon runner, an endless solitary run. Never seeing the finishing line. A bench.

A notice-board. Natasha's Friends. The Chamber Quartet. All Russians. What were they brought here for— they sweep streets, the one who washes the floors at the editorial is a philologist, Slavonic languages, absurd. Let them play Schubert. In "Tzavta". Russians.

"Tzavta." Eight and a half months back.

Mushmush's face in the lobby, eating some junk, crisps or something, discussion about image of homosexuals in media. A bore. Outed or not, Boyarsky whispers in my ear, "No hunks." For once he's right. Fed up with their discursive fucks. The militant holding forth on the stage bugs me, intense, where do they find the strength. All right, so he's young, the sonofabitch, social awareness, political awareness, seeks change. Me, I don't seek change in the public image, individualist. Unprincipled egoist, carrying a timebomb. Contaminated.

Stayed till the end. No choice—the militant owes me a hundred shekels. Borrowed a month ago, evasive, but this time he won't get away. Elisha the ruthless debt-collector. Bugsie Siegel. Go out to the lobby. Look around. A Society leaflet on the noticeboard: Emphasis on prevention, confidential screening for HIV. Know all this nonsense by heart, rubbish, "Many have succeeded in prolonging their healthy lives by a strict watch over their health. Please, inform your partner if you are carrying the virus." Oh yeah? Really? And then what? After the colour returns to his pale cheeks and he manages to control the staccato of his chattering teeth? And here comes the charming solution for those to whom bodily pleasure is no stranger. I'm singing the body electric, wait for it, science strikes again, hurray, here it comes!

Condoms.

There is not, in the full gamut of all the sounds invented by man, a more repulsive word. The essence of semantic grossness. But what to do, they said condoms, so condoms it must be. Elisha is a disciplined person, carries the virus with pride. A guy who's not afraid to challenge fate. Has this darkish sort of humour. For example he says to himself, "We were in Tzavta today," and at once asks, "Who's we?" What a question—me and the virus. Black terror begins to rise to the conscious mind, brake Elisha, distract the mind, can't withstand the fear, divert the mind, bloody leaflet, get off our backs. Some label they've tacked onto us: a high-risk population. "Inform your partner." Darling, I haven't been well lately, I think I may have caught AIDS, would you look in the medicine chest, see if there's any aspirin left. Righteous buggers, piss-ants, rubber merchants.

Ragged blue sweater, cropped nape, neck, feels the stare, turns, eyes.

Mushmush.

Nibbling crisps. Was inside, heard the discussion, got fed up, bored, what do you do? Came with friends, name age family status

Elisha.

Mushmush.

Twenty-two.

Forty.

A year in Tel Aviv, working, waiting tables, but will be a dancer. Not a bit late to start training? Started way back, classical from age nine, and on and off since then, but now continuously. Knows Elisha from newspaper, lives in Florentin with three others, real pain, no privacy. But wait, you and privacy?

Calmer now. Elisha. Pleasant reminiscences.

Memories are nice.

About love.

The warm bitter scent of Prinz cigarettes, Franz's hands.

Franz's white hands.

Elisha used to say, like white birds, flying seagulls.
Franz—You're a poet Elisha.
Elisha—Poet my arse.
The poem of my love for Franz.
He's gone.
Died.
Contaminated me.
Nazi.
He didn't know he didn't know he didn't know he didn't did know know
Enough!

    Must walk a bit, stretch my legs, soon it'll be possible to go to the shop. I'll find the punk, everything will look different. Cheer up Elisha. What's come over me today, wallowing in a moral puddle like that Olympic swimmer. If the cashpoint is open and working it'll mean that everything will be all right. Within reason of course. Within reason. A hundred and fifty shekels, three fifties. Flying high Elisha, beloved of the gods, Amadeus Fliedl! The machine's working. Hate cashpoints, enemies of humanity, computers, monsters, civilization will consume itself one way or another, the next deluge will be computerized. What interesting ideas you have Elisha, very nearly daring ones, what bold, unbounded thinking, you've overcome the limitations of the human mind, you think forward—you think of Mushmush, or you think to the right, and—surprise surprise! again you think about Mushmush, and likewise in all other directions. Spinoza. Jean-Jacques Rousseau. Kant. Hegel. Elisha. Genius. Ladies and gentlemen, allow me to

introduce, Elisha Fliedl, giant of the Arnon Street intellectuals, stormy applause, we're proud to present to you the principles of Fliedlian dialectics. A standing ovation. For a sample thesis we choose . . . Shut up, swallow your tongue! I'm amusing myself, it's a good sign. Perhaps I may yet recover. Hopeless optimist. A kiosk. Marlboro Lite, two, how much are the lighters? The lighters! No, not those, the transparent ones, give me the red one, no, actually the blue, and the evening paper and a Diet Cola. Give me two packets of Noblesse too. The Mushmushon always runs out at night, begs fags off me and curses because they're not strong enough. The Lites. How much is everything?
Got a bag?
Here's a bag.
Keep going.

E

Can see through the window.
He is not there.
Not there.
Itzik is sitting. A woman. Must be a customer. Too tanned.
Push door and go in.
A blast of air-conditioned synthetically scented air.
    I don't believe it, what a visitor, sit down matey, I'll be with you in a minute. These are from Paris, nix, you won't find it anywhere, personal import, the last one. I'm not trying to persuade you, you have to feel good about it,

gold-plated with carved ivory, art nouveau, a replica of a brooch that belonged to Isadora Duncan.

Oh you must know! An amazing dancer, terribly famous, a bombshell, she was the girlfriend of that poet, the blond hunk, come on Elisha, remind me matey, I'm no good at names, there was a programme about them on Channel Eight, he commits suicide in the end . . . ? Come on . . .

That's the one.

Nix, out of this world!

Elisha matey, do you mind not smoking here, it's killing me.

Congratulations. It's awesome, I'm telling you. You bet. Yah, it's a class by itself. Look, if you want the other . . . I feel this is more your look. You won't see anything like it on anybody, I promise. Elisha, old buddy, I beg you, put that cigarette out, I'm choking, I'll be with you in a tick, all right? Your receipt, next month I'm getting some fabulous merchandise, stunning art deco rings, would you mind shutting the door when you leave, otherwise the condition gets out . . . Piss on her mother's cunt, she drove me round the bend, coffee Elisha love?

Mushmush? How should I know?

Hey, you nuts or what? Guy hasn't worked here the past two weeks.

He was probably too embarrassed to tell me.

I sacked him.

Why? 'cause he's disfunctional, is why.

Never came on time, badmouthed the customers, went out

for a smoke every two minutes, I'm sorry, matey, but this is a business, not a playroom!

What, he said he was still working for me? I tell you, the guy's a pathological liar, when he says . . .

I don't give a damn about intentions, I care about what's going down. I don't have time for people like that, they're a waste of time.

Oh come on, matey, how should I know?

What, he doesn't sleep at home?

So why are you worried?

You got nothing to worry about, nix, I tell you he's simply irresponsible, that's all.

Right, if I hear anything.

No problem, buddy.

So otherwise what's happening, how's life treating you? You've gained weight.

Nix, you gotta watch it, me I've cut out sweet stuff. It's the calendar, matey, the calendar.

Hang on a sec, you're sweating, gone all pale, you should drink something, here, just a sec, I'll pop over and get you some mineral water.

All right, just as you like.

Bye matey, see you, be well.

F

Quick quick to the back yard, sit on the ground, have to cry, can't help it, it's in the chest, coming up, eyes stinging. Narrow passage, turn left into inner courtyard, strong smell of sewage, two stinking overfilled garbage bins, but in the shade, always look for shade, things are saner in the shade. Here in the corner, rest against the wall, it's cool, peeling, sewer lid nearby, green slime, small pebbles dig into arse. How I always notice the trivialities. Can't stop living for one moment, my worst guilt, refusal to stop living for a second. Ladies and gentlemen of the jury, the crime of the man standing before you is his total refusal to stop living, I am persuaded that you will give it your full consideration and sentence him with all due severity to the penalty he deserves, to be abandoned by the key factor in his life that answers to the name Mushmush.

Two weeks that he's been deceiving me, what do I know, I know nothing. Where to look for him. The mere hint that he may leave is too much to bear. Impossible. This fear of abandonment, where does it come from, I remember sticking to mum's arse all through childhood, so maybe from that first day in kindergarten, when I cried after she left, what crap, God, the sun's broiling and the ground is damp, that sewer must be leaking somewhere. If he saw me like this, sitting in a Tel Aviv back yard, leaning against a filthy wall, beside the garbage. He always teases—sterile, fastidious. Only don't let him leave, ever. Ever. I couldn't stand it, no, stop blubbing, revolting, passive, do something, what, can't stop crying, dirtied my hands, blow my nose, shirt, wipe my face. A little better. God, I didn't know such a pain existed in the inventory of mortal punishments. Utter despair. How did I reach such despair, the ghastly stench, Tel Aviv courtyards . . . It's not even a courtyard, just a little back yard, must take care not to let Itzik see me from his shop. Fired the kid two weeks ago, poor humiliated Mushmushon, didn't say a word. Maybe he had something in mind. There's no telling. Never any telling.

There was a similar smell in Tomas's yard in Budapest. Leaking sewer. They mustn't see me like this. My arse is wet. The balcony of the house opposite—spring onions growing in a window box, Tel Aviv types, probably have a pleasant apartment, clean with potted plants, aluminium saucepans, household cleansers, nice smell in the bathroom, light unmatching furniture, the Palmah Book, worn little Am Oved volumes, last weekend's *Haaretz* supplements, Bergner and Kadishman reproductions, relatives in Nahalal, a cookery book in English, speak proper unaccented Hebrew, hello Mum, you bitch, a long time since you crawled into my mind, greasy worm, wriggling, leaving a trail of slime on the whorls of my brain. You don't have light furniture, nor any pleasant chemical cleaning smells, mothballs yes, chests-of-drawers wardrobes dressers yes, a chipped Dresden figurine (Mushmush: Shame about the little duke's balls) again yes, and there are footstools, a mattress stuffed with horsehair, a smell of medicines in the fridge (so they won't spoil), a smell of urine on your underwear on days when you're too ill to bathe, ahh, let it all pass, my compassion is heavy, a weight. I wish I really did hate you, purely, one on one. The way I love him.

On Ibn Gvirol Street, ambling away from Tzavta.

The militant had returned the money. A hundred shekels. Mushmush in sneakers, hands in pockets, spilling to Elisha the story of his murky life, kibbutzim, "outside child", boarding schools, youth village, again kibbutzim, only because parents were abroad, diplomatic mission, secret you know. On behalf of Mossad, in fact.

Lies pouring out of him. His voice—Marlene Dietrich, callouses on the vocal chords, the kid says, but it's sexy, he says, consoling himself, that's what they tell me, anyhow I don't care, he concludes. Hungry? Don't know. What do you like to eat? Everything? What especially? Entrecôte.
White Hall restaurant.
Double portion of chips, he orders.
The little rubbish bin, the bottomless pit.
Can I have both a mousse and cake?
You may, my hungry scrawny little lover, all the mousses and cakes made within the bounds of the galaxy and beyond.
I'll walk you home, all right?
Starting to be dangerous. Take care, Elisha, take care.
May I?
Get with it Elisha, deep breath and send him to hell and gone.
Suddenly the despair.

Damp European air at five thirteen a.m., he looked,

he had to know precisely, the minute, the second. Fearful of forgetting. Must make a note, he thought, but did not move. The window's wide open, he's lying down, can't see the roofs, but the sky's getting brighter. In Franz's bed, in his clothes, orange corduroy trousers and an old flannel shirt, from New York days. Franz dying in my arms, like a wizened little old man, bald, I'm holding in my arms a tiny old man, the remains of his proud soul.

When he woke up, even before he checked, he knew it was all over. He remained lying on his side, holding the cooling body from behind, his habit in the past few weeks— let the patient sleep as much as possible, don't wake him. Only lifted his hand for a moment, to see the time, and carefully replaced it. Five thirteen. He lay there, watching frozenly the empty piece of sky, pressing the corpse to his chest, as if it were a sleepy boy picked up at the club the night before. Until Jap, the male nurse, arrived at midday and began to make the funeral arrangements with skilful diligence and a severe expression. Returned to Israel two weeks later, and the wait began. For dust thou art and unto dust shalt thou return. And who knows, he thought sometimes, maybe it will blow over, and at once smiled and said, "Sir, my intuition in this matters does not bode well," and waited. Alone. Two years. Till today.

May I? (pious Dietrich)
No. I've got to stop somewhere first. Maybe another time.
Can we meet again?
I don't know, maybe.
Can I call you?

(He's persistent)
No.
Why?
It's complicated.
You're living with someone.
You might say.
Then coffee, can we have coffee sometime?
(He's cute, no doubt about it, cute as hell)
It's starting to rain, you'll get soaked, go home Mushmush.
His neck.
To touch him, fuck him, tear him to bits, his skin, fingertips slightly squared, pale nails, his mouth, the upper lip arched, a chipped front tooth, broken, he said, a blow from a fist, liar, fuck him, in the mouth, his eyelashes, for months afterwards his name is lashlashes.
Skinny.
Levis 501.
What does he want from me?
Exploiter.
I do have my qualities, but he couldn't have discovered them in half an hour's polite chitchat.
Primitive
I'm no Apollo
That's for sure
Balding
Maybe he thinks I'll keep him. But he's sweet, sweet
Make no mistake about me
Mushmush
Stands in a puddle

Lunar Eclipse

Doesn't stop nattering
What's he saying
Holding my hand
Standing on Bograshov in the rain
Scene from a Turkish movie
Go on Mushmush or whatever they call you, scoot off home
What have you got in your pocket, little kibbutznik
Twenty shekels and ID
So take a cab and scoot off to Florentin, and buy condoms with the change and bring a note from the doctor, capish? Now what? God, that's all I need, blubbing, soundlessly, wipes his nose on his sleeve. Oh Suzanna, don't you cry. Can't stand it.
    Cold
Wet through
Stops a cab
Florentin
Take care Mushmush
Home
Turn on light, radiator, can't get warm, herbal tea, sleep, weakness, his eyes, drove me crazy. Fuck him and die. But Elisha, never mind fuck him and die, but fuck him and die with him? Not very nice Elisha.
    A decent sort usually
Wouldn't have thought it of you
With a condom
Okay then
Risky
That's not living

With a condom
All right
It's known
Use your hand and go to sleep
He did.
The next day he had pneumonia
He thought, here it comes.
Four weeks in bed, is what it came to.
Simply hung about in the rain flirting with you know who
Recovered.
Florentin
They said, he left, don't know where, don't know his full name, don't know his real name, don't know in which restaurant he works, don't know which kibbutzim he stayed in, don't know who he hangs out with, don't know where to ask, know nothing. Little fairies. That evening Elisha had supper at his mother's. Got home about ten.
    Surprise surprise
There he was waiting in the entrance
Mushmush
Found him
Said he missed him
Said, got preventatives
Said, he loved him
Loved Elisha
Said, he waited to see maybe he imagined it
Said, no he didn't imagine it
Said, he wouldn't leave even if he, Elisha, kicked him like a stray dog

Said, he'd begun to take ballet lessons, so he, Elisha, would be proud of him
And for himself too
Said he would get a proper job somewhere . . .

    Then he pushed Elisha gently against the wall and kissed him with his eyes wide open, pressed against him as if someone was trying to pull him away, and when Elisha's breath grew heavier and faster and his body felt charged and lost, he went down on his knees and did an act of love, till Elisha slid, drained of semen, down to the floor and sat down beside him.

    They smoked in silence
Went up to Elisha's flat
Had cocoa
Biscuits
Never parted since.

G

Straight home now, maybe he's been back for ages, crazy Elisha, totally self-absorbed, never imagines there might be other possibilities, not just the apocalyptic ones. Go on, chuck that tacky bag with the cigarettes and the newspaper, no, actually I need one packet, the open one, and the lighter. Clean yourself up, all mucky, sat on the ground God knows how long, take a cab, it'll be faster. Not sure. It's near enough, and on Dizengoff there's traffic lights every few metres, cab no use, go on, can't have heart-searchings over

every foolishness, stop a cab—Arnon Street, it's not far, driver doesn't know, he's new. You direct me. If I had a gun I'd shoot him, I'd shoot you, you hear, so drive to Ben Yehuda and Gordon, listening to a tape, cinema music, if only I had a gun, damn hot he says, shut up Elisha, sure Elisha will shut up! Yes, he replies politely, terribly hot, but the forecast says tomorrow will be cooler. The guy doesn't trust the forecast, he says, you can reverse whatever they say, but no, says Elisha, today it isn't so any more, today it's much more accurate, they have highly advanced meteorological instruments ... Stops. Has no change. Never mind, can I have a receipt? The printer's on the blink, he'll write it by hand, never mind, doesn't matter, no no, he insists, doesn't want any problems, you asked for a receipt you'll get a receipt. Mailbox, name slot says Elisha Fliedl and on the box in fading marker: Mushmush
Municipal tax
Plumber's flyer
That's all
Third floor
Right
Key
Maybe he's back
Nothing's been moved
Even the air
The molecules hanging in the exact same order
Sneakers
Worn
He isn't.

H

After showering he put on grey tracksuit pants, flung himself on the bed and let out some dry sobs, then pulled himself together. Misery needs witnesses. Like love, like beauty. Took Enid Starkie from the bedside. Know it by heart, I already know every detail of this biography as if it were my own. Do you really have to know everything about a poet in whose verse you're rummaging while trying to translate it into a revived Semitic language. Why bother to translate poetry. Who gives a damn. Who reads these things anyway, culture-vultures, intellectual snobs, students. A population utterly devoid of sex-appeal. Elisha's trying to be a solid type. With creative quality. Newspaper writing doesn't satisfy him on any level, while he himself pours out only blood, hieroglyphics and chicken soup. Translating Rimbaud, from French. Such exquisiteness! Paddled a bit in "A Season in Hell", loathed himself, stopped. Took a clean sheet of paper and wrote on it in rounded letters: "Dear Mushmush, I've infected you with AIDS. Now you'll die." Spent a quarter of an hour shredding the paper into tiny bits, finally went to the kitchen and fetched a saucer, put the shreds on it, set them alight and didn't take his eyes off the flame till they turned into a heap of fine ash. Suddenly he shook himself, took a clean sheet from the ream and began writing almost violently. When he finished he felt wrung out. He glanced at the paper and quite mechanically crumpled it and threw it into the metal wastebasket with

Bart Simpson painted on it. He sprawled on the sofa and fell asleep at once. Sank like a stone into a deep well. When he woke he sensed the darkness that filled the space without opening his eyes. How long had it been, two hours or maybe four. Amazed at his own indifference, he heard sounds from the kitchen. He's back. "Mushmush," he called out sleepily, his eyes still shut, "turn on the little light and bring an ashtray from the balcony." No answer. Maybe it isn't him but a burglar; mother's neighbours were burgled a couple of weeks ago, he recalled. Must move quietly, he opened his eyes carefully in the dusk, squinted at the kitchen. No light. Fuck, he thought. That's all I need, he'll kill me by accident. There's nothing to steal here. He'll get mad, you hear no end of such stories. A floor tile creaks. Fortunately the door is open, Elisha the experienced detective presses against the doorframe. Peers in. Bluish evening light from the window, and a silhouette.

I think I'll be able to identify this creature even if they tear out my eyes, even if he stands dead still and doesn't breathe, if apocalyptic darkness came down on the cosmos. His existence and my awareness of it are absolute from any aspect. Including the metaphysical. May I ask what you're doing in the kitchen in the dark, and why you don't answer when I call you. Is that the new style? Yes? Dark and silent? Shut up Elisha, something's wrong, something very very wrong, stop nattering obsessively like an old woman, you can't prevent the inevitable, he's about to drop a dreadful bombshell. I feel it in every cell of my body. It's quiet in the streets of my private Hiroshima. Shut up Elisha. I can't, the fear is burying me, an avalanche of fear, a storm of fear, the air is shrieking into my brain that something's happened. Talk to him rationally, be calm, start dealing with the facts. Mushmush, prince of darkness, what happened, problems at the ballet? That sonofabitch Itzik? Do you hate me? Do you want to leave? You have someone else?

Listen Mushmushon. I realize you have a problem but we'll have to talk about it eventually, unless you want to leave me without a word like a heroine in an old movie? Come off it, I'm too old for that kind of romanticism.

Mush, you're neurotic, talk to me, man, I hate what's going on here, try to drop this dumb manipulation you're into and start communicating. You ought to know it's getting on my nerves.

Okay, I've had it, when you decide to become a communicative creature again you'll find me during the next hour in the living-room of our shared flat. Turned nonchalantly, started to fumble for the light switch, light restores things to their prosaic proportions, when suddenly a quiet, dull voice, my life's melody—"I got tested. The result is positive. Final."

Elisha freezes in silence.

Again the dull voice, Dietrich dying.

"I'm sure I infected you. I mean you can get tested, but I think it's a waste of time. I mean you'll want to get tested I'm sure, but what I'm trying to say is that I must have infected you, you know, in the mouth, the arse, without condoms, I didn't think anything would happen, 'cause I never even looked at anybody but you, I mean from the time I met you in Tzavta and you took me in a cab to Florentin. So I guess it's from before. I'd have been careful, but you know there's only one safe way, doing it by hand."

Elisha is frozen, doesn't move, not to frighten him, only let him keep talking, he must not be startled.

"I don't really know what to say, you can kill me if you like, but I bet you won't kill me, it's scary to kill somebody like this, violently. It wouldn't be like you . . . I'm afraid to think what you must be thinking or feeling now . . . You didn't want me in the beginning but I was persistent, remember? I bet now you're saying to yourself, 'I should have kicked him out like a leper, I should have listened to my instinct.' But I invaded your life, and honestly I was sure I was clean 'cause I got tested six months before and it was okay, so I guess it happened afterwards . . . I'm trying to think who it was and when, but it's no use. That place in Florentin, so many people stopped there, and until I met you I was happy to offer my arse to anybody who noticed my existence. So I guess it was one of those times. I don't know. And the park, sometimes I hung out there every night for weeks, also for money and all that, so maybe then, or before, I don't know. And now I don't care, I don't care about nothing . . . Only that you'll hate me . . . I'm afraid you'll turn on the light in the kitchen, so don't. Good. I don't want to see your eyes looking at me . . . That's something I've always loved, the way you look at me, that's why I latched on to you from the start, it's the sort of look that makes a person feel it was worth it to be born into this world, like he's a beautiful fat baby with special diapers, really bright, the pride of the nursery . . . That's how you made me feel. That's how. Now it's all over. For what's left of my life I'll hate myself every minute that I didn't give up after that meeting in Tzavta. I'll leave tomorrow. As it happens there's a pad I can stay in, with a friend."

With Amir from the ballet? Elisha blurted

Mushmush was not surprised

No, with a couple of guys on Hess

Elisha moved slowly towards the window, sensing Mushmush shrinking into himself. Stood in front of him. Didn't budge.

They listened to the minutes trickling past. God, it's happened. It's here, it's ours, both of us. Now there's no escape. Now he'll never know. I've tied him to me nerve to nerve, vein to vein, blood to blood. Death to death.

The paralysing tension which had gripped Elisha for years began to ease in a gradual flow that washed over him and slowly filled him with a quiet delight, almost happiness. He said, Don't go Mushmush. You've nowhere to go and there's no need. The die is cast, and neither I nor you could control it.

The other remained frozen, unwilling to react.

Not even when Elisha lifted him in his arms and carried him to bed.

Oh Mushmush, velvety rag doll, let me undress you and put you to bed, now the pants, the T-shirt, raise your head a bit, fine, that's it. Covered him with a checkered cotton blanket. Take this, sweetheart, it's half a Valium, drink up, that's it, now try to sleep a little. All right? Me? I'm here. Yes, I'll go to sleep too in a little while, I'll just smoke a cigarette and come too. In a moment.

I

Sat in the armchair. It was nearly dawn, and he could make out the outline of Mushmush huddled in the cotton blanket. I'm thinking about you Franz, I keep asking myself endlessly whether I'd have changed anything if I could. A sterile, hypothetical question, and worse still—unanswerable. I'm quiet now, at long last, as I've never been before, and again I part from you, as I do from time to time, and in the flow of memories appropriate to such partings, there is always the warm bitter smell of Prinz cigarettes. Oh my lover, my brother, my disconsolate loss, I wish I could be with you again if only for a minute, at your bedside, to atone for having hated you, I'd kiss your gaunt arms, your head made bald by the radiation, and your agonized mouth. We'd talk about love.

Nightmare Poem, or The Unrealized Cure of Mor Alkabetz

Tonight I'm going to be good.

If I succeed in getting through tonight, tomorrow will be a lot easier. I'm hungry and dead beat. And I feel like crying the whole time.

I think about food almost continually. Hermetically sealed circles of thought. Not a crack in them.

Sometimes it seems to me that I'm already dead. My relationship with food is a sado-masochist kink, a necrophiliac romance. Perversion, disease, annihilation. Oh yes, there are lots of words to describe this aspect of my life. As if it were a poem. Perhaps it really is a kind of poem—an existential doggerel—a comic one. The secret nightmare poem of Mor Alkabetz. Graveyard tango.

Aren't I being pathetic! It's a lot of bull, anyway,

because in my case I can say categorically that I do want to live. Dying to live. I don't want to suffer. Don't want to be ill, to fall apart, to have an ulcer, rotten teeth, broken nails, falling hair, slack skin, boils in the throat, on the face. Like everyone else, I want to be healthy and happy. Nothing original about me in this. After all, everything's just fine, or everything could be just fine. I know that anyone watching me right now from the sidelines would think, life has really screwed up this woman, if this is what she's going through. A woman stricken by fate. And this is where the elements of surprise and mystery come into it. Why? Because, if nothing else, I'm a happy woman. It may sound pretentious, but it is a fact. I'm a woman who is living exactly the life she wanted and planned and shaped. I'm a woman who has fulfilled her ambitions. It hasn't always been easy, I admit. It was often a very tough struggle, but I won the exact life I dreamed of. I've got everything.

So why the tears? Why the suffering? Why a nightmare poem?

I don't know. Haven't the foggiest.

Perhaps fate doesn't care for perfectly happy people, so it finds a flaw, even in those whose lives are beautifully formed, to make the ungrateful buggers realize how good they've had it, in the widest sense of the term. Fate's psychological gimmick.

Perhaps I'm nuts, huh, and unaware of it? Crazy. Totally out to lunch. Bonkers.

I don't think so.

Nightmare Poem, or The Unrealized Cure of Mor Alkabetz

Pure reason doesn't let me think I'm any nuttier than your average citizen. Though it is the fashionable view that everyone in the Western world is crazy to some extent, isn't it? It's the accepted notion that everybody should have a go at getting professional help from time to time, if not a regular hour's session once a week. The world's full of loonies. It's a fact. I'm no prophetess of doom, it's an observation made by wiser people than me. Good people made movies about it, wrote books, and you see it in a cruder form but no less accurately in current events as covered by the press and television. One way or the other, it's perfectly plain that we're living in a problematic ambience! Therefore we need to see things in a different light, a more advanced light. The light of the times.

Everybody's trying to survive somehow. To get free of this endless tension that's filling our Western reality. To discharge the bad energies. No need to chew over all this vegetarian-spiritual-anti-nuclear rubbish. Everything's already known—values undermined by relativism, violence, hate, a hole in the ozone, intellectual decline, materialism, unemployment, upheavals on the stock exchange, crime among the Russian immigrants, discrimination against the Ethiopian immigrants, leaders without charisma, Arafat's impotence, religious parties' extortion, Arab extortion, bestial young people, fucking without condoms, tranquillizers, stress, tension, cable TV, cost-of-living index, the capital market, unemployment in border towns, air pollution in the big cities . . . So as part of the general atmosphere, I choose to eat. My way of achieving mental peace may be odd but it's legitimate. Our world, as bad as it may be, is a democratic one. A free world.

But tonight, as I've said, I won't eat. For days now I've felt an anguish beyond the actualities. Like a pebble in the shoe, it stops me moving on. And the pain is becoming unbearable. Small and sly, it tortures me, comes and goes, comes and goes, but never leaves off entirely. Tonight I'm going to stop the disease. Tonight I'm going to give up once and for all.

Bulimia is disgusting. It has a disgusting image. An image that suggests something swinish, smelly, out of control. Even the sound of the word is ugly—bul-im-ia. A crude, bubbling sound.

The anorexics have all the fun. What a life they lead, the dainty little sylphs. What style. Maybe I'm blinded by envy, but clearly their public image is a lot more positive. And image is a critical factor in an illness! The anorexics' nightmare poem is a lyrical variation on a spiritual-ascetic-agony theme, a bit like tuberculosis only less diseased. A sonnet on the death of the beloved. Nocturne. Picture it— Anorexia is the name of a beautiful woman in Greek mythology. The nymph Anorexia is hiding amid the laurel bushes from the fury of dumpy Aphrodite and Artemis, who envy her slimness. Horny Zeus, infatuated with Anorexia, is breathing heavily through the bushes, causing them to shed their leaves, thus exposing the nymph, then the two fat goddesses finish her off between them. Nocturne.

But bulimia? Bulimia is an altogether different story. Bulimia is disgusting.

2

A bad day. It certainly was bad. It all started with my assistant Peachy. Or maybe with the model. Or the meeting with Gadi. Whatever it started with, it ended with the rat. But I'm getting ahead of the story.

I'm a photographer. A fashion photographer. A profession I'd dreamed of, though I studied film making at university. But that's how it turned out. I'm making a lot of money. Not millions, but enough to lead the life I like. I have a gorgeous studio, from my flat I can see the white yachts anchored in the marina beside the Hilton beach. I like to drive fast and can change a tyre when necessary. I know what's going on in my bank accounts and I play the stock exchange when conditions are right.

I've had a lot of men, but never felt that their presence in my life was essential. They are always a pleasant addition to the autarky which is me. I've never needed their money, their support or any expression of their masculinity. I was glad when they were around, but I've always been an independent person. An independent woman.

Only once did I feel emotionally dependent, that was when I was living with Gadi, but I made sure to put a stop to it as soon as I saw it for what it was. Love, despite its fabulous reputation, can be a distressing, castrating experience, as any honest loving couple will admit. By the way, I met him today, the man I used to love, after not seeing him for ages. But I'm getting ahead again.

Back to Peachy. Peachy is my assistant. His one ambition (in contrast to that tart Ditti, my former assistant, whom I threw out when she got pregnant) is to be Mor Alkabetz's assistant for ever. And he's living up to it. That tart Ditti whelped her pup, then rented a studio of her own. A pathetic move, given the state of the market. In contrast to Ditti's ambitious mediocrity, Peachy is perfection. He takes care of me as if he were my wife. Sometimes he goes too far. Like today. Today we did a cover for *Woman's World*. Medium shot. Colour. Nothing out of the ordinary. When it came time to break for lunch . . . Here I have to break off and confess to a nasty little habit I have; sometimes I try to fantasize that I'm anorexic. Sometimes it actually works. For example, I come into the studio and say to Peachy, damn, again I haven't eaten anything for three days. He knows what he's supposed to say to that—what?! Mor, are you nuts? or—look how skinny you are, love, you've got to take care of yourself, it could be bad for you. I get a kick out of this little ritual of ours. For a few minutes it makes me feel naturally skinny. Peachy himself, I may add, is a devotee of Weight Watchers, which helped him to shed twenty-three kilogrammes, so his idea about slimming is moderation, moderation and again moderation. I despise moderation, and more than that, I despise Peachy, but I can't help myself—what can I do, Peachy, I don't feel like eating. It's a matter of character, you know, of build. Get me some mineral water from the kiosk, would you love, and make me a black coffee with half a teaspoon of sugar. I feel sick just thinking about food. A naïve little habit of mine. A caprice.

Nightmare Poem, or The Unrealized Cure of Mor Alkabetz

    Well, today I again insisted on playing this little game with Peachy. Who knows, maybe if I'd had something while everybody was eating, all this wouldn't have happened, or would have happened differently. But what's the point of these painful speculations. That's what happened. So then, today at lunchtime Peachy went out as usual to buy greasy, tehina-dripping shawarmas for everybody. Such plebeian grub may not harmonize with the glamour of the profession, but that's what we eat. It's satisfying, quick and near the studio. And since we're in a moment of truth, I love shawarma. Really love it. In ordinary times, in an ordinary spaz, I can put away four portions of shawarma. With cokes. Easy. But that's not the point.

    Peachy came back loaded with bags, handed out the dripping packets to the participants and rushed to the kitchen to try to remove the tehina stain which had blossomed on his new Moschino shirt. Those creeps from the PR firm, the make-up cow, the hairdresser and the model, all felt a bit uncomfortable stuffing their faces in front of me, but they did anyway. And how they did. Embarrassed by my abstinence, they tried to gobble quietly. I observed them with a calm neutral eye, as if they were electrical appliances in a show-window (oh the terrific slim photographer, oh wand-like Mor Alkabetz who is nauseated by this lowly food. Bring her a couple of oysters and a thimbleful of caviar!) Each of them in turn mumblingly extended their pittas to me, hoping I'd take a bite and relieve them of the awkwardness. Oh no no no, thank you darlings, I really don't eat these things (ho ho nymph!).

I looked at the model, that Sharon le Tampon, or whatever her name is. Sitting hunched over, crumbs dropping on her flat thighs, snuffling in her pitta, tearing out bits of tomato and meat, chewing slowly with the submissive expression of a cancer patient. What a waste. Corruption. The rot in the midst of plenty. An automatic reflex produces before my eyes the face of a brown child stricken by dysentery and covered with flies, and my own face, the face of a woman who loves shawarma.

The vapid feast ended, Tampon Sharon feebly shook the crumbs off and retired to the lavatory, leaving her unfinished pitta on the make-up table. I couldn't stop squinting at it. I thought to myself—maybe I'll be lucky and Peachy, who's also the head waiter, won't throw it out. Maybe he won't notice it and leave it on the table and then, when we finish the shots, I'll send them all away and celebrate with the remains of the pitta, as a symbolic compensation for my tantalized suffering.

But my hope was dashed. At the end of the break, when I started to photograph again, I saw Peachy, faithful slave to Weight Watchers' ethics, pick up that piece of shawarma with the secret loathing of a former fatty (the expression to be found on the face of an experienced hospital nurse withdrawing the bedpan from under an especially loose-bowelled patient), and taking it to the bin. It drove me mad. I wanted it as you want a man, as you want water in the desert. I desired it.

I went on snapping, but my head was full of shawarma portions, dozens of shawarma portions hovered, circled over and around me, like the stardust in Disney's logo, with the castle and Tinkerbell. I couldn't get them out of my mind.

Yes, beyond question, a lousy day. Fuck them all. Then in the afternoon, at the restaurant with that Yaniv guy from Barel PR. God almighty, the people I have to mix with! The lowest kind of urban trash. Tel Aviv trash. Ambitious cruds. But I got the Levis campaign! Then came the worst part. Returning from the restaurant in the evening, looking for parking space near the studio, I came across Gadi. That's right, the handsome slim Gadi I used to love.

Meetings with former lovers are a tricky business. For your peace of mind, try to be at your best when they they take place. We all want to be loved for ever. Especially by those who were smitten in the past. It's not a whim, it's an instinct.

Gadi didn't have this instinct. Or maybe he doesn't have any instincts. Perhaps he's been excessively cultured and socialized and lost that human impulse to revive the old thrill. He was cool and relaxed, as only someone who's learned to hate you over the years can be. He'd waited for this meeting from the day we parted. I'm sure of it. And me?

Like a wave of nausea, sudden and swift, came the need to inform him that he was speaking to a happy person. A successful one. To let him realize that my life had worked out just fine. Let him know what he'd missed.

That's pathetic, I know. The sign of a petty spirit? OK, that too. No matter how predictable, my behaviour veered with sudden violence right out of my hands. "It was beyond my control," as Glenn Close said to John Malkovich. This desire that the people who saw you in your weakest moments, at your ugliest, when you were skinless, should think that the passage of the years has changed all that, that your aspirations bore fruit and you became what you'd always longed to be. You want to scream at them to stop looking at you with superior knowingness. They know nothing! The extensive intelligence information in their possession is obsolete trash. Why? Because! Because you've changed from top to toe. It simply happened, far from their watchful eyes. You've changed beyond recognition, and your feeble nakedness is only a vestige from your naïve youth that they've retained, distorted and exaggerated, in their memory. Yes indeed, there are moments when the urge to shield yourself from other people's knowing you is more powerful than reason, just as there are moments when the opposite urge—to shed all protective shields—can drive you equally mad.

 I informed him about the Levis campaign. He always knew how much I wanted to make it big in my work. I explained the difficulties involved, the size of the competition. Fortunately, I was able to hold on to a smidgin of good taste and didn't mention how much they'd be paying me. He was glad to hear I was contented. I invited him to come in and see the studio. And all the time a sticky Japanese smile, like instant glue, stayed on my face. A horrific sight, I suppose, especially for someone who knew my usual glumness. I could tell that he was scanning my soul with his spiteful eyes and knew that while everything I said might be true, the facts might be true, but the spirit behind them was a gross lie, obvious and unsophisticated. A sitcom. A farce. A nightmare poem.

"No, I don't think so, Mori, I'd be glad to some other time." Mildly surprised, at ease. An elegant tourist who stumbled into an agricultural museum in a provincial town. I couldn't believe that this man had cried because of me, grovelled, begged, adored the black-and-white photos of old women I churned out by the gross. Wanted to have children with me.

What can I say—it broke me up.

My stomach shouted to me—stop, Alkabetz, you dumb suicide, watch out, you crazy woman, but the slope was too steep. It was beyond my control.

So I told him how much I thought about him. Sometimes. And about us. And how much I missed him. Idiotic, meaningless lies. And he, looking serious (only deep inside his pupils gleeful little demons were sniggering), yes, oh really, I see, courteous. Suddenly I saw the whole scene from outside. The entire gruesome comedy. But by then there were no handholds for me to haul myself up, and a voice in my head said, go for it, Alkabetz, go overboard, the way we like it—so I slipped a finger into his belt, gave it a little tug and said, come on, let's fuck . . .

After that things went very quickly. He backed away, said quietly, I don't think so Mori, really. But by now I was totally jagged (this is a falling-on-my-sword scene, sweetheart, on a fatal, total, terminal scale), come on Gadi, hey come on, trying to touch him again, on the neck, and he removes my hand and says, enough Mori, what's the matter with you, but I can't stop and try to hug him and bury my face in his chest and he has no choice left.

He gives me a shove . . .

Seeing all that, it would be reasonable for anyone with commonsense to ask, why do you do such idiotic things, Alkabetz, as though you hadn't felt that all the strings were out of tune thirty seconds into the conversation. Why didn't you arrest the avalanche of your pride after the first misstep, given that you were fully aware of the situation at every second. Well, the answer is simple, like the answers to all questions as to why humans act as they do. I couldn't stand the idea that he didn't care for me any more.

We all want to be loved. It's axiomatic. We all come to realize, after a certain cruel moment in our lives, having once discovered the existence of people other than our parents (the original and natural suppliers of love), that we would have to work hard in cold alien fields in order to win that love. That too is axiomatic. You will never be loved by all the people you meet, but that's all right, dear children, because it means that you have an independent personality, character, a moral backbone—so don't sulk! Yet despite this ancient wisdom, deep down in our greedy souls we still hope to win love for free. Why? Because. To be loved unconditionally is certainly worth a gamble. We gamble from hope, though it's gratified too rarely to add up to a law. We spin the wheel and wait for red seven to come up so we can sweep all the chips from the green baize into the pockets of our tuxedo. It does happen, sometimes.

Sometimes. It's like the classic figure of the eternal admirer who contents himself with the crumbs of friendship that you grant him, but deep in his heart adores you and is consumed by desire for you. Well, there are fewer and fewer of his kind. The heart is an organ that hardens with age, and anyway, the species is becoming extinct. Psychology's capitalist tendency—love yourself first—has reduced the occurrence of suicide from unrequited love to a literary minimum. It's old-fashioned and incompatible with the philosophy of the democratic West. It's passé.

Brilliant, Mori, you managed to develop a whole thesis, complete with sharp social criticism, the moment you got a kick up the arse from a former lover. But here's the heart of the problem. He, namely that Gadi, that skinny creature, was supposed to love me for ever. Didn't he? That's supposed to be the rule. Wasn't it I who threw him out the door? His love for me remained unrequited, and should therefore have turned into a bitter unhealing wound. But again I was mistaken. Several years after the separation, past facts become hazy—who left, who deceived, who humiliated whom. The present is a powerful factor. This time the present was ferocious.

I stood there in a daze and he muttered "Take care of yourself" and split, with that queer walk of his, cautious, slightly swaying, as if walking on a wobbly tightrope.

His fist of a rump. A tiger in flight. Loser, bastard, candy-ass, impotent. A nightmare poem indeed.

No, that's not how sudden encounters with former lovers should go. Not a bit like that. I should have found him burdened with three kids and a small bespectacled brown-haired wife with an intelligent but forgettable face. And in his eyes I should have read a gulf of longing, shallow but aching, for the madness of past times. That's how it should have been.

I'm so ashamed. Just thinking about it makes me cringe from shame. What a fool I am. A liar and a fool. Since when do I care about him, and why did I tell him I missed him when I hardly remembered him all those years—and what's worst, why oh why did I suggest fucking him, when nowadays I wouldn't touch him with a ten-foot pole. And he felt sorry for me. He pitied me!

I'd eat something. If I could. But—no no no . . . I'm as disciplined as a Prussian soldier. I'm as strong as the devil. The brave devil Schweik.

I went back to the studio. To function. Always keep functioning. That's the sacred mission. Soldier, halt, password! Sanity! Well done, dismissed. I had to do the two fashion pages of the supplement, but all I could think of was what I was going to buy in the supermarket and how much, and couldn't wait to finish everything and get home and eat and eat till I couldn't eat anymore, then throw up and feel a great peace come over my soul.

But sure enough, I got stuck till late at night with the paperwork for the annual tax return. Sitting and rootling in papers like a little municipal clerk, till I saw circles floating before my eyes. By the time I finished it was so late I didn't hear a single car passing in the street. After midnight. Long after. I went out into the landing, locked the door, and then it happened.

I saw the studio bin lying on its side, and beside it, amid the garbage, a big rat sat chewing the model's pitta.

My pitta.

I knew it at once, because of the lipstick smear on the bitten edge. I froze, and very slowly, delicately, careful not to startle it, I lifted a foot, took off my shoe and threw it at the rat with all my strength. I wanted to slash it open with the sharp end of the heel and see his insides burst out— guts, shit, blood and bits of the shawarma that belonged to me. I missed.

The rat scooted off into the night and I went to the bin, squatted down, picked up the pitta and ate it.

How did I get into this crazy state?

3

Have to calm down. That's what I must do, calm down. Take an inventory. Such morbid sensitivity. When actually everything's all right. I mean, all right when you look at the big picture. Problems? There are always problems. Hurts, difficulties, pains. That's the dark beauty of life. That's its power.

What's the matter Mori, you want to be always jolly? Are you a cow? A moron? You're an intelligent person, a complex one. There's always a price to pay for a complex personality. Would you rather live without any problems and be just anybody, a grey somebody, unimportant, ordinary. Normal.

Not on your life. Never. Never. I'd rather die.

I'll manage. Like they used to say at home—it'll be over by the wedding.

Wedding my arse. Home my arse, the whole fabulous Alkabetz family, including your classics degree from the Sorbonne, my precious papa, your degree's up my arse too. And mama's rich family in Casablanca my arse, and their textile plant, and my sisters Merav and Claudine, and your expectations and hopes and illnesses and worries and pride. Everything's in my arse.

All right, I take back what I said in the beginning. So I was putting it on, OK, so what. There's a reason. There's a reason for everything. Actually I do know the reason, all right, only it's unimportant. Bulimia is never without a reason. There you are—I don't want to repress anything. It's better to act in extreme ways than to keep things bottled up. So I eat, all right? It soothes me. Everyone has his little consolations. Some treat themselves to a pair of shoes from Tiffany's. I prefer the supermarket. And why not? It's like the garden of Eden. A vision from the End of Days. Everything I crave, everything I love, lying within reach. Dairy products? To the right. Cream cheeses—aha, that's the name of the game! Strawberry yogurt, the name of the next game. Pump of whipped cream?—a bit synthetic, but great for the girl in a hurry—to the left: ice creams, candy-bars, halva, marshmallow, biscuits, then—again to the right: frozen food! Not very healthy but travels well by microwave. Pies, pizzas, burekas, kubbeh, chips ... Complete meals ready for defrosting. Dairy here and meat there. We don't

Nightmare Poem, or The Unrealized Cure of Mor Alkabetz

want to bruise the sensitivities of the ortho-doxies and the traditionals. Hello hamburgers, hi steaks . . .

Young Mlle Alkabetz hovers delicately between the sausages and the delicatessen. How gracefully she pushes the trolley! Ice-skating champion of the Middle East . . . Oh yes, there's beauty to be found in anything.

By the way, I do my shopping at night. To avoid unwelcome encounters. Such as when I bumped into Rona, who was buying cottage cheese and a little box of cherry tomatoes. Talk about minimalism. For a long time now we've been chatting in a polite, jokey way which makes me want to die. As if we were old acquaintances without a grand history of love, betrayal and other melodrama.

Expecting guests, Mori? Parents about to descend? A green glance at the discordant pile in my trolley. Yes Rona, and Merav and Claudine with their kids, don't know what's come over them, want to have a fun day in Tel Aviv. How's the post-doctorate Rona? (Now that's really sick, a woman of twenty-nine completing a post-doc in physics. What'll be left for her to do in the long years before she kicks the bucket?) Doing fine, Mor. Any fucks Rona? There are fucks Mor. And love Rona? No love.

Well, at least my wonderful Rona has no love. I always have loves. I have everything.

I wonder what Ilana will say about it. Ilana's my shrink. She's supposed to be one of the top five in the country. For the past two years Ilana has been trying to help me solve the secret of my illness. I can just imagine her face if I walked in and said, Hi Ilana lovey, I'm cured. She'll be terribly sad—it will be the end of the Mor Alkabetz case and three hundred shekels an hour without receipts. Or perhaps she will be pleased—what a brilliant success, that Mor Alkabetz, bulimic-neurotic-hysteric-with-personality-disorders, and altogether a shitty character. And we thought she was a goner, men of little faith that we are.

I like Ilana, but lately I've had a sneaking suspicion that she's pretty stupid. Nevertheless, it's still one of my favourite pastimes to slump in the simple but costly leather armchair and gaze at her plump hands with a wedding ring that's much too thick for someone who has specialized in women's problems.

Ilana used to be a Jungian, but despaired of it and now she combines the dynamic with the behaviourist methods. It goes like this—first we talk a little about Papa Alkabetz, monsieur my father. I've always had a high regard for papa. Everybody has a high regard for papa, though he's only a French teacher at Alliance, not some brilliant interpreter of Plato. And papa, at least according to him and to his teachers at the Sorbonne in the year dot, had much to contribute about the works of that faggot philosopher. Oh yes, papa has a classics degree from the Sorbonne, but modernity or no, he still wished for sons, though was able to sire only daughters. Then we talk a bit about wonderful mama, madame the housewife Corinne Alkabetz, she of the undisciplined womb, who comes of a traditional family and longs to see me as a frothy bride under the canopy. Then, with Ilana's help, I do a profound self-analysis about my last ten attacks. What people did to me, hurt me, took away from me, didn't appreciate me, I didn't appreciate myself, didn't appreciate my crippled sister's cunt, and so on. I admit—I enjoy being especially disgusting in describing my attacks. I spare her nothing. Three hundred shekels an hour. Banal, isn't it? Come off it Mori, if you mind about the money don't go to a shrink. Fuck you. Then who will I talk to about my problems? To my assistant Peachy? To mama? Give me a break, I haven't talked to mama about anything more personal than income tax since I was in secondary school. I'm all alone at the front.

    Anyhow, how long can you go on delving into things. I'm fed up. Fed up with examining the past. Why things have turned out as they have. Why they happened this way and not that. Why me. Why one person goes nuts and another one, with the exact same history, does not. Natural predisposition, they call it. The gobbledygook invented by the doctors and shrinks to cover up the uncertainty gnawing at the heart of their theories. There's no deliverance in understanding how things happened, what damaged you in the past and why you've had it. They should drop psychology, it's a source of irrefutable arguments. It's nothing but moonshine and untidiness, this vulgar use of the study of the soul as a pill to cure the pain of existence. Perfecting a view of things as though there's no right and wrong and henceforth you are your own smug little god who decides what suits him and the hell with the world. Who is this world anyway? Who's ever heard of it? It's only a cosmic service office. God resolves. And you, pet, you're not selfish, you're not vicious, you're not cruel, it's just that you had problems in childhood and the suffering made you a bit difficult, a bit off-putting. Now you must take very good care of yourself, and love, not judge, yourself! That's the overall trend. Whatever you do is all right. We're only human, all of us. Flesh and blood and a handful of unstable emotions. Everything's human. As soon as you understand this and take it on board, you'll be free to sodomize little girls, murder old women, jerk off in the hall of the opera house, legislate capital punishment, and everything will be just fine. People dancing with themselves in the nightclubs. It's the age of the soloist. The age of Narcissus. You say I'm out of date? So what.

Sheet, what a misery merchant. She feels lousy about herself, her brain's all fucked up, she's obsessed with bulimia and whinges about everybody. Go on then, piss off to Somalia to look after children with swollen bellies, seeing you're so damn righteous and you know what's what. So live a moral life if you're such an expert on it, little bourgeois female, you hate yourself so you hate everybody else. Self-hate—the hang-up of women, slaves and blacks. That makes you a better person? Everybody knows that self-hate leads to more evil, fear and hatred. Anyone would think there's a bit of God in you, you liberal-lefty Tel Avivian bitch. Get off our backs. Aggression and alienation: naughty-naughty! Love and kinship: hurrah hurrah! War and blood: woe is us: peace and brotherhood: three cheers. All are equal—Eskimos, Red Indians, the Chinese and Japanese! . . . Put a sock in it, go help an old woman across the street, instead of wearing out our precious ear-drums with your embarrassing clichés. Shame on you, you demagogue! Go read a little Otto Weininger, such an original fellow, read Freud, Ericson, Jung, Marx. Learn something before you open your mouth to preach. Or better still, read a newspaper and spread your legs for some Arab from Jenin. That's more your style. Now piss off. You're getting on our wick.

It's all worn out, isn't it? Truth is worn out. Forgive me, dear truth, you are indeed true, but so trivial I feel like puking on you!

I feel like eating and puking on truth and lies and everything.

Must distract myself. That's the trick. Think about something good. In five hours it will be morning, I'll go to the studio and it will all be behind me.

Think about something different, something totally different.

Something good.

One example of something good to think about is achievements. Your achievements are your own, no one can take them away from you, they're inscribed in fiery letters on your personal history. Your achievements remind you in difficult moments, such as now, what you're really worth. That's Ilana's method, for example. She always reminds me of my achievements when I am down. Clever, isn't it?

The professional achievement that both Ilana and I like best is my year with the *National Geographic*. Hey, you can't deny that really is something. How many Israeli photographers do you know who can say the same? How many of them were women? Right. Not one, male or female. Except Mor Alkabetz.

But most of all, they're lovely memories. Sometimes when I can't sleep I lie in bed and think about Morocco, inject honey into my brain. That was my first project for *National.* I worked with the Leica I got from Gadi. The same model Capa used when he photographed the landing in Normandy. How symbolic. The Allies defeated the Nazis, and Alkabetz defeated her own mental illness. Temporarily at least. Two months are not to be sneezed at, and they were terrific. I returned to my roots. I did everything sentimental people do when they get to Morocco. Wandered about the souks, ate fabulous couscous, gambled in the casino, and above all—I didn't throw up. I was as calm as a Valium factory. And of course I took pictures. Mainly took pictures. The project was—woman. The universal nigger, the waitress at life's feast, the additional sex, that's what I photographed there. Hundreds if not thousands of women, perhaps an infinite number. From traditional ones like frightened black chickens to French-groomed bitches, filthy little snot-nosed girls, and of course old women. My great obsession. And what old women. There isn't a more photogenic creature than an old Moroccan woman! Wrinkled, perfect old females have always been known for their love affair with the camera. My eyes saw everything differently. From scratch. All the views, faces, buildings usually marketed as typical Moroccan sights in postcards and travel-books came out utterly different. Even the grumpy editor was tickled pink—"A lovely job, Miss Alkabetz." Such a fresh and

Nightmare Poem, or The Unrealized Cure of Mor Alkabetz

original treatment of a trivial theme (i.e., women are a trivial theme to this pompous fart). A brilliant and precise reportage. Seven colour photographs, all mine, in the September issue . . . Oh yes, Morocco is definitely a good thing to think about.

And then? well . . . then . . . OK, then there was Algeria, Kenya, and finally Tibet. By Tibet I was a total wreck. The downhill course started in the middle of the stay in Algeria, when I'd come down a bit from my initial high and simply had to work, and make it no less interesting than the Moroccan series, and keep satisfied. It meant wandering for hours on my own with a camera in a Muslim country, in dirty alien streets, and spending days upon days in a jeep, listening for the millionth time to the only Hebrew tape I had with me—"Pretend Games" by Allon Olearchik. Breathing dust, my skin coarsened by the sun, and not a soul in a radius of thousands of kilometres with whom to exchange a couple of words in Hebrew, only affected English and my halting French which was barely sufficient for survival, and all the people around me being Arabs and men and painfully alien.

I couldn't fall asleep at night. Warm air, oriental sensuality. My Israeliness was the obstacle. I didn't feel the slightest response to the male sexuality around me—moist eyes slithering over me from the moment they served my morning coffee and all through the day. A groomed doll in sunglasses, arms and neck bare, plainly a European cunt. An object. In Bertolucci movies and in novels by European writers who went for this kind of exotica, girls of the

Western, plastic sort, like myself, end by screwing the primitive natives and eventually realizing how sadly disconnected from the simple instinctual world they had always been. But I am neither this nor that, neither Western nor nothing. Needless to say that at home they were less than enamoured with Arabs, and in Israeli culture this is not really the sort of virile image that pulls the little bourgeois gals. Our relations with the neighbours are too problematic, on a stressful personal level, for nice gals to indulge in fantasies about construction workers.

So I started to eat. Wild fits, sometimes three a night. I thought it was a phase, but it got worse and worse, and by the time I reached Tibet it was horrendous. I was out of my mind, sick, and the work only wore me out. There was no joy in it any more, what with that Steve keeping after us the whole time. Why was it necessary to send the deputy editor to the site? The argument was that the Himalaya project had been his baby all along. So he went with us everywhere, passing comments, sometimes even asking to see the frames. Practically sitting in the camera. He knew nothing about this kind of work.

It was difficult to throw up. I'll never forget how I tore my throat with my fingernails that night outside the stinking village of the polygamous women. In total darkness. Heaps of rice that I'd got out of the landlord after the general supper. Such terror that it might not come out, that I might not be able to vomit all the Asiatic shit that was filling my stomach, heaps of unused energy threatening to blow me up from within. At a certain point, when I was

Nightmare Poem, or The Unrealized Cure of Mor Alkabetz

near despair, I pushed three fingers as deep as I could and rattled them in my gullet like an epileptic. It did the trick, but left a tear in the oesophagus. And the following weeks, when the wound became infected, it was bad. In the end I resigned and returned to Israel . . .

All the same, in the final count it was a success, that year with the *Geographic*. Despite the difficulties. They were experiences, weren't they? Everything's part of life.

Anyhow, the best part of it was when I was told I'd got the job. What a joy that was. Right on the button, and unplanned. I knew that the portfolio I sent them was impressive, and my résumé must have really turned them on—an officer in the Israeli army, an athlete, BA in film and television, experience in press photography. I remember Gadi coming in with the envelope and I saw right away that it was from abroad and I knew, I sensed, that it could only be from them. What a triumph. Of course there was no question of going, I could hardly go trekking in the wilderness with the pregnancy and all our plans.

In the end I went.

Maybe I should have something to eat after all. I must. I can't stop thinking about all the food I got. Maybe it was a mistake, what kind of nonsense is that, buying seven hundred shekels' worth just when you decide to kick the habit. Maybe to beat the devil in his own presence? Bullshit. Why make it difficult for myself, why put such temptation under my nose?

Can I throw out the food?

Oh sure. You don't throw out food.

Throwing out food is like murder. When you throw out food it's like you tore it out of the little hands of all the African children. It's as if you killed children with your own hands. You don't throw out food. Period.

Maybe one little thing? Something very small. There's no getting away from the weakness.

What bliss. I eat, therefore I am. I make choices at every moment. The dark beauty of existence.

4

But I'm happy about that year. If I hadn't taken it up I'd have regretted it all my life. I can't deny that the abortion was a very sore business. Actually, more than the pain of the abortion itself, I was hurting for Gadi. Isn't it ironic. Always outside myself, even in the most difficult personal situations. Gadi was all that mattered to me throughout that business. After two months of pregnancy he couldn't get over the fact that we already knew the baby's sex, and were planning to name him Cain, as in Byron, after the first rebel against God (poor papa and mama, their frozen faces when they heard the name of their future grandson!), and knew that he would soon have little eyes and a real prick, and we got incredibly excited, or at least, Gadi got excited, because me, I already knew on a deep level that the whole scene was not for me.

In actual fact, I started out with good intentions. Everything was going well with the studio, and the terrific

Nightmare Poem, or The Unrealized Cure of Mor Alkabetz

equipment I got for a song. And I did want the baby. Then the doubts came—Rona was about to leave for Harvard and I felt it was burning me up, I wanted so much to succeed, but in a big way, like her. To be what I always wanted to be—the best. As I often was. Suddenly the studio seemed parochial, pathetic. A little Tel Aviv photographer. And the pregnancy—superfluous, too soon, destructive. I looked at myself from outside and saw a measly housewife, someone who rushes on Fridays to buy the local papers to read about other people's fabulous doings, which makes her sick but she reads on. I wanted to break out, fly like an arrow, do something really astonishing, something that will leave even papa open-mouthed, and he'd say to mama—what do you know, Corinne, our Mori is better than ten sons. And mean it, for a change.

All the same, I kept thinking, maybe I'll keep the baby.

Wanting it got on my nerves.

But everything was getting on my nerves then. I felt that even the fact that I loved Gadi was pinning me down. Sometimes I wished he'd leave me, so I'd be alone again. Or that I'd stop loving him and then split. But I didn't stop.

I remember perfectly well when I decided to get rid of the embryo . . . I remember it very clearly.

It was a few days after I got the letter from the *Geographic*. I'd sworn to Gadi that I wouldn't throw up while I was pregnant, but it was a nightmare. At first I didn't even try to control it. I lied in my teeth. I had to wait till he went out and then I'd rush to the far grocery on Mapu and buy pittas and a kilo of ice cream and half a kilo of pastrami, coffee-cakes with cheese and poppy-seed, Bulgarian cheese, two smoked herrings and five packets of milk chocolate, and fly back home. I'd wolf it all down till I felt I couldn't manage another bite, and then eat a little more, just to feel the limit, then of course drink the required three glasses of water and crouch in the lavatory over the bowl. Narcissus gazing enthralled at his reflection in the lake . . . Two fingers down the throat, retching in quick spasms, till the vomit begins to spurt.

Then I'd flush the toilet, making sure every last scrap was gone, then scour the bowl and spray air purifier to cover up the traces, and quickly to the bathroom to brush my teeth, the next anxiety already squeezing my chest—what will it do to the baby, poor creature. Mental retardation, a heart defect, soft bones. How he will suffer from his future mummy's shenanigans in the toilet. Poor little lump of protoplasm, why should he suffer.

It tortured me. I decided to stop vomiting.

I succeeded. It worked perfectly well until the day I went to the pharmacy to buy shampoo and in a fit of kamikaze self-destruction went up to the electronic scales. Pushed a coin into the slot, stepped on, and saw—sixty-two kilos. More than I'd ever weighed in my life.

The air suddenly felt heavy and thick, as if all the oxygen was pumped out of it. From that moment I knew nothing would ever stop me. I am fat.

Fatso. Butterball. Hippo. Bomb.

Nightmare Poem, or The Unrealized Cure of Mor Alkabetz

That was too a high a price to pay. I went home. Took a tranquillizer, washed my face. It was obviously time to get reorganized.

First of all I phoned Stern, who happened to be on duty at Assuta Hospital, and fixed a date for the abortion. At first he was shocked, but I said, do me a favour, don't ask too many questions, believe me I have a good reason. He insisted on being a humanist and refused. Didn't want to be a baby-murderer. I searched for words, I was so taken aback by his refusal I couldn't say anything only gasped like a fish, till at last I burst into tears and then it came— I said, my Gadi's in love with someone in Haifa.

That was an argument that convinced Stern, because everybody knows there are some real sharp chicks in Haifa. He said, oh all right. Just keep cool. I'll try and get an anaesthetist for Wednesday.

Funny—later it turned out that Gadi really had somebody, and from Haifa. You have to admit it's exactly the sort of thing people call an irony of fate. Gadi explained that it happened because the abortion shook his faith in our relationship. Gadi said he'd never looked forward to anything as he looked forward to our aborted baby. And in the end Gadi said that now, when we were both wiser, he wanted us to start again from the beginning and begged me to forgive him, because he'd forgiven me.

At which point I threw all his belongings out of the flat.

Oh my dear Gadi, how very naïve. He really tried to reach me, in his selfish way, but clearly those were arguments that never stood a chance of arousing my compassion and forgiveness. I don't like it when people betray me. I truly hate it when people treat me badly. I have no psychological and philosophical resistance to such things.

Bravo Mori. How very original. So what. So what if my pain is not unique. My pain bears some very ordinary features. I've already said that with regard to wishing to be happy I'm not a bit original. Of course the reason you treated me badly, darling Gadi, was because you yourself were distressed. All the evil in the world comes from distress. That's how our enigmatic God Almighty created the causes of evil, this fascinating phenomenon in the realm of human morality. There is no pure, Hitlerian evil, as we'd like to believe. Everybody acts from a desire to make things better, especially those who didn't have it so good from the start. I know all this. I'd yawn, if I weren't in such pain.

Gadi's shirts flew down the stairwell like the banners of an unknown revolution, fluttering easily on a light breeze. In the first weeks I clung to Rona, to her mother, and to former lovers, whom I screwed with a will and even managed to comfort myself a little. But then, just when by all accounts the mourning process should have eased and begun to peter out, came the great depression. I stopped leaving the house, didn't shower or change my clothes, ate, vomited, and mainly lay in bed in a state of exhaustion.

I don't know how many days passed like this. Probably less than I thought. I had to save myself.

The first morning I managed to get out of bed I went to the post office and sent a long wire to the editor of the

National Geographic. Twenty-five words in fluent English. I apologized for the delay in responding, and announced I was taking the job.

5

All right. So I did eat. I had to. It was such a long day, and all of it haunted by Gadi's insult. By the feeling that anybody who feels like it can come up and hurt you, and there's nothing you can do except think philosophical thoughts about the human condition. And eat. You're exposed as you move through the world, surrounded by people who want to do bad things to you. Not because they have anything against you, they don't, it's because of their own psychological and moral problems. And you're supposed to understand. You're supposed to understand them all not because you're a saint, but because there may be some consolation in it.

There isn't. I understand everybody, but it hurts me when I'm beaten. My understanding has its limitations.

All right, I also hurt people. There isn't a person in my life whom I haven't hurt. For instance? For instance, my dad. For instance, when I yelled at him that the reason he was so keen to have a son was that he himself hasn't been a man for a long time. I saw mum's face turn white as a pitta, because nobody, but nobody, talks like that to Papa Alkabetz, certainly not in our family. I saw papa shrink, and suddenly noticed his drooping shoulders and the grey hairs peeping out of his pyjama top, and saw how he'd aged in recent years, and felt a wave of guilt wash over me, not because I offended him, but because I didn't feel any love for him, only pity, like for a dog that's been run over. The worst of it was when he looked at me and said quietly, Hard, you're hard, Mori. You'll have a hard time with people ... I wanted to hug his neck and kiss his old cheeks, but I couldn't, because touching him always disgusted me, and he said, Well, I'm tired, and went to rest in the bedroom.

We never mentioned this incident, as if he simply forgave me, but I remembered it for years afterwards, and felt the guilt pressing on my heart. Another one of the obstinate incidents that refuse to dissolve in the memory with the passage of time. All the same, the subject of the son he'd always hoped for was never raised again, at least in my presence.

And mum, with her submissive eyes and vast rump. I think I loved her when I was quite small, though of course I wanted to be like papa. But even in those days I sometimes wondered what the hell made him want her.

Papa met mama in Paris in the sixties. How touching—he was at the university and she was visiting relatives. Material for a Louis de Funes romantic comedy. At home everybody knows that to have been a student in Paris in the sixties is the coolest thing. Of course papa was politically engaged. Papa was no sucker. Papa took an active part in the student revolt, was a leftist. In those days Reich was the latest thing, and I suppose young papa boned quite a few pussies, though I admit I can hardly imagine him in the role. Understandable, isn't it? You'll agree that visualizing our dear parents engaging in sexual activity, even the most ordinary, is an easily avoided undertaking.

But despite the sexual and political joy that swept over the young Parisians in those days, papa did not marry some hot-headed, crop-haired student, but mama, an innocent maiden with religious-domestic leanings—definitely non-educational.

It seems that even in the sixties, the symbol of rejuvenation, equality and sexual liberation, certain men wanted to marry virgins. As they say, *c'est la vie*. Revolt or no, Algeria or no, we'll stand under the canopy with a kosher Jewish maiden. And papa, for all his qualities and obvious originality, was no exception. I bet you'll say, you don't understand, Mori, that's how it is, it's another aspect of life's dark beauty, of its hidden laws, of the divine order. You think only special, interesting and enlightened people are entitled to fall in love and be fruitful and to all the rest of the earthly delights? What, are you a fascist? The last time someone upheld such a view and worked to disseminate it, it ended with the systematic extermination of several ethnic groups, to one of which you happen to belong . . .

All the same, for long stretches of my childhood I liked mama. I didn't know that there were other options. I thought it was the same with everybody, until I met Rona and her mum. Before that fateful meeting, I used to picture the children I'd have when I grew up, hoped for a boyfriend who wouldn't be disrespectfully horny, and didn't let the boys press against me when we danced slow dances at class parties.

Oh yes, mama is almost a caricature of a typical mum. A character out of a non-existent but perfectly possible Israeli comic strip—a warm and pious personality with hennaed hair. A Mediterranean version of Edith Bunker.

My greatest fear since I was a teenager was that I'd grow up to resemble her. To me she was the embodiment of the ghastly female. The ultimate housewife, the ultimate mum. I did everything possible to escape this genetic-cultural destiny hanging over my poor head and body. I'm sure she sensed my contempt for her, though of course I never said anything specific about her, only talked endlessly about other women, other mothers. At times quite viciously. I remember with what obvious pleasure I told her about the abortion. Or about the men who came and went. And how much I admired Rona's mother. I got such a kick from the gluey worry in her eyes, the destruction of her little hope that I would eventually settle down and live with a man like an ordinary human being, and breed his litter, and wash his smelly socks, and fry his eggs. Not that she ever permitted herself to say such things to me, but I read her like a book. She was not sufficiently sophisticated or intelligent to hide her baboonish drives—husband, children, food, womb . . . She didn't even try to adopt a more reasonable worldview if only to please me.

She very much wanted to please me. She wanted so much for us to be a mother-and-daughter act like in the soap operas. I remember my astonishment when I met her

Nightmare Poem, or The Unrealized Cure of Mor Alkabetz

relatives that time in Casablanca. Her cousins and all the rest. They seemed so enlightened and cultivated. I couldn't understand how she came out such a chimpanzee, until I perceived that it was all an illusion, that those women were just as messed-up as she is, except that they wore dresses by Lagerfeld and studied at fancy universities in Europe— not to make them independent, but for their family's stupid prestige, for their husbands' stinking pride, and to make them into exquisite, cultivated maidservants, but maidservants forever.

Everything changed when I met Rona. It was like hearing such a beautiful melody that you feel deep down in your mind, in the depths of your archetypal consciousness, that you must have heard it before and that it's the essence of truth. The first thing Rona taught me was how to vomit. It was a worldly lesson, but an important one for my future life. I close my eyes and see us standing on the shore of the Sea of Galilee, in Ein Gev. It was during a class trip to the Golan that our friendship was sealed. I had on a black swimsuit with white polka-dots from David's brassière shop, and Rona was in a scrap of spotted Gottex and a baseball cap worn back to front.

"The Greeks were the cultural flash of genius of all time."

She stressed the "the" in a low voice.

"They invented everything that was worth inventing."

Rona dipped a translucent violet foot into the chilly water and at once pulled it back.

"Though their democracy was crap, since it didn't

include women and slaves, otherwise they were real champs. Art, philosophy, mathematics. Compared with them, the Romans were militant beasts, though they did hatch some clever ideas in the political sphere which males of all sorts still admire to this day. But like any system run by males, that one also destroyed itself. They wanted to rule the world, and in the end they rotted from within, because that's what lust for power always does. Nero, that fat psychopath, played the lyre while watching the flames that were consuming Rome and colouring the dawn. They destroyed themselves, and that will also be the end of our civilization if men continue to run things. Where did you get your swimsuit?"

Rona admired everything to do with ancient Greece and dreamed of doing classical studies at university, but already in ninth grade she knew she'd have to give up this dream for carefully considered reasons. It was simply a terribly impractical subject.

"What would I do with it afterwards?"

Rona sighed and tugged the spotted swimsuit out of the crack of her arse. She gazed at the Sea of Galilee through narrowed eyes and looked like a lean, pampered leopard cub.

"Anyway, in the final analysis, Classical Studies, like Philosophy and General Literature, are lousy departments, designed to produce cultivated housewives, high-school teachers and journalists for the local press and women's magazines. Hanging around all day in the Humanities cafeteria, hoping to get laid."

Rona remained true to herself. To the best of my

knowledge, she never hung around the Humanities cafeteria, though it was the natural hangout for such a brilliant and beautiful creature. When the time came, she opted for physics. She had the requirements for every possible career, but most of all she had style and a profound understanding, backed by aesthetic, political and social views, of what constitutes true good taste.

"You know," she said to me on that annual trip, when we were bundled in our sleeping-bags under clear April skies, and I was moaning about the quantities of sweet corn, hummus and tinned peaches I'd gobbled with youthful lack of restraint in the alfresco supper, "you don't have to leave it all in your stomach."

She permitted herself a charming pause, during which we listened to the crickets and other nocturnal sounds, and continued in a thoughtful whisper, her face turned upwards.

"The Romans used to hold amazing feasts, and when they were too full to go on eating, they vomited into special silver buckets held for them by cute laddies, so they could go on guzzling."

She fell silent, still looking at the sky with dreamy concentration. I turned to her, waiting for the rest. In fact, I'd read something like it somewhere, but it had struck me as totally fantastic and impossible. The only times I'd ever thrown up was when I came down with summer food poisoning.

"You have to drink and then move away."

She slithered out of her sleeping-bag and I saw her sculptured form hiding the moon.

"Come on, get up."
She was perfectly serious.

". . . They also poked the laddies in the arse," Rona whispered when we were groping our way back through the raspberry bushes, after the first lesson she gave me had ended successfully.

"What laddies?"

The taste of vomit filled my mouth and I longed to press my lips to the water cantine we'd left behind in the camp.

"The cute laddies who held the buckets for them"— the historical context was always as important to Rona as the fact itself.

It was impossible not to fall in love with Rona. She never tried to talk me into anything, but it was enough to observe her to know which side the butter was on.

But I even managed to abuse Rona, although she was perfection. From the moment we met, every new discovery of her personality and views only reaffirmed the premise of her perfection, time and again, almost without reservation. Her figure was slender and perfect, her head clear and perfect, her values sublime and perfect, and so were all the other attributes of her person and belongings.

Not to mention her perfect mother. Oh indeed, Rona's mum! Rona's mum was of course the total opposite of good old Mama Alkabetz—a flat-chested blonde, a successful real-estate lawyer. The only food she knew how to prepare were tiny sandwiches with smoked salmon or imported cheese. Divorced, fluent, the right universities, the right books, the right acquaintances. Everything in proper measure, not a trace of the snobbery or *nouveau riche* flavour that often accompanies this set of qualities. For example, she was wild about classical music, was personally acquainted with Zubin Mehta and Perlman, but did not have a subscription to the Philharmonic orchestra—for reasons of style. She was unquestionably the real thing.

I'll never forget that woman. She would sit curled up on the expensive sofa in their living-room, an outsize cat, peroxided, smoking unfiltered Pall Malls, and talking about imbecile men she'd met in the course of the day who were pathetic enough to come on to her. From time to time she'd send me or Rona to refill her glass with neat Black Label, and I remember watching this woman, the ash dropping from her cigarette on the carpet, her long bony toes twitching restlessly in the stockings, and thinking, that's how I want to be. Exactly like that. In my mind she was like one of those Olympian goddesses that Rona was interested in. Athena maybe. Yes, Athena. Certainly. I remember how shocked I was the first time I came across a sign of her common humanity. I went into their lovely bathroom, full of mirrors, bottles and vials sporting the labels of Lancôme, Van Cleef & Arpels, Issey Miyaki, Lancaster, Dior, Guerlain and Kenzo, and after washing my hands and peering at the pimples on my face, I suddenly noticed a green Clinique soap on the edge of the bathtub with a long black pubic hair stuck to it like a mark of Cain. In retrospect, though, even this minute awkward incident only made her more concrete, her small faults underlining her powers.

And Rona was so like her. Brilliant and thin. Though I knew she had a long history of anorexia, and that she had financed any number of youth shrinks and experts on eating disorders, but it made no difference. She was thin, she was exceptional and charming, and a wonderful student. And a loyal friend. Everything a woman should be.

I hurt Rona too. How else. That's the way the cookie crumbles. The wicked way of the world. It's not my fault, it's the world made by men.

But as you know, my friends, the circle has been breached—very slowly we began to resemble them. Commonplace but true—the oppressed take on the qualities of the oppressor. Given half a chance, the slave becomes a merciless ruler. It's well known that many of the women who fought so desperately for their equal rights concluded that it was simpler to adopt the masculine doctrine than to risk trying to impose the feminine principle upon the world. They botched it in a big way. Are you listening, my liberated, independent, progressive friends—you really botched it. The liberty you achieved is a makeshift one. It's insufficient. To me it's insufficient. I want the genuine good, the genuine humanism. I want feminine wisdom to rule the universe, to erase every vestige of the thousands of years of disgrace that the human race has brought upon itself.

I want a big womb to shelter us all. That's what I want . . .

Funny, Rona's mother was a great feminist, but she always said she preferred to work with men. Surer, more reliable, and they don't get pregnant. I also prefer to work with men. Natch. I get on fine with them, I can speak their language. I'm familiar with power and I like it. And of course Rona's mother was right—they don't get pregnant . . . We despise them and wish we were like them. Such a lousy dissonance. Feminism has betrayed itself. Women betrayed themselves. And darkness was upon the face of the deep and the—certainly masculine—spirit of God moved upon the face of the waters.

I took Gadi away from Rona. The joy of conquest. Like a Russian tank in the streets of Prague. I wasn't even interested in him that time when he came to dinner at her mother's and she invited me too, to show off. I saw right away that I could swallow him whole. They didn't have much of a chance against me. Rona was looking pale from nights of revising for her second degree exams. She was fiddling with the food on her plate, while I wolfed mine and drank wine and laughed the whole time, and whenever I turned to him I touched him lightly, accidentally on purpose, on the knee or arm, and asked him a million questions, about himself and his studies and what he was writing. Till I swallowed him up.

The only thing that made this incident morally tolerable is that at a certain stage I really fell in love with him. Then even Rona had to shut up as far as I was concerned, because who can stand up against the real, grand love, the mythic encounter between cock and cunt? The grand union? That what we've been brought up on and looked forward to all our lives. Salvation through love for a man. Even anarchist Rona knew and accepted it.

I swallowed slim handsome Gadi, and then I vomited him in my usual way. So I also hurt Gadi, and the baby, though he was still only a tiny lump of flesh.

So I have hurt everybody. Why am I whining then about the hurts other people inflicted on me? That's the bloody, masculine, way of the world. And having hurt others, I should be able to understand them. They don't want to hurt you, they just want the best for themselves, and you happen to be in their way. So they move you aside. Some do it gently, others roughly.

Sometimes I wonder if perhaps all the victims of Mor Alkabetz, both relatives and strangers, don't say to themselves, it's because of Mor's problems, she didn't really mean it. She is a sensitive person. Maybe they're understanding and psychologically empathic.

Fuck their mothers. I have no problems. I have a problem. A single problem. It's bad, but there's only one. Good Lord, why have I suddenly plunged into all this soul-searching, this gobbledygook? They did this to me, they took that from me, and I also did, took, beat up, sinned. It's sickening. To be precise and call a spade a spade, the whole thing can be summed up in a few words. I have fits of eating after which I have to throw up. Big deal. It's a well-known psychological problem. Many people suffer from it, many women. Everything goes back to women, to the heavy cross of femininity that I have to bear. The personal Via Dolorosa of Mademoiselle Alkabetz.

A feminine problem, right.

I'm going to solve it. Cigarette? Cigarette.

Luckily there's food. So I'll eat. Anyway I've ruined everything. So I'll eat.

Eat eat Mori, and you'll grow up big and strong like daddy, like Rocky, like Schwarzenegger and that handsome President Kennedy.

It was really comical at lunch yesterday with that jerk Yaniv from Barel PR. We were sitting in Aharoni's Golden Apple, and I tucked into their terrific business lunch. He was going on about his great plans for the promotion of some snack-food or other, and suddenly said, "I bet you think I'm terribly ambitious," when all I was thinking of was how soon I could nip off to the toilets and throw up. When I'm in a good mood I am fairly tolerant about this belief of the average Western male, that having been born in a democratic country he too, with his hidden potential, may become president or chief-of-staff, and it's only because he hasn't taken the trouble to fit into the appropriate system that he hasn't done so yet. Another sweet illusion of the democracy that nurtures ambitious little male minds.

I went to the toilets and threw up. The scent of their air-purifier—Forest Air, it said on the container—filled my nose. I puked the trout in butter-almond sauce with baked potato in two great barfs. Quick as a wink. No hassle.

As a rule, I try to avoid eating in public places. I avoid eating in company. It's years since I've eaten in order to satisfy hunger. As soon as I've taken the first bite, I know I won't be able to stop. Like right now, for example. But that time I had no choice. I wanted the Levis campaign and he wanted to dine me. So I agreed. The lavatories in a first-rate restaurant aren't bad. Clean, big mirrors, marble. The best.

Mind you, there too you can run into problems. You can easily find yourself besieged in your cubicle by an artsy-fartsy Tel Aviv female popping in to powder her renovated nose between the main course and the dessert. Then you must lower your head right into the bowl so she won't overhear the strange noises and won't tap her manicure on the door to ask if you're all right. It has happened. But this time there was nothing for it. To make a good impression on PR executives you really have to eat with them in fancy restaurants. Some business has to be done over a meal. That's the business way of the world. The path to a man's heart lies through his stomach, and so on and so forth.

When I came out of the lavatory I couldn't stop the tears. I was sweating. The make-up was all smeared, eyeliner, mascara. Forget the lipstick. I looked in the mirror and saw an ugly clown with streaming eyes and a little piece of fish stuck to the chin. I wiped everything off somehow with toilet tissue and went back, trying to look cool . . . Then came the funny bit. The idiot gave me what he must have thought was a piercing look, and winked! For an awful second I thought he too throws up after meals, and he's showing understanding. But he only swung his chin from side to side and said, "It's unkind not to share with a friend," and twitched his nose like a rabbit. Then I understood that he thought I'd gone to sniff cocaine on my own. I was so relieved that I spent the next ten minutes persuading him that I'd caught a chill because of the air-conditioning everywhere. Finally I said, in fact, I'm opposed to drugs. That type of escape from reality is not for me.

6

All right, so I couldn't resist, so what?
    But all is not lost.
    I'll simply leave it all inside. I won't vomit. That's what I'll do.
    This is the real test. What's so clever about not eating? Sometimes I don't eat for days, but it's no therapy, because it's always followed by a spaz.
    No no no. I'll leave it all inside.
    What if I get fat?
    I won't be able to stand it.
    I won't get fat. You don't get fat in one go.
    The main thing tonight is not to throw up. That's the assignment.
    If only I could sleep. Time would pass more quickly. Not a chance. Not with such quantities of junk in my stomach. So I won't sleep.
    I'll stay awake and won't throw up. Either it's a cure or it isn't. All the way.

7

They say that physical activity helps to suppress pain. Diverts the mind from the craving to throw up. From fear. The brain releases endorphins. A natural high. I should do what the orthodox do—start to sing, and the gladness will come by itself. Can hardly do ten press-ups . . . Hey hey hey, yababam yababam yababam, the Lord bless you in Zion . . . oh the great try on, oh the randy lion . . . oh the Lord in Zy-y-on . . . shit. Can't go on . . . How do they do it in the Marines' training camp in those Vietnam movies? Ah, if only I were a man . . .

At some stage in my childhood I began to think I'd like to be a boy. Not because I was a mischievous tomboy, streetwise and athletic. On the contrary! I was rather a feeble girl. And feminine. Oh so feminine. I developed early and well. Period, tits, the works. Mama always took pains to dress me well, despite our limited means. Oh Mori, you ungrateful pig! Look back with longing on the little denim skirts you inherited from Merav and Claudine, the pastel cotton-knit dresses, T-shirts with yukky Mickey and Minnie Mouse, the pencil-boxes with pictures of princesses on the lid, and pink "perfumed" erasers that you and your little girlfriends used to inhale, as if the cheap scent was the great promise of womanhood, about to spread its legendary wings over you. All right, all right, I remember!

It was nice, being a girl, but oh to be a boy!—Now that, my friends, you have to admit smells of real power.

Nightmare Poem, or The Unrealized Cure of Mor Alkabetz

Even warm loving mama always told me how much she hoped I'd be born a boy. She thought it was amusing to tell me about it over and over again . . . The tiresome old family myth of the House of Alkabetz. Mori's papa and mama always dreamed of a son. Baby-boy Alkabetz, equipped with a potent little cock. Securing the continuity of the race. But what did they get? Only girls. Matronly Merav, cute Claudine, and mental Mor. Tuviah the Milkman's quandary. Never mind, said Papa Alkabetz to Mama Big-arse Alkabetz, but his heart sank with grief.

    Am I being obsessive? Keep blaming Mummy and Daddy for my own psychosis? Oh right, here comes the psychological element again. The patient's history. Her relations with her parents. An unresolved oedipal desire for the father. Penis envy. Then the unfortunate upbringing— the destructive effect of the mother's suppressed libido, the traditional conservatism. Tough, tough. Incidentally, it's great to have a suppressed libido. I wish I had a suppressed libido. No no no, stop here Mori, you're getting away from the subject. We're discussing the psychological factor, trying to examine the patient's childhood, and you're off again about your fucks. Wait, dear heart, we'll get to it, how else. There's hours to go to sunrise, when you'll take a shower, shave your underarms, slip into clean clothes and escape from this dangerous place, telling yourself over and over, I got through the night, through the attack of feminine feebleness. I'm cured.

    Now is the time to open a serious discussion about childhood. Perhaps the secret lies in there? Ah, childhood,

childhood. That impossible time that artistic people like to wank over when they think about it. Nabokov's *Speak, Memory* is my favourite example. I was so excited when I read about all those beautiful boys in sailor suits, and fragrant, cropped-hair girls in lacy knickers. How those descriptions thrilled me! How they fondled each other's crotches on starry nights on the French Riviera. Sensuous children, intoxicated by the scent of the lilac, jasmine and orchid blossoms surrounding their parents' summer houses—wealthy Russian nobles fleeing from the raging storm of the October Revolution.

My childhood too is engraved in me with the same sensuous intensity, but I am free from nostalgia. At this moment I am dominated by rage. Rage over the mental and physical particles I was forced to absorb into my blood, as though they were an organic and inseparable part of all that I am.

Mounds of garbage. Truckloads of spiritual trash. The dump of the soul.

Here is an almost reckless summary: childhood, adolescence, youth, newspapers, weeklies and monthlies, thousands of good books and a considerable number of bad ones, often just as pleasurable. You can reel out the names of the giants of literature as if they were Marines on morning parade, but what's the difference, in any case all Western literature was written by white Eurocentric males! Cases like George Sand, the Brontë sisters, and all the literary ladies of the twentieth century are mere drops in the boundless ocean of creative masculine thought.

And what about the movies? An art form that

developed in our enlightened, humane century? Who are the main makers of cinema, that great and cruel god? "What do you want to be when you grow up, little girl? A brain surgeon? An astronaut?" "No mama, I want to be Robert De Niro!" Oh De Niro's Vietnam exploits, De Niro's mafia exploits, De Niro's taxi, De Niro's mole, De Niro's guns and grins. What a man, Jesus Christ, what a man.

I'm not talking about the standard Hollywood crap. I've never given a toss about it (though I suppose even this crude, low-grade and banal nonsense has done its sly work on my raped consciousness), no, I'm talking about quality. I'm talking about people whose work will be engraved in golden letters in the history of human civilization. I'm talking about Jarmusch, Tarantino, Coppola, Cimino, Scorsese, John Houston and Altman.

I can't leave out another little example—rock 'n' roll. The testosterone-charged glamour of rock 'n' roll. The phenomena that produce a hard-on, both physical and mental, in both sexes. Jagger's balls, Morrison's buns, Springsteen's energy, Prince's exhibitionism.

And those skin-tight trousers! And the women they ran around with!

And the money. How much money washed over them, how many kilos of white powder passed through their nostrils, how much eccentric style, how much independence, and above all—how much freedom. And power.

All these and many others pierced my mind with their talents, leaving it indelibly, seethingly marked. Bewitched and cursed forever. These ambitious men ravished my soul, squirted their mental seed into every dark corner of my brain. I didn't even try to resist. My mind lay down under them, submissive and splayed, like the Apache's virgin bride when he comes home from the hunt with a still-warm antelope carcass slung across his shoulders.

And on the other side—the great feminists. The first books I read, the things I began to comprehend with intense excitement. I'll never forget my amazement after reading Marilyn French's *Beyond Power*, in which she deals so persuasively with the condition of women in the world, with the history of woman, her terrible trap, the white male's dominance. She spoke directly to my heart. She knew me. I wanted to be like her.

Deep down I knew it was best to be a man. But if you're unlucky enough to have been born female, you might as well be a first-rate one. Fly right off the scale. A perfect blend of all the options available to us at this stage of human history.

I realized that for me there were only two options. One was to disappear, avoid everything, fix my eyes on the night sky and stare at it for ever, till redemption came in the form of death. The other possibility was to let everything that is seen, heard and felt to seep into me, to poison every cell in my body, confuse and rattle me, till my insides became a vast, abstract kaleidoscope. I opted for the latter, or rather, I imagine that I opted for it. The pure merciless truth is that the second option chose me. And from that eclectic womb I emerged into the world, baked and with a raisin on top for decoration.

The new woman . . .

8

Tomorrow is going to be tough. Very tough. A stomach full of rubbish. The Triumph underwear catalogue. I shall spend the day photographing chicks wiggling in bras and panties in front of me. Why did I choose fashion photography? It's the sexiest thing to photograph. And the best paying. Money matters. A woman needs to have money. A woman, to be worth anything, must get somewhere. Otherwise she's nothing, zilch, the weaker, inferior, lost sex!

Going to photograph models. Sharon Abu Snit, Tampon Abu Split and Bonbon Abu Tit. Smiling constantly, like mongoloids. They all have low brows, a smooth skin and glass eyes in various colours. They're all young, all slender. Lumps of meat, rubber dolls. Coathangers.

Hate. Hate that obsessive preoccupation with the body, with beauty.

When I was their age it didn't occur to me to be a model. And nobody would have thought of employing me as one. A plump girl, an unhappy girl. I fought hard to win my place. The first boys I laid. Talk about disaster . . . I wanted sentimental, naïve love, but I already knew that a woman had better be liberated.

The new woman loves sex. A liberated woman must love sex. Take charge of your orgasms. Masters and Johnson, *The Hite Report*. Most women don't come in the act of fucking, Shere Hite concluded in her book, which was considered revolutionary in its day, though apparently it didn't revolutionize much . . . She published it in the seventies. How is it that so many years have passed, so many people have read it, and nobody has learned anything. Neither the women nor the men nor me.

Sex is cool. It's also easy. I know how to do it, I know how to be sexy. When you meet a man who turns you on, fuck him quick. What, are you a shy sentimentalist? Answer: no. You're bold. You're fiery, you're pleasure personified. When I meet a man who turns me on, I try to fuck him without delay. I know how to do it. So does he. I'm not some backward conservative. I'm a sex kitten, I am. A wicked beast. The code is so clear and plain. I'm liberated. I'm free.

The men didn't read *The Hite Report*. I reached that conclusion long ago. It doesn't really interest them, though it's packed with useful information that could turn them into much better lovers than they are now. They're supposed to be eager for such information, are always trying to obtain it from any source, from porno movies to stressful personal experience. The man is always convinced that he's as keen to pleasure the woman as himself. But that's the fallacy. When you fuck a man he does not honestly and sincerely try to give you pleasure. No, when you fuck a man what he wants is to prove himself.

That's what's really in his mind.

It's the same in life generally. Your pleasure only interests them as evidence of their marvellous abilities. Your pleasure is a mirror reflecting their virtuoso potency. Many of them don't know, and actually don't care to know, what really gives women pleasure. I mean real, live women, not organic copies of film heroines, lusty Bobolinas out of magazines, advertisements and all kinds of porn. I discover to my dismay that even those who've indulged in extensive sexual activity with countless women are incredibly ignorant about the basic facts of female anatomy . . . They want to skewer you on their phallus and watch you moaning with delight, like Sharon Stone, in soft light, eyes half-shut, an expression of pleasure tinged with pain on the half-opened lips, painted a natural colour.

 I know how to fuck like this. No problem. I've seen the movies. From behind, no problem, from the front and on top, legs over shoulders, in the mouth, in the arse, in every known and possible position. No problem whatsoever. I am the ultimate voluptuous woman. I love sex and have no inhibitions.

 Now you'll say, oh that daft Mori, she's so frustrated, so vulgar. What does she know. With us it's not like that. Not exactly like that. My man spends a full half hour on foreplay before he sticks his dick between my legs. Sometimes he's kind enough to lick me down there for ten whole minutes. Not that he knows how to do it exactly, but at least he tries. Let's face it, it's not easy . . .

 We can understand him, can't we, girls? A woman's cunt is a problematic thing. Desire, liberation, daring or whatever—in the final analysis it's a moist unprotected hole, an exposed opening of the body. Leading to the insides. It's small animal with a strange smell. And woman should smell good, my friends. Should smell great. Even down there. She isn't a fishmonger, is she. Rona told me that she got some liquid at the pharmacy which she squirted in there. A kind of hygienic douche that makes the thingie smell of violets, she said. How fortunate we are that progress and science are taking care of us. They invent all kinds of devices so that our anatomy won't disturb the civilized world. Disinfectant liquids smelling of violets, special soaps for every orifice of the body, deodorants for the mouth, the cunt, the armpits, the brain.

Have you ever seen a man rinsing his precious cock with violets before he comes to stick it in your mouth? Ah but that's different, isn't it? Say it—a different anatomy. Go on, say it.

Madam, the system is perfectly plain: you're supposed to enjoy it when someone shoves his dick into you and fucks you lustily and well. That's all there is to it. Well, sometimes it is fun. Sometimes. But mostly it isn't. Not a bit. I need tenderness, genuine liberation, concentration, shyness. Yes, shyness. I'd like to allow myself to be shy, to feel shy, to experience it. To let shyness exist, just as I treat my lust to this fine, wet, untrammelled experience.

I want to kiss someone for a whole year. Let them kiss me on the eyes and forehead for a whole goddamn year. That's what I want.

9

I'm dying to puke . . . absolutely must puke . . . can't hold out. What ghastly shit. Utter crap. I want to die. Want to die, to end this nightmare, this stinking night, this idiotic cure. Who needs it. What's the urgency? So I have a weakness, so what. Does everything have to be perfect? So I'll throw up. What can happen. I can get cured some other time. It's only a matter of resolution. Why did I have to do it today, when tomorrow I've got to do the catalogue. It's a twelve-hour shooting day. Nobody does things this way. What awful idiocy. Best to wait till I take a few days off. I can't stand it, this food inside me, in my stomach, rotting, being digested, breaking down into sugars, carbohydrates, fats, becoming absorbed into my body, into my cells, pads of fat growing on my thighs, around my belly, on my arse. I'm heavy, everything hurts, pain everywhere . . . Let me die and have done.

I want my mum. I want to go back to being small, a foetus, to be sucked back into her womb and not be born for years and years, until this new age is over, these bad years, until civilization falls apart, destroys itself with nuclear weapons, with damaged ozone, hate, famine, AIDS, floods.

Then I'll be reborn. The big woman of the tribe. The big mother. And there will be no death, no competition, no pride. I'll gather herbs, bear children and educate the men of the tribe. A sweet smell of salvation will hang in the air, and the sky will be black and clear under God's gaze. And His spirit will fill every grain of dust, every leaf of grass, and a great, solemn quiet will come down on the world, from here to Japan.

10

For the failure of my cure I accuse the producers of preserved foods, the producers of unpreserved foods, the producers of food as a whole. The inventors of the baguette, whipped cream and steaks.

I accuse the media, the advertising world, the faggot fashion designers who created the cult of the underfed female as a metaphor for the boyish arse of their fantasies, the white male dominating the globe, the feminist revolution of the 1960s, the post-feminist revolution of the eighties, the benighted nineties, Freud and Marx, Kevin Costner, Axel Rose, the male model for Levis and Eitan Dahan of class Nine Three.

I accuse all who tried directly or indirectly to define my human and feminine identity and to imprison me in their limited conceptual world. All who taught, influenced, vanquished, impressed, fulfilled ideals and trained others to fulfil them.

I accuse all who tried directly or indirectly to turn me into an object upon which to hang purposes, aims, qualities and other characteristics intended to make me into the perfect handmaiden of civilization. An honorary member of capitalist society at the end of the twentieth century. An equal contestant in the great contest. A survivor.

I accuse my parents, my primary-school teachers. Ilana the shrink. Gadi.

I accuse the men I've fucked, I accuse the men with whom I had relationships, I accuse the men I did not fuck and with whom I had no relationship, but who never missed an opportunity to tell me how to be the right kind of woman at this time, in this crumbling century, this rotten age which is post-everything.

I accuse the women who told me the same things. I accuse the women who accepted the role and thereby forced me to emulate them. To seek to be like them. I accuse Meryl Streep, Devorah Omer, Jessica Lange, Susan Sontag and Ora Namir. Cindy Crawford. The lipstick and tights models, the manufacturers of lipsticks and tights, my sisters, the women neighbours, all the orgasm-fakers from Chicago to Sderot. All the women who really do come, from Chicago to Sderot. The whores, lesbians, drag queens, career women and housewives. Golda Meir, Yonah Wallach and Madonna. The pious old women and bold young ones, the kindergarten teacher Rena, and mama.

I accuse MTV, the press, the mass of images, the system, the Army Radio, cable TV, the Second Channel, Dan Shillon, the Moses family, American cultural imperialism, Zionism, the Labor Party, the Opposition and the Government.

I accuse the idealists and the cynics. The bourgeoisie. The orthodox, the lower classes, the Palestinians.

Lunar Eclipse

       I accuse myself of not making my life into a turning-point, of letting myself go and allowing the great current to sweep me along.
       I accuse everybody.
       I hate everybody. They're all sons of bitches. Everyone in the world is a whore and I'm the biggest whore of all. I'm the new woman.

About the author

Alona Kimchi

Alona Kimchi was born in Russia in 1966 and emigrated to Israel with her family in 1972. She graduated from Beit Tzvi Theatre School and began an acting career, then turned to writing. This collection of short stories, originally published in Hebrew as *Ani Anastasia* in 1996, was awarded the prestigious ACUM Prize for Literature. Kimchi lives in Tel Aviv, working in the theatre and as a journalist.

Israeli critics acclaimed her work: one called it a kind of "linguistic laboratory" and another described the language as "fluent, vulgar and sometimes manic". "Each of the stories astounds in its own particular way," wrote the reviewer in *Iton Tel Aviv*, "exposing another kind of unhappiness or misery, yet all have a quality of acute, venomous humour and superb verbal brutality."

The fonts used in this book are from the Garamond and Gill families.

15-95